The Silence of Medair

Medair: Book 1

Andrea K Höst

All characters in this publication
are fictitious and any resemblance
to real persons, living or dead,
is purely coincidental.

The Silence of Medair
© 2010 Andrea K Höst. All rights reserved.
ISBN: 978-0-9808789-0-5
EBook ISBN: 978-0-9808789-1-2
www.andreakhost.com
Cover art: Julie Dillon

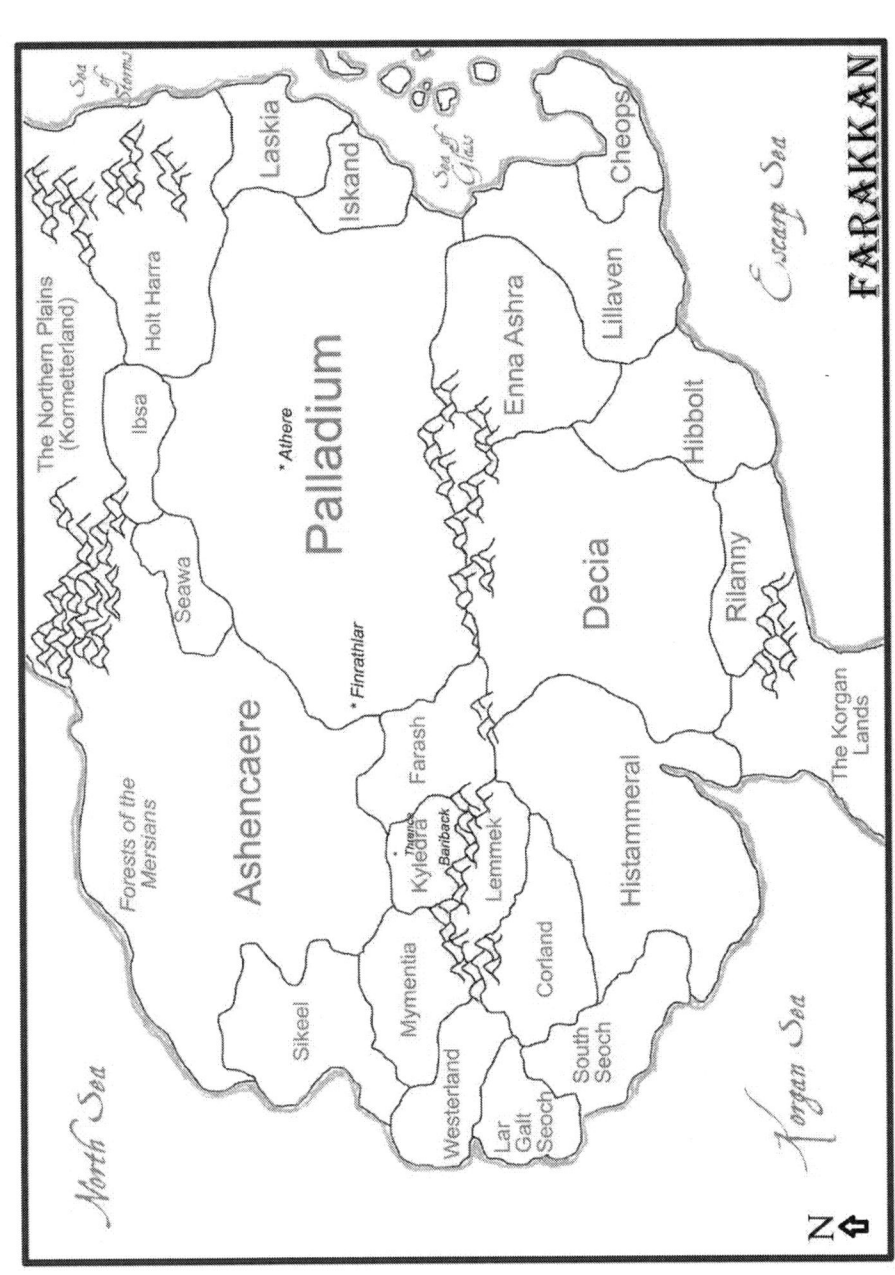

ONE

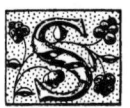Sunlight on metal. A flash on the lower slopes, gone before she looked up, but enough to leave Medair staring down beyond the trees which hid her cottage. Had she imagined that momentary brightness, caught only in the corner of her eye, or was there truly another living person on Bariback Mountain?

She was keeping company with the wind, high on a slope where goats had once been taken to graze. The idea of movement did not fit with the drowsy scent of Bariback violets, the drone of the bees, and the way the breeze dried the sweat on her skin. The sky was an eternal, unblemished blue which gave no hint of the storm that would inevitably follow so many damp, sticky days, and the whole world must surely be dozing. It had been her imagination, nothing more.

Oblivious to Medair's opinions, the flash came again. Feeling abruptly exposed, she stared down Bariback's northern face. The mountain did not bother with foothills, rising directly to a blunt peak, with only trees to break up the incline. At its base, past the wooded middle slopes and patchily cleared lower reaches, a river snaked through farmland long left untilled. Beyond was Bariback Forest, so useful in ensuring Medair's isolation.

There was no sign of movement in the vista below, but she couldn't stay up here without checking. Swiping sweat-damp blonde hair off her forehead, Medair started down.

Still not entirely convinced that the flash had been real, she dawdled, the usual reluctance she felt when returning doubled by the oppressive warmth of the day. Even when the weather was not this humid, the cool and splendid solitude of the heights had become something she craved. Needed. She could not run from her memories, but the vastness of the upper slopes somehow kept them at a distance.

Medair halted at the sight of a line of horsemen below. Six riders, with two sturdy donkeys trailing on lead. They were too far away to make out more than the vaguest details, and she wished she hadn't fallen out of the habit of taking her little spyglass with her on trips up the mountain. But hindsight was no benefit to the ill-prepared.

Remembering who had first said that to her, Medair cursed all White Snakes, and one in particular. No matter how she tried to cast it out, that soft, level voice would insinuate itself into her thoughts. Thrusting unwanted memory away, she watched the line of horses disappear into the trees. They were heading directly for her cottage.

Could these be settlers? A group of survivors returning to the village decaying on the lower slopes? Or newcomers to the area, made homeless by unrest elsewhere and lured by tales of deserted farms? She was surely not the only person in Farakkan desperate enough to risk lingering disease. There had been that trapper on the slopes in Winter. Perhaps he had spread word of the same discovery Medair had made: the plague had gone.

Six horses and two donkeys didn't suggest poverty or desperation. A prospecting group, perhaps, uncaring that centuries of delvers had declared Bariback worth no effort? Or something else? Disquiet gripped her, not least because she didn't think she could face people of any kind.

She wouldn't find answers standing around like an idiot. And it was important to reach the cottage first, because she hadn't brought her satchel with her, had thrust it under a bench at the beginning of Winter in some vain attempt to erase what it represented simply by hiding it from sight. Despite all that had happened, she couldn't leave the Emperor's gift there for strangers to find.

Setting out at a trot, Medair estimated how long before the riders would reach her cottage, and pushed herself hard to make sure she was there before them. It was not home, but she had made the place hers. She had patched the holes in the walls, replaced the mattress with something bearable, had eaten her meals at the scarred table, and buried the former occupant out the back. A stupid risk, when the local mages evidently hadn't been able to combat the disease which had killed the village. But she hadn't cared.

Nor did she care to wait meekly at the cottage for these riders. Even if they didn't happen to be bandits, the idea of talking to people seemed impossible. Not when they would ask questions, or say devastating things quite unintentionally, and look at her with eyes that tried to guess her place in the world.

That thought reminded Medair of her worn boots, inexpertly patched trousers, the grey colour of once white shirts, and her unfortunate hair, which she had decided to leave alone rather than try and trim with a knife. She had truly not been prepared for the realities of life when she went into self-imposed exile, was ragged in a way she had once never dreamed of being. If the riders were settlers, she might be able to trade for a few essentials, perhaps even allow herself to become part of a community. If. If they were settlers. If she could stand their curiosity and the mute pressure of her own shame.

※

Panting after her run, Medair strode into the cramped room which had been her Winter home and snatched her satchel from beneath the workbench. Sturdy, adorned only with a small embossed scroll on the flap, it had once been both a symbol of achievement and a practical tool of office. Five hundred years ago, before the Ibisians had destroyed the Palladian Empire. Gripping the familiar leather, she tried to decide what to do next.

The memory of what had happened the last time she'd told someone her name was enough to push Medair toward the side of caution. She would hide until she knew if these newcomers planned to stay or go and if they stayed, perhaps she would go. It would be easier to travel than to try and belong.

Her decision made, Medair hurriedly snatched up loose possessions. Knives, blankets, clothes, canteen, whatever food came to hand. She drained a water jug before thrusting it in after the tools she had gathered from the plague-gutted village, then glanced about for anything else which would fit through her satchel's mouth.

Having shoved three times its volume into the satchel's cool interior without distorting the leather in any way, Medair slipped the strap over her head in a move which remained instinctive. The satchel swung innocuously against her hip. If she were to start travelling again, she would shorten the strap and wear it on her back, so it would not disturb her stride with its slight weight. Just now it was at exactly the right spot for her to reach down and open it, dip her hand in without having to stretch.

She brought out a ring, gold twined with some black metal, of a size for a man's hand. Standing in the doorway of the cottage, she studied it for a long moment, this tiny representative of what was hidden in a satchel which had lain under a bench with the dust mice because she couldn't bear to think about it. The rings – for there were more than a dozen – had been laid out in a glittering line on an ebon-black table. They had not been her goal, but she'd taken them, along with all the portable magical relics which had been in the cave where she'd spent that long night. She'd planned to give them to the adepts to study, to turn to the cause which had sent her searching out their hiding place. The cause she'd betrayed in sleep.

Medair had learned the function of three of the rings through trial and error, since she wasn't mage enough to do a proper divination. Invisibility, strength, animal control. They had been useful in occasional times of need, but she'd only used the fourth once. After the fourth, she hadn't been fool enough to put any others on her fingers.

Now, she slid the black and gold ring over the knuckle of her right thumb and studied her hand as the weed-studded dirt became visible through her flesh, then grimaced at the uncertain quaver of her stomach, which did not at all appreciate whatever it was invisibility did to her. But queasiness seemed an easier thing to deal with than people.

Standing by her cottage door, Medair caught her breath as a man stepped out of the trees. He was wearing a fur jerkin too warm for the weather, and she recognised the trapper she'd glimpsed on the lower slopes in winter. Those who followed were not quite so cat-quiet, but they were good, and Medair breathed more shallowly, willing herself into utter immobility. Not settlers, not prospectors: warriors.

As she watched armed men stalking her empty cottage, Medair had to grit her teeth to stop herself from bolting. It had been a mistake to wait, though there'd been no way she could have anticipated this. She'd never had anyone come after her with swords. Never. The idea made her cringe.

There were five men in the open now, the sixth rider perhaps remaining with the horses, back where any noise they might make would not disturb this hunt. The trapper dropped to one side, allowing the others to do the stalking, and these four crept toward her in a way which was both unnerving and ridiculous to watch.

They were too uniformly equipped to be mercenaries. Mercenaries usually supplied their own armour – hotchpotches of plate, leather and chain scavenged, inherited or purchased. These men all wore leather, well-fitted, over dark grey clothing. A uniform, despite the lack of any insignia of rank or mark of allegiance, and they displayed practiced team-work as two stalked the door direct, the other pair circling to prevent escape from any windows or rear exits. One of the men was ginger-haired and freckled, with a tilt to his eyes which suggested Mersian blood. The rest were tanned and had the dark brown hair and hawk-nosed profiles of Decians.

The tiny hand movements they used for communication told her they were no ordinary soldiers. Scouts? Some sort of elite squad? She closed her beringed hand into a fist. None of them looked like a user of magic, but it was not as if they were Ibisians with their earrings to declare status. If they were anything like the Black Hawks, the Special Assignments Division of the Emperor's armies, there would be magi among them.

It was very difficult not to move then, as the Decians crept towards her. A magic like the ring's would not trumpet itself, but if a mage came close enough to touch her, he would feel an echo of its power. Even Medair's negligible abilities would alert her to an invisible person standing a foot away. Farak, they could probably *smell* her if they paid attention: she'd sweated more than enough coming down the mountain, and hadn't bathed daily for centuries.

The contents of her satchel were her advantage: they would surely not have anticipated an invisible target, any more than she had expected soldiers. She couldn't guess how anyone knew to look for her.

What *they* were expecting was the important question. They could not possibly know. Her hand brushed the leather of her satchel, and at the thought of all it contained she shuddered. How could these men be looking for her, Medair an Rynstar, and the prizes of her wildly successful, fruitless quest?

Decia, largest of the southern duchies, had always been stalwartly loyal to the Palladian Emperor, and the kingdom it had become was still at odds with the Ibisian conquerors. But Medair knew she couldn't become part of that struggle, even though she hated what the Ibisians had done. If these people really were looking for her, knew who she was, what she carried – she had to get away.

Medair noticed another man standing at the forest's edge just as the lead two rushed the cottage, swords drawn. Another Decian, he was dressed like the rest, a light sword at his side. His eyes were on the door as the man whose commanding gestures marked him as leader emerged, frowning, and shook his head once. The five gathered together, only the trapper standing apart, watching with wary interest. Two feet away from the nearest man, Medair practically stopped breathing.

"Looks like she's run," the leader said, with just an edge of anger. "Place has been emptied. How long before you can locate her?"

"Half a decem or less, with a hair or some personal item – presuming she's still within range. If she's more than a few miles away, a different, less precise trace will be needed." The latecomer raised an equivocal shoulder.

"Likely she's hopped just before us. Go to it, then."

The latecomer detached himself from the group, then hesitated at the threshold. "She's a mage," he said over his shoulder, closing his eyes and holding his head to one side, listening to something only mages could hear. "There's traces of power lingering. Possibly something to confuse her trail. It's very, very recent."

"Seb, Norruce — a quick circle, if you will. Try and isolate her most recent movements, the direction she went."

Touching hands to foreheads, two men with a distinct, brotherly resemblance began an intent study of the ground, moving in outward spirals. Medair tried not to think what their tracking would reveal.

"Glyn, send our guide on his way," the leader ordered.

The Mersian nodded, but lingered. "Could she have been warned?"

The leader shrugged. "It seems unlikely. We were exposed more than once on the trip up — if she's as valuable as it sounds the sight of any stranger might well send her skittering. She won't get far."

"She better not. We've only the vaguest idea what she looks like, Sir! We don't have the resources to track her if she reaches a more populated area and even if the Kyledrans were of a mind to cooperate, how would we know if they found the right person when no-one's come close enough to know her face? We don't even have a *name!*"

"You underestimate us, Glyn," the leader replied. "Go."

"Yessir," muttered the Mersian, rebuked. The leader entered the cottage and Medair took the opportunity to move after the Mersian. She'd almost caught up with him as he politely thanked the trapper and hinted at the possibility of a bonus.

"Now, that's good of you, sir," the trapper began, then sighed, eyes widening. For one astonished instant Medair thought that the man had seen her despite the ring. Then he fell. The Mersian bent to wipe a blade on the fur-lined vest, replaced it within a sheath hidden at his wrist, and strolled on into the trees, humming softly.

Shuddering, Medair followed as close on his heels as she dared. They didn't know who she was, didn't know what she looked like. Were about to use magic to locate her. She didn't have any protection against a trace.

The Mersian whirled, knife in hand. Freezing, Medair swallowed her breath and watched him searching the trees. He was thorough, standing as still as she, eyes roving even up into the branches. Of course he saw nothing, but he was not convinced and began walking at a much slower rate, placing his feet with care. Invisibility was no protection against a knife, so Medair circled, guessing the most logical place for horses to have been left and coming up even with him some ten feet to his right. She tried to match the careful placement of his feet, putting hers to earth at the same time he did so that he would not be wholly certain any slight noise she made was not his own.

When he reached the cluster of mounts tethered in a small clearing, he appeared to shrug off his concern and bent to examine one bay's hoof. Not accepting this clear invitation, Medair picked up a fallen branch, concealing the eerily floating object behind the nearest tree while she waited for the ring to include it in her invisibility. The wood was mouldering, unpleasant to touch, but testing revealed that it hadn't rotted to the point of being unsound. It would do, presuming she could bring herself to hit someone.

Medair watched as the Mersian became more businesslike. He was still alert, still watching, not ignoring the signals his instincts were sending him merely because no attacker had rushed to take him so before moving she squatted to her heels again and palmed a clutch of walnut-sized stones.

When she had approached as close as she dared, just as the nearest of the horses was flicking an ear in response to the scent of sweaty human female, she tossed the smallest of the stones far across the clearing. The Mersian pivoted at the muted impact and Medair took those vital two steps closer. The horses reacted, snorting and shifting, so she didn't hesitate in sending the rest of the stones up in a high arc, then immediately gripping her weapon with two firm hands.

Her timing was good. Moments before she estimated the stones should land she tensed, began the last step forward, swinging the hunk of wood back as the knife reappeared in the Mersian's hand. He was starting to turn towards her, then there was a thumping patter of stones landing and he hesitated long enough for her to solidly dint his skull, knocking him to the ground.

Face-down, the man was still groggily conscious, but Medair dropped her weapon anyway, revolted by the idea of hitting him again. As the horses crowded away from them, she pulled off her black and gold ring and groped in her satchel. The animal control ring was a small braid of silver, and she jammed it on her pinkie finger, wishing that it were possible to wear two rings at once, wishing this wasn't happening.

The horses immediately stopped jumping about. Medair hastily unlooped all but the two donkeys, then hoisted herself up onto a grey. Questing about with her toe for the other stirrup, she cast one anxious glance back toward her cottage, then led an equine stream away from the dangerous men who had been sent, for whatever reason, to capture her.

Away from solitude.

Two

edair rode at a speed both reckless and unkind to her mounts, all the way down Bariback Mountain and far along the neglected road toward the forest. The thought of those five men, of the noise her lump of wood had made colliding with the head of the one called Glyn, was a hound nipping at her heels and she would not stop to do more than water the horses until she was certain they could not catch her that day. It was only when she had forded the Sorbry River and was faced with the forest that she thought beyond simply 'away'.

With the sky darkening, and her heart finally easing out of her mouth, Medair looked about for a grassy verge, then stripped the gear from five of the horses and sent them scattering toward the river, impelled by the ring. Guilty over not having rubbed down their sweating flanks, she lavished attention on the last horse, a sturdy bay, cosseting him and securing a tether while the ring kept him complaisant. Then she slipped the circle of silver from her finger and replaced it in her satchel.

The bay immediately sidled away from her, but, as she had hoped, he did not consider her quite so much a stranger any more. He was more interested in cropping grass than escaping. Turning her attention to the sky, Medair frowned at the clouds crawling south. The long-brewing storm wasn't far away: tomorrow, if not that night. She would get wet before she reached the nearest city, Thrence, nearly three days' ride away.

More information was what she needed before she began making choices, so she turned to the stolen saddlebags. Only a small amount of food: most of that must have been on the pack animals. She had six bedrolls, which guaranteed a relatively comfortable mattress for the night, even without drawing on the resources of her satchel. Five canteens, various items of male clothing, oddments like little pots of oil and saddle soap. A scattering of coin minted with the crests of a half-dozen kingdoms. No insignia at all, no documents, no neatly packaged explanation of who and why and how.

Having sorted out the gear and stowed what she considered would be of use, Medair cooked herself some dinner and sat back against a tree, thinking.

They had not known what to expect, that elite, unscrupulous little group. They had approached with caution, but had not known she was mage until the second Decian had misunderstood the traces of power given out by the ring. They knew neither her name nor her features and, really, considering what she carried, five men, only one a mage, seemed a little...inadequate. If they had taken her by surprise, then yes, they could have had her. But with the contents of her satchel, if she were desperate, she could fight off a great many more than five, no matter what their skill. With what her satchel held, she could bring down an army. That was irony.

Did the one who had sent them know? "If she's as valuable as it sounds," the leader had said. If whoever had sent these people knew who she was, what her satchel contained, why not adequately prepare those set on her trail? Why not a greater effort at secrecy in their approach? She couldn't think of any reason for them to come after her if they *didn't* know.

"I am Medair an Rynstar, Herald of the Empire," she said to the dying embers of the fire.

She had been one of the two heralds Grevain Corminevar had sent to greet the Ibisian refugees when they'd appeared in Kormettersland. Wild magic, forbidden in Farakkan, had destroyed the Ibisians' island home. Not with the massive Conflagration the mages of Farakkan warned would be the consequence of wild magic slipping from control, but by a creeping blackness which melted the land from beneath their feet. As Sar-Ibis dissolved into nothing, the Ibisians had fled to Farakkan through arcane gates; an incredible feat of magic.

Riding through their camp that first time, she'd actually been glad to see how organised they were. Their tents were in orderly clusters: small suburbs in a city of cloth separated by securely penned animals, crates, carts and carriages. Even saplings, their roots bound in sacks. With their own supplies, the hundreds of thousands of refugees would not be such a strain on the north-east as had first been thought.

She'd felt desperately sorry for them, before they'd declared their intentions. She'd wanted to reach out and help, to show them the bounty of the Empire, wondering what she could do to make it easier for them. Their alien appearance, so tall and bleached of colour, only made her feel sorrier for their displacement, for the desolation they had to feel.

Trained for her memory, Medair could not wipe out any part of that first day. She would always remember riding through that endless camp of white-skinned people, and how glad she'd been to carry a message of aid. Try as she might, she could not forget the first time she'd seen the Ibisian ruler, that cold statue of a man framed by the graceful black heads of carved ibises. She could even recite every word of the message the Emperor had sent to his homeless counterpart, the message her teacher, First Herald Kedy, had delivered:

"Words are small things," Kedy had said, his voice an echo of the Emperor's deep, measured tone. "They cannot possibly carry the weight of events, or convey anything but an outline of thoughts and feelings. My sorrow and dismay I must give you in words, knowing that nothing I say can begin to alleviate your loss. Instead, I offer you my welcome, people of the Land of the Ibis. Farakkan is a wide and varied realm and the Bountiful Lady will gladly receive another people into her fold. The Palladian Empire will give you a home."

It had been a message of sympathy and understanding, full of generosity. Medair had been so blindly proud as her mentor delivered it. She'd stood there in the tent of the Ibisian ruler – the Kier – conscious of the image of strength and security she projected, willing to do whatever it took to make loss easier for the Ibisians.

Then the world had changed forever. Kier Ieskar, the Ibisians' implacable, incomprehensible leader, had declared war and waged it with total efficiency. Farakkan hadn't seen a battle fought primarily with magic since before the Fall of Tir'arlea, and the Empire had been woefully unprepared. Massed spells cast by hundreds; Ibisian adepts whose strength dwarfed their local counterparts; their damnable geases solidifying their victories; and, behind it all, the relentless brilliance of the Ibisian Kier. The White Snakes were close to unstoppable.

But the invaders had been hopelessly outnumbered. They couldn't have won. Couldn't, shouldn't, wouldn't have won if the West hadn't betrayed Grevain. That had been the worst moment of the war, more horrible even than that first battle at Mishannon, when the White Snakes had taken the city without losing a single warrior. Destal an Vesat had delivered the message, unable to hide his gloating. The western kingdoms were throwing off the 'yoke' of the Empire. They would not support Palladium against the Ibisians, for the Ibisians were now their allies.

It had become only a matter of time before the White Snakes took Athere, Palladium's capital. Unable to bear the destruction of the Empire whose peace she had been raised to venerate, Medair had turned to the past, when mages more powerful than any White Snake had waged their own battles. Those mages might have long since departed Farak's breast, but the artefacts they'd created remained, at least in legend. There was one which would surely save them: the Horn of Farak, hidden among the Hoard of Kersym Bleak. Medair's Emperor had given her leave to seek it, but few had thought she had any chance of success.

Telsen, half-delighted, half-angry, had turned up from nowhere the day before she'd left. The last time she'd seen the man she no longer loved or hated.

"You're not really going to chase that children's tale?"

"You have an unfailing ear for gossip," she'd replied. Maintaining her dignity around Telsen had always been of primary importance. If he knew how much he'd hurt her, he'd probably work it into his music and she'd find her heart being sung to the world. Such had been her logic.

"You can't know that the Horn still exists, Medair, if it ever did. Can't know if it's in Bleak's Hoard, can't possibly hope to find the Hoard just when we need it most, when so many have sought it before you."

"You've always told me to trust in coincidence. That Farak will provide."

"Maybe." He had smiled, tilted eyes lighting with that particular fire which told her he was inspired. "Maybe. What a tale it would be! The Horn of Farak, fashioned from the bones of the Goddess Herself. Athere under siege, surrounded by White Snakes, and you appear, raise the Horn to those kissable lips, summon a mighty army and save us all."

He'd hugged her enthusiastically, as ready as ever to forget that he'd fallen out of love with her years ago, and gone through a dozen women since. She'd answered half his questions, only hinting at the clues she'd discovered in the archives. She knew better than to tell him her conclusions. He'd been planning verses for her epic when she left him.

During the long journey north, Medair had daydreamed often of the song Telsen would write for her victory. The Hoard of Kersym Bleak was legend, true, but legend based on fact, and she'd planned to destroy the White Snakes with what it contained. She was not certain if even Telsen could put into words how she felt when, in the heart of a dripping limestone maze, she'd lifted the Horn from a cushion of silk and quailed to think how many deaths would stain her hands when she used it.

She still blamed that moment of self-doubt for the disaster which followed. If she'd been more certain, more eager to strike down the invaders, she would not have rested at the heart of the maze, and slept away any hope of success.

It had taken two days after leaving the cave for Medair to realise the cost of that night. Her missing horse she'd put down to an inadequate knot. The confusing, indefinable difference of five hundred years of forest growth she did not recognise for what it was until after she understood what had happened, until after she'd reached Morning High. Never before or after would the sight of a ploughed field bring such confusion. She'd stared at the neatly churned earth which had not been there two of her days ago, and stumbled on to discover a village she knew full well didn't exist. And people who were strangely tall and blond. Her reaction to their concerned questions – uttered in a mix of Parlance and Ibis-laran — had nearly caused her to be locked away as a madwoman. Because one night in the maze had become five hundred years in Farakkan, and the world had moved on without the victory Telsen had prematurely set to music.

That had been last Spring. She'd travelled blindly south, heading toward the city which had been the Emperor's last defence: Athere. By the time she'd reached the old capital of the Empire, she was sure she didn't want to see it. The whole north-east of Farakkan was under Ibisian control, and White Snakes were everywhere, calling themselves Palladians.

But, because she did not know what else to do, because she had to look, Medair had walked through the city she had thought to return to in triumph. There were more walls, but the palace still stood, and much of the city was all too familiar. A Corminevar even sat the Silver Throne: a pale-skinned, snow-haired descendant of Kier Ieskar and the Emperor's only daughter. It was unbearable. She hadn't been able to stay more than a day in that monument to defeat.

Medair hated the White Snakes, for it was impossible to feel anything else for the people who had wrought such destruction in the Empire. Not that it had been difficult to hate: they were arrogant and over-civilised, mannered and cold. Despicable in their greed.

She'd been told her own history in Athere, even listened to stupid tales about how she would be reborn, would come back to save Palladium from the White Snakes. The ballads knew the start of the story well enough. Two years after the Ibisians had arrived on the continent of Farakkan, it became obvious that the Emperor's armies could not hold. In a month, perhaps two, Athere would surely fall. So Medair an Rynstar, Imperial Herald, had left to find the Horn of Farak.

They couldn't tell the end, those ballads of futile heroism. Only Medair knew that her quest for a weapon to defeat the White Snakes had been successful. She'd found the Horn of Farak and brought it back to the Emperor's city. Five hundred years too late, five hundred years after Grevain Corminevar had lost.

How easy it would be to use it on the White Snakes anyway, in memory of the Empire she had served. She'd certainly considered it, after buying an afternoon of answers from a scholar, and listening to the facts of the fall of Athere in the driest and most enervating of terms. She'd stood just within Cantry Wall and stared up at the White Palace and pictured herself taking the Horn from her satchel, raising it to her lips. No-one, nothing could have stopped her. And the White Snakes would have died.

But it was impossible. During the war, she would have done anything to defend her home from the Ibisians. She had dreamt of a world where White Snakes did not exist to destroy her peace, where she had never heard one voice in particular: cool, tranquil, hateful. But to use the Horn on the Ibisians who now dwelled in Athere? Who were Palladian?

She'd run away from the desire to do just that. Away from White Snakes and the part of her which demanded that they be driven out of the city they'd stolen, that they be punished, wiped out of existence. Because no matter how much she hated them, she'd known it was wrong.

After she left Athere last Summer, Medair had carried the Horn with her and tried not to think. The Duchy – now Kingdom – of Kyledra had been her first home, and she had travelled to her family lands north of Kyledra's Bariback Forest, only to find no trace of the Rynstar demesne. From there, stewing in hatred which no longer had a true focus, she had ignored warning of plague and headed for the mountain. Its lofty solitude had been a balm of sorts, and, until now, a refuge. With these Decians on her trail, she needed to find somewhere else.

Medair's oath had been to the Empire's heartland, Palladium, and to the people who had, over the centuries, mixed blood with their invaders. She could not let herself be involved in Decian plots, when Decia intrigued against Palladium. She could not use the Horn without killing the descendants of true Palladians. Perhaps – perhaps she should return the Horn to the place she had found it, deep in a maze beneath the far northern mountains, out of the reach of anyone searching for her.

Medair nodded to herself. Yes, it would be safest to put the Horn and everything else out of the reach of these Decians and whoever had sent them. And, just maybe, she would go to sleep there again and dream away another five hundred years, until the world had become wholly unrecognisable, and not quite so painful.

Or she could sleep forever and be done.

Three

ramatic thoughts of suicide were nothing new to Medair. Waking early, she set about packing in the relative cool of dawn. The pile of saddles and bags she had taken from the other horses would mark the place she'd spent the night, but she didn't think it worth the effort of hiding them. She would do better to simply stay ahead of her Decian pursuers.

The bay had almost chewed through his tether overnight and eyed her sidelong as she approached. He knew she wasn't his usual rider and didn't seem as indifferent to the fact as most horses she encountered. She offered him a dry biscuit, which he lipped eagerly, consenting to stand still long enough for her to heave the saddle onto his back. Then, when she was distracted trying to tighten the girth-strap, he stood on her foot. Her boot saved her from more than a bruise, but it was hardly endearing. Cursing, she gave an admonitory jerk on his bridle, and he blew his ribs out in retaliation. Now she could barely get the girth fastened, let alone safely tightened. Nasty creature.

She considered continuing to wear the ring. Animal control was not a quiet magic, and the ring would act as a small beacon for any mages in the area. But she had no wish to fight her mount for the entire day. After a moment's hesitation, she used it long enough to get the bit and saddle properly settled and herself securely on the bay's back. The gelding snorted and surged a few paces down the road when she slipped the ring back into her satchel, but, though his ears were back, he didn't buck or bolt. That would be enough.

Bariback was a forest of low, dark trees: tight, close and secretive. It had never been a friendly place and, beneath the tallest mountain in Farak's Girdle, it felt crushed and sullen. The road was well supplied with fallen logs and encroaching saplings, and on top of that it was an awful day for any sort of travel. The air was treacle, buzzing insects pestered, crawling over sweat-soaked skin and making determined attempts to fly up her nose. The bay's tail flicked in constant punctuation to their progress and Medair spent half her time pulling at the collar of her greying shirt, which was sticking to her in the most uncomfortable manner imaginable. She made a note to cut her straggling hair, plastered with sweat past her nose and down the back of her neck. A year's untamed growth, when she'd once kept it almost daily trimmed.

Despite the circumstances and the heat, Medair was feeling almost cheerful. Her tentative decision to return to the cave where she had found the Horn was now a definite goal. Whether she would stay to sleep was another matter, something she doubted she could decide until she was there. But giving up the burden of lost hope which was hidden within her satchel was something she was certain was a good idea.

Late morning, and the bay's head suddenly came up, ears pricked forward. He stuttered to a halt and sidled sideways when Medair tried to urge him on, nearly dislodging her on a low branch. Pacifying him by agreeing not to go anywhere just yet, she stared along the overgrown road, wondering what had set him off, and spotted a dozen thin streamers of smoke dissipating in the muggy air to the north. Camp fires? A forest fire? It was big, but didn't seem to be getting any bigger.

She couldn't go back. Nor did she want to leave the road and risk getting completely turned around in the forest. It was important to get to Thrence quickly, so she could lose herself in the crowd and try to find a solution to the Decians' trace spell. The bay made his opinion clear by backing down the centre of the road.

Exasperated, Medair hauled out the silver ring again. Enough was enough. If it were an early summer fire, she needed to be past before it really caught. If it were more strangers, then she could always try and outrun them.

Under the control of the ring, the bay went forward, jerky and reluctant. By the time they were close enough for the smoke to be making her eyes sting, he was inching down the road, sweating and blowing. The ring gave him no choice but to go on, but his extreme resistance was making Medair wonder if going around might be the better option. It wasn't just burning wood she could smell. It was the rank, sickly odour of scorched meat.

Then she saw the bodies. A fat man dressed in comfortable robes lay on the road in a position which spoke eloquently of attempted flight. The back of his skull was a black depression. A short distance away lay an armswoman with a red snake insignia on her shield and flies rioting in the blood drying around her. Medair had seen death before. She had witnessed the slow defeat of the Palladian Empire, stood impotently on the sidelines of too many battles. Toward the end there had been heavy losses. Dead people still made her sick to the stomach.

Dismounting, she led the bay carefully around the bodies. His ears were flat back and his eyes showed white, but the ring held him. She wouldn't try its control by taking him directly toward whatever was up ahead. Instead, she led him off the right side of the road and made a short, arduous journey through the trees until the smoke streamers were behind them and the air untainted. Then, leaving her slightly less frantic horse securely tethered, Medair went back.

She had stumbled onto slaughter. There were bodies in all directions, centred around a circle of char about a hundred feet in diameter, intersecting with the road along one edge. It looked like a prelude to the Conflagration and had probably been burning merrily yesterday afternoon or evening while she slept at the roadside. It was fortunate that the fire had not spread far outside the blast area, or she would have woken to a more pressing problem than a fractious mount.

Dotted among the fallen trees and charred remains of shrubs were blackened lumps. Large ones for horses, smaller for people. Medair made a complete circuit of the ashes first, a cloth held over her face as she worked to keep her stomach under control. An adept had done this: killed so many so quickly. An adept of immense power, for the blast to have been so large, which likely meant an Ibisian. What had she stumbled into? What were the White Snakes planning now?

A pale, mask-like face turned to look at her out of every corner of her memory. She could almost hear that soft voice make some particularly hateful comment about unfounded assumptions.

Shaking distractions out of her head, Medair looked about for a key to this carnage. Half out of the circle of char lay a man wearing a familiar outfit of grey cloth and sturdy leather, no insignia visible. Bariback seemed to be infested with Decians. She had to force herself to check the body over for identification, but found only his hawk-nosed profile to proclaim his allegiance.

Reviewing the uncharred bodies, she found Decians, Kyledran guards, the badge of a merchanter house, and more snake-shielded fighters. Mercenaries. The mercenaries were probably connected to the merchants, hired swords. But here was another, this time with a silver horse on his shield. Very well, four or five distinct groups, out here in the middle of nowhere, fighting. Over what?

Being familiar with spells that exploded, although unable to cast them, Medair walked gingerly to the centre of the blackened ring and sighed through her teeth and the cloth which was wholly inadequate at blocking the stench. Fire was a dangerous weapon in close combat – it killed so indiscriminately sometimes even the caster fell.

Uncharred, a woman in a brown travelling dress lay crumpled atop a circle of green grass. She'd been wounded, Medair guessed, and her body hadn't been able to take the stress of the spectacular casting she'd released. It was hard to guess from her appearance, but Medair thought she might be linked to the mercenaries. She was too blonde to be a Decian and didn't seem to be a Kyledran official.

There was an inexplicably strong and distinct aura of power lingering about the fallen mage. Medair, investigating tentatively, discovered a purse tied to the woman's belt. She opened it and shook out onto her hand a cluster of faceted stones, clear with a tinge of yellow. Each was about the size of a pigeon's egg.

Disbelieving, Medair almost dropped them. This explained the span of the fire and was most likely the reason behind the battle, as well. Rahlstones. Not incredibly powerful in their own right, but they magnified a mage's power tenfold. Her eyes went to the dead woman's hand, clenched into a fist, and she carefully prised it open. Another clear stone. After a brief hesitation she added it to the rest.

A dozen rahlstones.

"Just what I didn't need to find," she muttered, surveying the carnage. These people had killed each other, almost certainly over the contents of the purse. None had survived to take the stones, but there would surely be many more eager to ride right over Medair to take possession. She wanted nothing to do with what could only be a major intrigue.

But it seemed stupid to leave them lying in this blackened clearing, so she dropped them into her satchel, where the power-shielding would hide their presence. A contribution to Kersym Bleak's collection, unless she found something more positive to do with them.

Turning to leave, she literally stumbled over a figure curled at the base of one of the smouldering trees. A boy of twelve or thirteen, only singed beneath a thick coating of ash. Alive.

Wide-eyed, Medair lifted him from the ashes and staggered out of the circle, checking for wounds and finding none. He was breathing steadily, but his temperature was high and he was obviously dehydrated. There was the scent of power about him, too. Not as obvious as the rahlstones, but a lingering suggestion of depth.

Except for that trace of power, he was not difficult to puzzle out, especially with the blue circles beneath his eyes and that temperature. The boy was a mage. Strong, since he'd been able to protect himself against the fire. In the brief moments between realizing what the brown-clad woman was casting and the set-spell being released, he must have drawn the sum of his strength up into a shield of pure power, the simplest and most exhaustive of magical manoeuvres. So now he was in spell shock, having overextended his considerable abilities.

Spell shock was not fatal, if you survived the actual casting. The boy would be weak and feverish and thirsty and would doubtless sleep a great deal over the next few days, but he would not die. Unless she left him out here in the ash, with a storm coming. She would not, of course, but she grumbled beneath her breath, mind on the five men who thought she must be valuable, none of whom were likely to cherish kind thoughts about her after she had stolen their horses. How far behind were they now? How much would this boy slow her down?

Medair was able to hook him over a shoulder and stagger back to the horse, where she pulled water skins from her satchel. The bay was grateful for the drink, but the boy only feebly swallowed without waking. He did not so much as move as she struggled to keep him slung across the bay's withers while she mounted. She didn't need a dependant, no matter how forlorn he looked, and would leave him at the first convenient village.

∽∾

Thunder accompanied her on the awkward ride which followed, and an early green-grey twilight descended. Then the rain arrived in force. At first the huge, heavy drops were a relief after the relentless humidity of the last couple of days. It quickly became an annoyance, then something to make the situation wholly miserable: riding through a forest on a mean-tempered, stolen horse, clutching a dirty, feverish little boy, and hunted by five killers.

Drenched and battered by the force of the downpour, vision obscured, she could think of nothing to do but travel on until she reached the ramshackle wayfarer's shelter she'd used on her way to the mountain. It couldn't be more than a mile or two, and she used the time to speculate about the boy's role in the battle. He was dressed in plain trousers and loose shirt. Perhaps he was a servant of the merchant, or even the son of the mage. When he had recovered she would at least be able to ask him what had happened. An exchange of the precious stones, interrupted by – one? two? – sets of thieves?

The current political situation was not particularly stable – or had not been in Autumn, when there had been talk of a trade war between Decia and Palladium. A dozen rahlstones would be a spectacular advantage if it came to war. Used together, a group of adepts could cut a swathe through enemy forces or maintain defensive spells against all but the most persistent attack. Their stock of rahlstones had been one of the things which had made it possible for the Ibisians to wage war against an entire Empire.

The shelter proved too small for the horse, but she was sure it would mind the rain less and, besides, it shouldn't have stood on her foot. Medair tended to the animal before the boy so she wouldn't have to venture back out into the rain and by the time she staggered inside with the tack she was shivering.

The single bedroll she had kept was soaked, but she made do with a pile of the many blankets she had stowed in her satchel. Stripping the boy, she dropped him on the pile beneath another blanket, then chanted her way through a fire charm, wishing she'd had the foresight to ready a few set-spells before being forced to flee Bariback Mountain. Finally, she started a watery vegetable stew and changed into dry clothes and considered the boy.

He sounded suitably alive, groaning and twitching as she wiped traces of ash from his face. She patted a streaked cheek consolingly. Not a particularly taking lad, with little chin and a nose which would be impressive when he was fully grown, but he'd survived that fire, so there must be something to him. When the stew was done and she had eaten, Medair eased him upright, and rested him against her chest. Time to try to coax him awake, enough to accept a spoonful of savoury liquid.

The role of nurse was new to her, and she was uncertain if she was doing all she should, but the boy's response to the stew was at least encouraging. He was sluggish and only half-awake, but if he could eat he mustn't be too deeply spell shocked. His skin was still fever-hot, but he did not drop immediately back to sleep. Blinking ponderously at the ceiling, he lay frowning at something, then focused on her when she sat back down.

"A few days abed and you'll be back on your feet," she told him. "You can rest properly at the next village along the road." And out of her fumbling hands, Thank Farak!

The sandy brows drew together as he blinked at her again. She wondered if he was short-sighted. "It's spell shock," she informed him, attempting a soothing tone. "Not too serious. Don't worry, you'll sleep it off before the week's out."

Definite perturbation. He turned his head to look at her better, then abruptly lifted a hand and held it over her face. Medair flinched instinctively, but he compensated, the base of his palm pressing against her chin, fingers splayed towards her brow. Before she could do or say anything there was a huge surge of arcane power and the boy said, "Take me to Athere," in a hoarse, barely audible voice. "As directly as convenient," he added, then sighed and passed out.

Medair gaped.

"You little *wretch*!" she gasped, not believing what had happened. A geas. He had put a geas on her. This scrawny, filthy, half-dead *scrap* of a boy had geased her!

Medair's vision swam with unaccustomed fury. It was a spell the White Snakes had introduced to Farakkan. They had geased their prisoners in droves, bound them with magic so the invaders need not fear the conquered. It had been in many ways a merciful approach, but Medair would never forget the frustrated impotence in the eyes of the people of Mishannon, the first Palladians bound not to harm Ibisians. One of them had described it as living with your heart in a cage.

Trembling with anger, she paced about the confines of the shelter, glaring at the grimy face above the matching grey blanket. A geas. The little rodent had geased her. Geased her!

Eventually, since the little rodent was now both defenceless and unconscious, she calmed down enough to sit sulkily on her own blanket, still glaring. There had to be a way out of this.

The geas had not been spur-of-the-moment. He had had it set, just waiting to spring on someone. Not an uncommon practice – many spells took too long in the casting to be useful, but they could be prepared, set, ready to be triggered, and would last up to a couple of weeks before they had to be renewed. She couldn't tell a great deal about the geas which he had placed on her, though she could feel the power of it like a snake coiling about her spine. She doubted it was as simple as the verbal command he had given. Very likely it had the usual clauses about not harming the caster and so forth, so she couldn't kill him to free herself and she could not break it. Medair was too minor a mage to even begin to cast such a spell, and the Empire had learned some hard lessons about how much stronger than the caster you needed to be to break a geas.

Despite her limited magical defences, she might have been able to withstand the geas if she'd guessed for one moment that he could or would cast such a spell. Instead, having nursed this viper back to relative health, he had surprised her with a bond she didn't have the ability to break.

Medair grimaced. Relative health indeed. He looked on his way to giving up the ghost. Most of the power for the geas would have been in the preparation, but what he had used in triggering it had obviously sent him close to the brink. Well, there wasn't anything she could do for him. He would die or he wouldn't and it would serve him right if he did!

After a further spate of glowering she pulled another blanket from her satchel and tucked him up more firmly. There was still a hint of power about him and, at this stage, she wouldn't be surprised if he had a whole sackful of tricks ready and waiting for unwary rescuers.

"A twelve year-old adept. My luck is running true to course." Medair stared out at the storm, which was now driving in through the door. With difficulty she shut out the weather, and carefully fed damp twigs into the fire to alleviate the gloom. Smoke lurked about the ceiling, but didn't grow too suffocating. Small mercies.

Medair wasn't particularly good at being angry, so she grew resigned instead, plotting her course to Palladium's capital on the map she kept in her head. The quickest route would be east from Thrence through Farash, but nothing was ever that simple. As Herald she had been used to travelling without bar or threat through an Empire where quarrels between duchies were settled in the Silver Court. Now Farakkan had broken into myriad little kingdoms clustered into alliances about four major realms: the Ibisian Palladium in the north-east, Decia to the south, Mymentia in the west and Ashencaere in the north-west. Kyledra, Lemmek and Farash enjoyed an uneasy existence in the centre of these four groups, battling not to be swallowed up or overrun in the hostilities between their powerful neighbours.

Strange to think of the once ardently loyal Duchy of Farash at odds with the Empire's heartland, but she'd found on her way to Bariback that the border between Farash and Palladium was not an easy one to cross. She doubted it would be any simpler on the way back, especially with a semi-conscious mage-child in her care and who knew how many different groups searching for someone with rahlstones.

Grumpily, Medair decided on a route north to the generally neutral Ashencaere, which had remained inward-looking since the fall of the Mersians – a kingdom far older than the Palladian Empire. There was nothing else to do but go to sleep. Resisting a geas once it had taken hold usually resulted in painful bouts of nausea, headaches, all manner of nasty maladies right up to total paralysis. If she didn't take the boy to Athere "as directly as convenient," she'd have cause to regret it. Fortunately the wording of the compulsion wasn't wholly unreasonable. She would not be forced to travel through the night until she dropped in exhaustion, but she doubted she would be given too long a grace period.

Nothing ever seemed to work according to her plans. She should stop making them.

Four

he boy was still alive, and even looked a little healthier, when dawn and dripping leaves woke Medair. He wasn't inclined to respond to her attempts to rouse him however, so she ate and cleared the shelter, then attempted the novel task of dressing an unconscious child in almost dry clothing. The weather had turned cool in the wake of the storm, so she kept a blanket out to wrap about him and, with an efficiency born from a desire to get the business over, had them underway while the air was still in the half-tones of very early morning.

It was awkward to go at speed with him cradled against her chest, and she experimented with various positions until noon, when they reached Nodding, a tiny village centred about a farm which had once been a Rynstar holding. Medair had established on her trip through in Autumn that there was no trace of her family home, and today she refused to be sidetracked into thinking about the fate of her mother and sister after the war.

With a few casual questions Medair learned that a great many people had headed into Bariback Forest recently, but none had returned. Nor was anyone interested in whether they did or not, so long as they didn't linger in Nodding. Fear of years-old plague made the villagers unwelcoming and she realised it would have been difficult to leave the boy in their care as she'd originally planned. She was not quite run out of town, but no encouragement was given for her to tarry. It was only when she was back on the horse that she realised that she'd talked with someone for the first time since Autumn. If nothing else, being geased had distracted her from her empty misery.

Thrence was at least another day's travel. Surely the geas would allow them a day there to rest and recover, so that the boy could ride his own horse? But then there were the Decians. Was Thrence big enough to hide her?

Mulling over alternatives, Medair was surprised by a curl of power emanating from her charge. He groaned, and raised his head. Really, he must be a phenomenal mage indeed. Spell shocked people were supposed to be days or weeks in recovering. Power would accrete to them only slowly and relapses were common if casting was attempted. He'd be mad to cast now.

The boy muttered something, lifting a hand. But not summoning power. Some sort of spell was disbanding, wearing thin through lack of renewal, like a set-spell. Not her geas, unfortunately. She reined in as he shifted against her chest. How many pre-set spells did this boy have on him?

"Bratling," she said, as he slid to the right, "stop wriggling about or you'll – "

Medair broke off, jaw dropping for what seemed the tenth time in the last few days. The boy was growing as she held him!

Having in moments gained considerable height and a mass of white hair, the boy – man – did as she had been warning and overbalanced them both. Medair impacted first, discovering wet stony ground. The man – the Ibisian – landed on top of her with a complete lack of grace, bruising those portions of her anatomy which had so far been neglected. Gasping for breath, she blinked through tearing eyes as a pale face wobbled before hers.

"Clumsy," said a wry, soft voice.

She hit him, landing a creditable right direct to his jaw. His head snapped back, then he collapsed again. On top of her, of course. Sobbing more than gasping now, Medair rolled him off her and struggled to sit up. She stared first at him, next down the road, then put her hands over her face and indulged in a brief but violent storm of tears.

It wasn't so much that the tiresome boy who had geased her had been a shape-changed Ibisian, or that he had fallen on her, or that they were both mud-coated in a puddle, or that her back appeared to be one hundred bruises, loosely joined together. Nor was it the sight of her mean-tempered steed galloping gleefully riderless down the road. Rather, it was that soft voice and the particular shape of this Ibisian's face. For a brief, anguished moment she had seen and heard Kier Ieskar and been caught between believing that she had gone mad and trying to comprehend how he, too, was living five hundred years after his death.

She'd first seen the Kier at the heart of the massive Ibisian encampment, in an elaborate tent; a palace of cloth. Its throne room had been large enough to hold two or even three dozen willowy Ibisians. They shimmered in silk of colourful if muted hues, and all seemed to have acres of straight white hair flowing down their backs. She had followed First Herald Kedy into the room, had been distracted by the height of the Ibisian nobles, then transfixed by the one who sat at their centre. Ieskar Cael las Saral-Ibis.

White on black, a striking image after the colourful sea of the court. Ebony birds with long necks and longer curved beaks had framed the head of the Kier, and he had sat as statue-still as those carvings. His slender hands had been curled over the end of the armrests of his throne, his white robe was arranged precisely about his feet, and that moonlight hair had been divided neatly into twin falls past his shoulders. There had been only three points of colour anywhere about the man: a single fiery stone hanging from his left ear, silver in his right, and pale blue eyes which cut straight through Medair's composure and left her awkwardly trailing in Kedy's wake instead of striding proudly forward on behalf of her Emperor.

They had made their bows and the Kier's response had been to lift one long finger a tiny fraction from the black wood of the throne: a minutely eloquent signal for Kedy to begin. If Medair's mentor had felt at all unnerved, he had given no hint of his discomfiture. That professional poise had been something Medair longed to own, continually attempted to emulate, but in that throne room of cloth she had felt it forever out of her reach.

Kier Ieskar had been much younger than Medair had expected, at least a year or two her junior, barely out of his teens. His hair had been waist-length, and cut to neatly frame a slightly pointed face. A small nose and precisely formed lips afforded him a hint of prettiness which was almost entirely lost beneath his eyes, ice-blue and penetrating. He had not moved at all as Kedy addressed him. He had listened in silence to the faithfully repeated message, and sent them away without a word.

Medair didn't know precisely what the Ibisian court discussed after hearing the Emperor's offer. She and Kedy were given an introductory language lesson, a meal, and had no intimation of how wrong things were going to go when they were brought back to the throne room.

Nothing had altered. The members of the court remained on either side of the entrance, allowing the Imperial Heralds unimpeded passage to the throne. If even Kier Ieskar's eyelids had changed position since they'd been dismissed, she'd not been able to tell it as they bowed before him. She had seen his chest move slightly, and taken a breath of her own in response. It felt very much as if it were an event for him to inhale.

"I have considered your Emperor's words," Kier Ieskar had said, speaking Parlance without the slightest trace of an accent. "It is an offer of great generosity, and does him honour. I will not do my people the disservice of accepting it. If there is a home for the Ibis-lar in this land, it is one which we must take by force of arms, not as a gift."

The Kier had a soft, very measured voice which effortlessly commanded attention. His announcement had been delivered with such tranquillity that it had taken Medair a moment before she understood the import of his words.

"In five days," Kier Ieskar had continued, as the world dropped out from beneath Medair, "we will march south. Those who do not stand against us will be spared. That is the answer I must give, in return for Grevain Corminevar's noble offer."

The man lying tangled in a blanket in the mud, his shirt shredded and his trousers split, was not Ieskar Cael las Saral-Ibis. In other circumstances, she would not have mistaken them, though there was resemblance enough to think them brothers. The voice had been the thing, that soft voice so like the long-dead Kier's. Ieskar had not often been wry – never while he sat upon the Ibis Throne – but sometimes, over the marrat games he had required her to attend, his voice would take on just the tone, the very inflection, this man had used. It was the most expression Medair had ever seen the immensely controlled Ibisian ruler allow himself.

Five centuries later, having stopped weeping soon after she started, Medair sat on wet, stony ground, knees held to her chest and studied the unconscious White Snake and the cloudless sky and the grass studded with flowers on the verge. The drifting seed of a dandelion caught her attention and she watched that until it had floated beyond sight. Then she listened to the lowing of cows, and birds calling beyond the field beside the road. Distantly, something clanked and she had the impression of voices. They must be near the next village. The horse, typically, had run back toward the mountain.

Rising to her feet, Medair began to walk: away from the forest and the horse and the White Snake. The day was beautiful, the sky washed clean by the storm, the air filled with birdsong. Bucolic bliss. Almost two hundred feet down the road, just after Medair turned a corner to discover a glimpse of buildings, the ever-increasing tightness in her chest became too much and she dropped to her knees, gasping. Spots fuzzed her vision and she wondered if she could be drowning in nothing but twisting coils of magic. She closed her eyes, trying to overcome the pain with hatred. White Snakes. The pale invaders. She would have no truck with them, would not aid one of their kind. Cold, arrogant, unforgiving Ibisian destroyers.

A pathetic and futile gesture. The geas was just as effective, whatever shape the caster wore. At least this explained the twelve year-old adept, which Medair had thought abominably precocious. Eventually, weary and calmer, she stood and wiped her hands on mud-smeared trousers. Sucking a bleeding knuckle, she walked back to where she had left the White Snake.

He looked worse than she felt, not even counting the rapidly darkening violet bruise she'd given his jaw. If the geas had punished her for that blow, she had been so busy hurting everywhere that she hadn't noticed. The circles beneath his eyes were equally striking, and he looked drawn and wasted. An unravelling transmogrification would have drawn on his reserves whether he willed it or not. And his reserves had to have been as good as empty. If she could overcome the geas, leave him in a ditch by the side of the road, he would probably die.

Deliberately, she turned her back on him. White Snake. She opened her satchel, found a water-skin, and emptied it over her head, trying to sluice off the mud. Clean clothes were the next step, pulled on hastily, though there was no-one in sight. She left the mud-caked garments abandoned. She would buy new ones. Somewhere on the way to Athere.

Slowly, she turned around.

Problem. Large, good-as-naked, unconscious man. White Snake. He might be willow slim, but six foot whatever was definitely not going to be as easy to handle as the undergrown boy he'd been pretending to be. With considerable distaste and just an edge of curiosity, she cut away the shirt and ruined trousers, then stopped to look. So it was true that Ibisians had a thick blue line running the length of their spines, a curiosity which had been the subject of much discussion in Athere during the war. She sternly tried to ignore the naked male factor and treat him as inconvenient cargo. Tried to ignore the way her skin crawled when she touched him. White Snake. His pubic hair was downy-fine corn silk.

He was incredibly dirty, mud completely overwhelming the last remnants of the layer of ash. Even if she'd had trousers which would fit him, she wouldn't have grubbied them by the association. Instead, she knotted the equally filthy blanket about his waist and draped another one over her shoulder before drawing a simple iron ring from her satchel. Medair and her bottomless bag of tricks. This was the third ring whose function she had discovered, and it had an unfortunate side-effect.

Knowing what was to come, she decided that she couldn't deal with him waking up. She glanced down the road toward the village, then drew a glyph on his soft, hairless cheek. Much better for his health if he has a long, uninterrupted sleep, she told herself – and the geas – piously as she chanted under her breath. And doesn't have to wonder how someone at least seven inches shorter than his six feet whatever could manage to pick him up with such apparent ease and set off at a trot down the road with him slung awkwardly over her shoulder.

Along with physical strength, the ring gave her an emotional buoyancy. Her problems became petty things, and what was important was that it was a glorious day. Having to deal with a White Snake was a minor matter, a trivial problem she'd soon have out of the way. She jogged along hoping to meet a traveller just to see the look of astonishment. The initial drunken recklessness which came with the strength was one of the reasons not to use the ring, but she couldn't say it worried her at the moment. Even the pain in her back had gone.

Hiding the Ibisian under a hedge outside the village, Medair walked in with a swagger and spent an unnecessarily long time haggling over the few riding animals available, merely because their owner had a fetching smile. Neither of the two she could convince them to spare were nearly fine enough to match her spirits.

She also bought some clothing to fit her burden, but did not dress him until she had found a horse trough to dump him in. The ring was handy for overcoming her distaste enough to scrub him thoroughly, until the water was polluted with mud. She laughed at the disgust of the yearlings which investigated the trough after she lugged her now slippery-wet Ibisian away to a bed of chewed clover.

He really was like Ieskar. Something wrong about the cheekbones, and the jaw was a touch stronger, but he possessed the Kier's small nose and there was only a slight variation of the precisely-cut mouth. Those white-lashed eyes would probably dominate his features as the Kier's had, if they were open. This man's long, delicately-boned hands were just as fine as those she had watched move marrat pieces over too many games, though the right lacked the thin scar across the back of the fingers. And, of course, he was tall and slender and pale. Ibisians simply didn't come in short, stocky or dark variations.

His hair was much longer than the Kier's had been, quite past his knees, though very damp and tangled at the moment, the drying strands like spun silk to the touch. Immensely impractical. She sorted it absently into a braid, wondering why this Ibisian adept had been masquerading as a Farakkian boy.

Athere was the last place Medair wanted to go, and certainly not in the company of an Ibisian. To be obliged to shepherd a man who reminded her of Kier Ieskar was a cruel twist. She had had too much of him.

When Herald Kedy had died during the early stages of the war, while the Ibisians had been taking Holt Harra and Laskia with an ease which was almost insulting, Medair had been the only envoy to the Ibisian court halfway fluent in the language. The Kier would not again condescend to speaking Parlance during official audiences, though he was perfectly capable of using the Imperial tongue when he wanted. Instead, he'd had one of his court, a woman named Selai las Dona, teach the Imperial Heralds Ibis-laran.

Medair's training had been tested to the limit listening to the Kier's exquisitely polite words of war, whatever language he delivered them in. It had been so much worse when Kier Ieskar had departed from the formality of his throne room and decided to play marrat with the Imperial Herald. He'd just summoned her one day, at the beginning of the first winter, and informed her that he would teach her the game.

Medair had lost count of the times she had matched with him during the months after the first stage of the invasion. Often the games had been completely silent, as they concentrated on the complex patterns of disks. Infrequently, Kier Ieskar would ask her a spate of questions on some facet of life in Farakkan, so that he could "know whom he must rule". Once, having observed that the Imperial Heralds wore different colours according to the kind of message they carried, he asked her what colour she would wear when she brought him words of surrender. She had managed a courteous reply even to this, unable as ever to read the thoughts behind his pale eyes. And silently prayed to Farak that she would never again wear anything but the mulberry-red of war in his presence.

She never had. Athere, betrayed by the West, was finally overwhelmed by the invaders, but Medair was not there to witness the defeat. Herald Jorlaise had carried out the formalities of surrender. Jorlaise had been the last person Medair had seen before heading north, rueful with the necessity of improving her Ibis-laran. "If anyone can pull this off it'll be you, Medair," she'd said. "You've always had the luck of a cat. We'll be waiting to hear from you."

Had Jorlaise thought of her as she'd stood before the Kier wearing black, delivering the words of surrender? Luck of a cat. Medair had seen too many cats starving on the street to see that as the compliment Jorlaise had obviously intended. Her luck to rescue a shape-changed Ibisian adept.

It was much more difficult to dress a damp, fully-grown man than it had been to deal with a dirty, undersized boy. His skin was very warm beneath her fingers, but she kept to business, trying to estimate the extent of his spell shock and puzzle out his role in the battle which had left so many dead. Tranced into deep sleep, he did not so much as stir.

His presence was doubtless something to do with the rahlstones. That made possibly six interested parties. Well, the rain would have washed away the physical traces of her foray through the charred circle in the woods, but there was always magic. More pursuers? She sighed, wondering if she could keep ahead of the Decians and whoever else without killing her charge.

This Ibisian was older than Ieskar had been. The Kier had been a mere twenty-one when he'd declared war on Palladium. And dying. She'd learned that on her visit to the new Athere; that he'd taken some sort of wound involved with the destruction of Sar-Ibis. He had been slowly failing all the time he'd been conquering Palladium, a fact which cast a new light on some of his comments over the marrat table. Dead by twenty-three.

Her helpless captor was nearer thirty, perhaps four years Medair's elder, though several centuries her junior. He looked about ready to expire at her feet. The lobes of his ears caught her attention and she silently counted the number of currently empty piercings which had been made to hold the earrings Ibisians used to signify rank. The right ear of every Ibisian she had ever seen sported decoration of some sort, for ornament or to signify ranks of magecraft. The second piercing in this man's right ear meant he was married.

It was the left ear which told her that he was an important Ibisian. There were six major gradations of rank below the current Kier and her heir. A Keriden, the lowest titled noble, would wear a single polished bloodstone; the next rank two, the next three. They were fixed to studs or dangled from silver chains according to the obscure dictates of fashion and taste. The fourth highest rank wore only one left earring, but of a stone they called tiger's eye rather than bloodstone. Medair had never seen a tiger, but it apparently had some resemblance to the banded gold-orange and black stone she knew as charlamine. The Kier had worn a single fire opal.

There was no further system to delineate differences of rank within rank. Children, spouses, anyone who could claim nobility without currently holding a title, wore a single piece of pale green jade. They were addressed with an honorific similar to "lord", and did not strictly outrank any other wearing jade. Only the Kierash, the son of the Kier who now sat the Silver Throne, was a titled heir and Medair understood that even he would still wear only the small carved piece of jade which proclaimed him 'of cold blood', as it was called. Ibisians placed a great deal of emphasis on the difference between one who held noble office and those related to that person. With three piercings, it was evident this man held a title. Either Kerikath or Keridahl, depending on whether he wore tiger's eye or bloodstone.

Fascinating as it was to be able to learn so much from an unconscious man, Medair would rather he still wore the shape of a boy. She would so much rather not have anything to do with Ibisians.

Would she have helped him, if she had found him in this form? Or left a white-skinned man to die in the ash? The Ibisians of this time had done her no harm, but it was impossible for her to divorce them from their ancestors. The idea of having to travel with a White Snake, all the way to Athere, made her sick to the stomach.

But the geas prevented her from abandoning him, and all she could do was get the journey over with. His change had made it necessary for the second horse, since it would be too cumbersome to try and ride double with an unconscious person bigger than herself. She had no wish to be dumped into every second puddle all the way to Thrence.

Manoeuvring him into a sitting position on the big grey, she wondered what people would think when they saw an unconscious Ibisian with his arms tied around his mount's neck. Kyledra was not officially hostile to Palladium, and she could not hope to get through Thrence without someone taking an interest. She'd have to find a place to rest and hope that after another night's sleep he'd be able to ride on his own.

Setting off at a spanking pace, she made the next town – a real town this time, not a cluster of buildings servicing surrounding farms – before dark. With a choice of two inns, she picked the one closest to the northern edge of the town, and asked the ostler and a stable boy to carry her friend upstairs, not making an attempt to explain his condition. They were not eager, and the silence which fell over the public room when he was carried through spoke its own story. Every eye was upon them as they mounted the stair. To Kyledra, Ibisians were a symbol of the threat of war.

As she had requested, there were two beds. Medair covered the Ibisian with a light blanket, and muttered a quick charm against infestation over both beds. Then she abandoned her boots, and took off the ring. And groaned.

She was not as spent as she would have been, attempting the day's feats without magical aid, but this particular item took a great deal out of her in compensation. Bruises whose presence she had entirely forgotten reminded her of their existence, but she was too tired to investigate them. Sliding the ring into her satchel and sealing it firmly, Medair climbed into the second bed, tucking her satchel between her shoulder and the wall. After punching the lumpy pillow, she grimaced across the darkening room to where the Ibisian was little more than the gleam of pale hair in the darkness. A White Snake. The sooner she was rid of him, the better.

Five

Waking to a thump and a headache, Medair squinted across the sunlit room. The White Snake had collapsed near the window and was attempting to lever himself to his feet with as much success as a turtle flipped on its back. Hating that this stranger had been moving about while she slept, she watched his silently determined attempts until the pain in her head intensified.

Sitting up allowed her to fully appreciate her bruises, but it was the geas which was punishing her with a headache. It must be nearing lunch, and the innkeep would probably be on the verge of throwing them out or demanding more money. This was not so bad a thing as the memory of five men in pursuit, who by now would doubtless have found transportation.

First she pulled the Ibisian to his feet and dropped him back on his bed, noticing that he'd successfully used the chamber pot before collapsing. Despite herself she felt a brief sympathy for his situation. It did not succeed in making her forget her headache, the geas, or her reasons to hate his kind, but did keep her tactfully silent in face of his weakness. Ignoring his attempt to steady himself upright, she splashed some water on her face, then sat down to push her feet into her boots and run a comb through her hair.

The Ibisian managed to prop himself against the wall while she cleaned up. When she next glanced at him, he was studying her. Grey eyes. Ieskar's had been an icy blue, but the different colour did not mar the resemblance. She had no doubt that he could, like the Kier, make a person incredibly uncomfortable simply by watching out of eyes which seemed to take in everything and give nothing back.

Resentment swelled, and she decided to put off conversation. Flipping the comb onto his tumbled blankets, she slung her satchel across her shoulder and went out to order them breakfast. A handful of the Decians' coins stopped the innkeep's complaints, and a few more were sufficient to arrange for the Ibisian to be carried down later.

In a foul mood which seemed likely to only get blacker, Medair checked the sparse midday crowd for potential trouble, then took up a tray to the Ibisian. He was sorting his tangled hair into a slightly less haphazard braid, but there was far too much of it for him to hope for more. She certainly wasn't going to groom him.

Putting the tray within his reach, Medair retired to her own bed, taking up a bowl containing steamed grain and slivers of meat. Chewing a brown shred, she watched him pick a long string of dark green out of the snarled braid and drop it to the floor.

"Water weed," he said, the soft voice neutral rather than wry this time. That only made it worse, even more like Ieskar's. "I am sure there is a reason for that." He gave up on his hair and took up the second bowl in a hand which shook, his every action exuding a fragile dignity.

"Horse trough," Medair explained, and found herself abruptly amused. Already she could see that the man was used to command and comfort both. Most adepts were, and this one – there were surely few people who could manage to be at so bedraggled a disadvantage and still appear in charge of his situation. Those grey eyes flashed up to meet hers, then he returned his attention to eating, apparently requiring all his concentration to not drop the bowl. The bruise she had given him stood out shockingly against that white skin.

A part of her wanted to fling out of the room again, to get away, to not have to deal with this at all. But the geas removed running away from her choices. Trying to force herself out of her sullen temper, Medair finished her own bowl while he was still only halfway through his. She had only once been spell shocked, and had been among friends while she recovered. That weakling helplessness would be hard to bear for an Ibisian adept, especially when health and safety depended on a total stranger who had no reason to be kind about things like dropped bowls of stew or the necessity of relieving neglected bladders. She was almost as glad as he must have been that she'd slept while he attended the chamber pot.

And he would only have had a few disjointed moments of consciousness since the fire. Waking to be fed and to geas her, and next on the road when she'd hit him. Now here. She wondered if he was surprised to still be alive.

Two men from the stables had been given the job of carrying him down, and she was relieved to see them before the Ibisian had quite finished his meal. She hardly felt inclined to small talk. The stablemen were no more enthusiastic and made little concession to Ibisian dignity as they got him to his horse. All that loosely braided hair swung as he struggled to remain in the saddle, and his face was particularly expressionless. Not at all used to being heaved about like a sack of rotted potatoes, or being unable to fend for himself. She kept a sharp eye on him as they rode out of the town, wondering how long it would be before he fell off.

"Ebbsy," he said, correctly identifying the town as they left it. It hadn't been a question, so she didn't bother to reply, only just controlling her reaction to that damnable voice. "We will need to press hard to reach Thrence today," he added.

Medair slowed her dun and looked at him. Grey eyes swung to meet hers and she noted that he was ready for an argument. And here she had been wondering how far she dared press him for speed, her mind on five men in leather.

"We'll get there well after dark on these nags," she replied, rigidly keeping an indifferent note in her own voice. "Would you like me to tie you to your saddle now, or after you've been flung into the mud a few times?"

Lashes momentarily veiled the pale eyes, then he smiled, throwing her completely off balance. She'd never seen Ieskar smile. The Kier's voice had changed inflection at times, but his face had been a stone mask which she had thought might crack rather than alter in any way. This man's slight, very natural smile was like waking up to a lime-green sky.

"Now," he said, in that unfortunate soft voice.

He was not Ieskar. Medair told herself that over and over again as she obediently stopped and, much to the interest of a passing farmer, tied the Ibisian's legs firmly in place. Accepting his statement that this was all which was needed, she took the reins of the grey, lengthened them and tied them to her own saddle. Then she looked up at him, feeling a pang of conscience. He was a White Snake, and he had geased her, and there were the Decians to worry about, but–

"Isn't two days to Thrence better than pushing yourself to the point where you might be bedridden for days?"

He studied her. Definitely used to command. Even though she was long-practiced at shrugging off that Ibisian air of superiority, she suddenly felt like an errant serving-maid who had asked her emperor why he had directed his last war so badly. She would wager her satchel that this man wore tiger's eye.

"I knew complete obedience without question was too good to be true," he said. The tone was perfectly grave, and Medair tried to decide if he was truly that arrogant, or if the White Snake was actually making a joke.

"Very unlikely, at least," she replied. "Though trying to interrogate someone when I've a geas-inspired headache would make me snappish, at the least."

"A necessary evil," he said, without any hint of apology. "I do not have time to be established in any villages. As for today – I have people I hope to catch in Thrence. They were meant to leave there this morning, if I did not communicate with them, but I suspect that they will have lingered. They, too, have their problems with unquestioning obedience." He paused. "It will be a bad day for me, yes. I might not be particularly lucid by nightfall. If I am not, go to an inn called the Caraway Seed, which is near the centre of Thrence. Ask for Jedda las Theomain and tell her 'the nest was robbed'. Repeat that back to me."

"Caraway Seed, Jedda las Theomain, nest was robbed," Medair repeated impatiently. She eyed him without favour. "There were Kyledran guards among the others. Could you be recognised and linked to whatever all that death was about?" She, too, could be sparing with the information she chose to give. So he thought someone else had made off with the rahlstones, did he? Well, they could bide a time in her satchel.

He started to shake his head, and stopped, holding himself still. The refusal to wince was typically Ibisian.

"There is no reason I would be connected with what happened in the forest," he said, subdued, she diagnosed, by a spinning headache. "But I could well be recognised and my condition would give rise to a good deal of unhealthy speculation. It cannot be helped."

Medair made a noise in her throat, then turned away. It was pointless questioning him. White Snakes never told you more than they wanted you to know.

"We'll buy you a hooded cloak somewhere," she said as she climbed back into the saddle. She didn't know who this man might be, how many might be chasing him, her, or the rahlstones, let alone what she could do to prevent the Decians from catching up to her. Her bag of tricks, unfortunately, did not contain anything to foil a trace spell. Well, that she knew. There was a great deal she'd left untouched, but now was not the moment to experiment.

Digging her heels into her mount's sides, Medair set them off at a slow canter towards the city which had risen from the ashes of her birthplace.

Medair's headache vanished as soon as they started out, but she was soon thoroughly sick of the chafing saddle. Her charge was unconscious by mid-afternoon and caused considerable interest among passers-by, even after she'd covered him with a hooded cloak. And the gates had been closed for the night long before they reached Thrence.

Banging on heavy wood only produced an exhortation to come back in the morning. Centuries ago, Medair would have called back: "Open in the name of the Emperor!" and the gatekeeper would have seen her Herald's garb and hastily let her in, but she now resorted to a small bribe to crack the gate. Money was an authority never overthrown, and she was glad to own it on arriving at The Caraway Seed, which proved to be a very large inn in the wealthiest section of town. When she rode into the well-lit yard, the stares of the ostler and attendant stable boys immediately made her aware of her much-neglected appearance. Not to mention the clod-hopping animal she was riding. She acted as if she hadn't noticed, sliding off the dun and handing the reins to the nearest stable boy.

"I'll be a moment, finding out whether this is the right place. If it is, they'll need oats and warm mash. It's been a long day."

The foyer was warm and clean, with stairs straight ahead and a dining room to the right. For a moment the squat, burly man who emerged from a back room looked inclined to send her straight back out the door. "May I help you?"

"I hope so," Medair replied. "I have a message – and a delivery – for a woman called Jedda las Theomain, who has been staying here. Is she still here?"

The man seemed puzzled by her voice, which was neither coarse nor uneducated. In fact, the faintly outdated way she had of speaking gave her a certain air of aristocracy. Or so she'd been told by a young man with bed on his mind. The accents of the highest nobility, he had assured her, not knowing that she had been on nodding terms with half the ruling families of the Empire, even before she became a Herald. And that she'd practically had to relearn Parlance on her return, because people insisted on pronouncing words in the strangest ways, besides mixing it freely with Ibis-laran. She'd found him trying to cut open her satchel the next morning and had thereafter not attempted to find oblivion in the arms of attractive men.

"Keris las Theomain does indeed extend us her patronage," said the innkeep briskly, apparently marking her down as a messenger. "I will pass on any deliveries."

"I'm afraid I have to talk to her myself. And her package is still out tied to the horse. She'll probably want to look at it before accepting delivery." She smiled, feeling quixotic. "I'll need a room for a couple of nights, by the way," she added, catching sight of a pale, silk-clad woman watching her from the stair. There would not be many White Snakes in Kyledra, so the odds were good that this woman was Jedda las Theomain herself.

"Ah..." She waited while he decided whether or not he wanted to have her lingering any longer than necessary. "Of course, madam," he said, apparently preferring to err on the side of caution. "One gold half-nedra per day for a three-room suite."

Dropping two gold coins in his palm, she informed him she'd be seeing to her horses. "And Keris las Theomain's package," she added, and told herself the situation wasn't funny. It felt so very strange to be dealing with *people* again. To be arranging meetings with White Snakes who didn't have the least idea who she was.

"–it *is!*" she heard a boy's voice insisting as she returned to the yard. She found the ostler and stable boys gathered around the grey mare. They all started and looked towards her with wide wary eyes, then towards the unconscious Ibisian. The hood was partly drawn back from his face.

"You can put the dun to," she told the ostler. This was beginning to turn into a farce. "We'll have to get him off before the grey can be stabled. Do you have a knife?"

Medair reached up and checked the adept's pulse, finding it faint but steady. She rubbed her fingers on her trousers, frowned at herself for feeling a need to wipe the Ibisian off, then looked toward her audience. "Did I not tell you to stable the dun?"

Two of the boys hastily led her mount away, but the ostler's fumbling for a knife was interrupted by movement at the doorway of the inn. Medair turned to face three people: a pair of Ibisian women, and one sandy-haired Farakkian man. Two of them had their hands on the hilts of swords, the third was the woman Medair had seen on the stair. The White Snake had apparently thought it best to muster reinforcements before joining Medair in the yard.

"I am Jedda Seht las Theomain," the woman said, jade in her ear and disdain in her eyes. "What is your message?"

Irritated, but not anxious to deliver even silly cryptic offerings before an audience, Medair settled for stepping to one side so that the group at the door could see the adept more clearly. The response was quite satisfactory.

"'*Lukar!*'" gasped the second woman, who was in her early twenties, her hair white-blonde and her skin tinted with too much colour to be pure Ibisian.

In an instant they were clustered about him, cutting him down. Medair waited patiently, keeping her nervous desire to flee under control as Jedda las Theomain had her escorted upstairs.

The White Snakes had engaged half the second floor. Inside the main suite were four other people, three Ibisian. Two were obviously servants. The third, an elegant youth in white silk, stared intently at the adept's still figure, then withdrew to stand near the window. He also wore jade in his ear, a tear-drop depending from a thin chain so long it almost brushed his shoulder. The last in the suite was a Farakkian woman, her flaming hair as startling as her clothing was subdued. A sword rested at one hip and she touched the hilt lightly, then stayed in the background, watching Medair.

The adept was taken away to the depths of the suite, while Medair was directed to a chair in the well-appointed sitting room, and set there to listen to people moving about behind closed doors. Travel-grimed and tired, stomach beginning to rumble audibly, Medair wondered just who "Lukar" was. These people were acting as if they'd found Farak herself tied to the back of the grey.

Eventually, Jedda las Theomain returned. She did not take a seat but stood examining Medair minutely. Medair compensated by staring back just as directly. Full-blood, as Medair guessed 'Lukar' and the youth by the window were. There weren't that many full-blood Ibisians left, she had found. You could usually tell mix-breed by the blond hair or the skin, which lost the precise paleness of a full Ibisian. This woman's eyes were blue, the jade in her left ear proclaimed nobility, a single silver in her right meant she was an adept, unmarried. Lady las Theomain – or, more correctly, Keris las Theomain. Keris for 'lady', Kerin for 'lord'.

"Tell me your message now," said the woman, not even clothing the order in the stark Ibisian courtesy which had made the invaders seem so bloodless.

"He said to say 'the nest was robbed'," Medair replied, stifling her resentment. Perhaps she might be released from the geas now that the Ibisian had a whole group of people to run after him. Behind her, someone cursed, but neither Medair nor Jedda las Theomain reacted.

"That was all? You are certain?"

Medair nodded slowly.

"Where did you find him?" asked the younger Ibisian woman, seating herself on a brocaded couch to Medair's left. Medair shifted her gaze, and found concern instead of hauteur. Part of this White Snake was Farakkian.

"Bariback Forest," she said, keeping herself factual. She'd known she'd be interrogated, and it was no good glowering at them. "I saw some smoke and went to investigate and found...a lot of dead people. A couple of different mercenary groups, Kyledrans, Decians, merchants. A blast of fire had taken out about a hundred feet of the forest. It looked like they'd been fighting before that, though, because I found bodies at the edge with battle injuries. Your adept was in the circle but unburnt. Spell shocked and wearing the form of a Kyledran boy. The shape-change wore off yesterday and he...obliged me to bring him here and tell you that."

"Your mishandling of him may cost him his life," las Theomain informed her in a cold yet absentminded voice. "He is not fit to travel."

Sweet, Medair thought, lifting a shoulder. "He wanted the speed. Something about people being due to leave this morning but having problems with obedience."

"Indeed?" Jedda las Theomain asked, her full attention shifting back to Medair. She lifted a hand and began speaking words for truth and binding. Medair hesitated, her fingers closing over the arm of the chair, but she didn't move. The spell could not force honesty from her, only indicate when she lied. And protesting might prompt them to lock her up somewhere.

"Did Co – did the Kerin say anything else of what had happened?" las Theomain asked.

"No."

"'The nest was robbed' – those are the only words he said?"

"That was the only message," Medair replied, putting all her effort into a display of being helpful. "Do you want me to repeat everything he said about going to Thrence and things like that?"

"No. He did not give anything to you? You spoke of a package."

"I meant the Kerin," Medair replied. "He didn't give me any packages. He didn't have anything on him to give, only the clothes he wore and they were shredded when he changed shape."

"I see." The woman produced a small purse, which she tossed to Medair. Catching it automatically, Medair felt the weight of metal. "Your word, if you please, that you will not speak of these events to anyone." When Medair did not immediately respond, the Keris made a small gesture of impatience. "Come, that is more, I am certain, than anything the Kerin promised you. Your word."

Medair lifted the corner of her mouth in an awry approximation of a smile. She hoped her fury didn't show. "Yes, it is certainly much more than anything the Kerin promised me," she said truthfully, and stood. "You have my word, Keris las Theomain, that I will not mention these events again unless you or the Kerin bids me otherwise. Good night, gracious ladies, kind sirs." After a painfully controlled bow, Medair walked out of the room. No-one tried to stop her. Apparently they thought her adequately dealt with.

It had been a long day. She was tired, her back ached abominably, and all she wanted was a bath, food and bed. And to shred Keris las Theomain to quivering gobbets of flesh for the insult she'd just dealt. Medair's jaw was clenched so tight it ached, and she found that her hand trembled when she opened the door of her room.

The White Snakes had judged her small indeed, she thought, standing before a mirror in her room. There were circles under her eyes, muddying the light tan she'd cultivated during the Spring. Her hair was tangled and needed a wash as much as a trim. Her clothes declared their heavy use and she supposed she must smell of sweat and trail-dirt. She'd never been a beauty, but she was tall and slender with delicate bones and pleasant features. As Herald, she'd always been particularly careful of her appearance, to the point her sister had claimed she'd grown vain, conceited. It was odd to see how dull and plain she looked after a Winter's neglect, and she forced herself to see what the White Snakes had: a scruffy little vagabond. Someone who might place gold over anything.

Medair sat down on the invitingly soft mattress and emptied the purse onto the coverlet. Fifteen gold coins. Not an incredibly large sum by today's costs. A fortune only to a dirt-scratcher. Why hadn't she thrown them back in Jedda las Theomain's face?

Because I wanted to leave, she told herself, and if I hadn't gone then, there would have been more questions, more truth spells.

Perhaps because I was too surprised.

With slow movements she pulled her satchel onto her lap, sent a questing hand inside, fingers closing briefly around the rahlstones before seeking another prize.

One of the satchel's many virtues was that you did not have to search about for things. If you knew what you wanted, it would come to hand as obediently as a well-trained falcon. Medair drew out two bulging leather purses and a small velvet bag.

From the largest purse she spilled out gold Imperiums. There were about four hundred and fifty coins. This was her unspent wage for the years she had served. Born to a wealthy family, she had never needed to draw on it. She selected a coin imprinted with the profile and crest of her Emperor, the man to whom she had given Oath, who had made her Herald. He had died from wounds before Athere had surrendered.

The second purse contained gemstones. These had been a gift from her mother, compensation of sorts for the fact that her elder sister would inherit the Rynstar lands and title. They were worth a great deal more than the coins. Not nearly so much as twelve rahlstones.

With delicate fingers Medair drew a badge from the velvet bag and touched its shining silver as reverently as she would the cheek of a new-born babe. The insignia of an Imperial Herald, once more precious to her than gold and jewels combined. Two crossed crescent moons: one etched with the same scroll which decorated her satchel, the other with the Corminevar triple crown.

Suddenly impatient with herself, Medair packed everything away, ordered a bath and scrubbed herself shiny clean. Dirt was an easy problem. Returning to the mirror, she inspected the bruises on her back. There were only eight, not thousands: small and dark purple. The bruise on her hip probably came from the Ibisian's knee. Another grudge to hold against him, along with her shoddy treatment here.

She needed to decide what to do with the rahlstones. There were certainly enough who appeared to want them, but who actually owned them? The Ibisians? The Kyledrans? The Decians? It seemed that the best thing she could do was work out who they belonged to and give them back. Not because her pride had been wounded when someone had paid her coin for aid freely given then forced from her. Not because of the geas, or her bruises, or because a White Snake had looked at her and seen the smallest thing she could construe. Just – because.

She could, Medair reckoned, safely leave the adept and his offensive friends alone for a day or so. Whoever he was, he could not possibly travel for at least that long without *really* risking his health, so the geas would surely not bother her. It would give her a chance to try and find out if anyone in Thrence was missing twelve rahlstones.

Tomorrow, she told herself, she would go shopping.

Six

With breakfast under her belt, and a chestnut gelding fresh from the markets on lead, Medair made her way to the centre of Thrence and a building all tricked out in vast columns and tremendous arches. In her time, mages had apprenticed to masters or attended the Circle in Athere. There had not been a truly formal system as there was now, with an Arcana House in nearly every large city: a mixture of teaching school, place of research and consulting chambers. Those who wanted to buy the services of an accomplished mage visited their local House and were assured of finding a competent practitioner. Kyledra was unlikely to boast the most powerful mages in Farakkan, but she hoped that there would be enough to serve her purpose.

Since she needed to see an adept and Medair had failed to make herself appear important before asking for an appointment, she had to wait quite a long time before being received. Her stomach was making faint suggestions about lunch by the time she was ushered down a high-vaulted, badly lit hallway. Her guide took her through brass-bound double doors into a large office piled high with manuscripts, curious items in cloudy glass jars and other mystical paraphernalia, most of which had more to do with impressing the credulous than any serious pursuit of the arcane. Here, an angular man sat behind a monstrous desk swept bare of any encumbrance, eyeing her over fingers steepled together. He was all in black and cadaverously thin, a beaked nose giving him a resemblance to some great carrion bird.

"Please be seated, Miss," he said, in a surprisingly pleasant voice, all smoke and molten honey. "I'm sorry you've been kept waiting so long. It's been a busy morning with much to-do. I am Adept an Selvar. How may I serve you?"

Warming to genuine courtesy, Medair smiled. "It's a two-fold problem," she began. "The first is a trace. I have reason to believe a trace was set on me some days ago. I'm not certain where the one who has set it is, precisely, but I would like to purchase a charm to obfuscate matters."

Dark eyes narrowed, but his voice lost none of its polite regard. "If the trace has already been established, it cannot be broken – not without interference with the caster."

"I understand that. But a well-away or something which will off-centre the trace, so that I cannot be precisely pinpointed – do you have anything of the sort available?"

"You are a mage, Miss...?"

"ar Corleaux. I have studied, but do not have the strength for most of the spells, unfortunately."

He nodded, still watching her with dark, probing eyes. "An invested spell is no little thing. Will not one of ordinary duration suffice?"

"Not really."

"Very well. You would like this immediately, I gather? It will not come cheaply."

Medair shrugged, dipped a hand into her pocket, and placed a sapphire on the desk. His brows rose. "As to the other task," Medair continued, placing a ruby beside the sapphire. "There is a geas on me. I would like it broken."

The Adept gazed at the two gems, which winked like mismatched eyes. He probably thought her a jewel thief, fleeing from justice. "Would you prefer gold instead?" she asked. "I carry gems, since they are so compact, but if they're not suitable I can arrange for coin."

"Not at all, Miss ar Corleaux. These are, in fact, more than generous." He reached out a long, bony arm and scooped the red and blue up. "I believe there is an invested spell of the type you desire in storage. If you will follow me, we will fetch it and then see about the geas."

With a certain amount of caution, Medair trailed him through the House. Her reward was a circle of malachite depending from a thin leather cord, which she immediately hung about her neck. Catching the Adept's eye, she found him smiling with full comprehension.

"It's not a perfect cure," he warned. "This would spread a trace focus out over perhaps a five-mile area, but only so long as the caster is not in your presence, whereupon the misdirection would become plainly obvious. Now we shall see to your geas. I will need much help, depending on the strength of the caster. Follow me."

He collected four women and two men, a couple of whom were in the middle of instructing. They invited their classes along, rather as if a geas-breaking were some rare and amusing game. They took her to a large empty room with a high roof and no windows, and Medair was directed to stand in the centre of a star chalked on the floor.

"The problem with the geas," said Adept an Selvar to the assembled audience, "is that it takes on a dimension which far outstrips the caster. Even if one of you –" he looked at the students with a humorous eye "– were somehow to successfully fumble out the casting, I doubt that I alone would be able to break it. I see you smile, whether with derision or disbelief, I do not care to speculate. But simply put, if I were to cast a geas, it would take at least three of me to break it, perhaps four. Thus I have gathered seven together and we shall overwhelm by force of numbers."

"Please, Sir," said one of the students, a snub-nosed youth with merry eyes. "What's the geas making her do?"

"Manners!" snapped one of the mages, cuffing the boy, which he bore with the grin of one who was willing to take the rough so long as he got what he wanted.

"Would assuaging young Bartley's curiosity be too much to ask, Miss ar Corleaux?" an Selvar asked.

Medair summoned a light-hearted amusement she did not truly feel. "Oh, it's ensuring that I don't spend two nights in a row in the same bed," she said, to the amazed delight of the youngsters. "By forcing me to travel almost continuously," she added. "I wouldn't be overly surprised if I were in the Korgan Lands by the end of Summer, the rate I'm going."

She laughed with them, as the mages each took up a position at the points of the star. Then she sent a silent prayer to Farak. This would work, and she would be free to go her own way.

"Now we shall test the mettle of the geas' caster," said an Selvar. "The first step is to make the power of the spell visible. This is a standard task, but you might wish to watch how we begin melding our power as we perform it. Miss ar Corleaux, it would be best if you left the charm I gave you outside the star."

Medair removed the necklace and deposited it and her satchel over a chalked line. She watched with interest and admiration as they smoothly opened a flow of power between each point of the star. It was a delicate task, this melding. She had seen it often fail, but these six performed the feat with ease, and soon she began to glow. The geas manifested not as the snake she had imagined coiled about her spine, but as a network of silvery lines beneath her skin, patterned like veins.

"Now, a geas can be badly cast in numerous ways," an Selvar continued. "It could be poorly 'claused', as we call it, allowing the 'chanted person to merely perform the letter of the task and not the spirit. It could even allow the 'chanted person to kill the caster, which would be unfortunate – from the caster's point of view. It could be sloppily set, but as we can see, this geas has hold of Miss ar Corleaux very thoroughly indeed and I assume, since she needs it broken, that she has not been able to escape the punitive effects. What we will do now is simply pull the power out, as if we were uprooting a weed. The question is how extensive is the root system and whether we are strong enough to pull it up. It is always best to use more magi than is likely needed in a geas-breaking, so that much energy is not expended to no profit." The adept smiled at Medair. "This won't hurt," he promised, then signalled to the other mages.

It was fascinating to watch. Lines of force erupted from the six mages as they began a low-voiced chant. The power lines curled about Medair, then attached themselves to the silver beneath her skin, which began to lift out of her flesh. It was a curious sensation, a little as if someone were pulling out hairs all over her body, but, as promised, without pain. The magi gradually increased the pull and she watched their faces, noting that concentration had turned to a more intense effort. The pull on her decreased and she felt distinctly lop-sided.

Then the lines of force snapped. Medair staggered, pain blooming behind her eyes, and she lifted a hand even as two of the magi fell over. The audience burst into noise, a confused babble of surprise. Covering her eyes, Medair saw wriggling lights and tried to block it all out.

A touch at her elbow preceded Adept an Selvar's warm voice. "I am sorry, Miss ar Corleaux," he said. "Whoever placed this geas on you is obviously an adept of great power – probably one of the most powerful. We cannot break it."

Medair fought the throbbing which seemed intent on bursting her head and, after a sentence or two more, an Selvar evidently realised that she was barely taking in what he was saying. He led her to a cool dark room where there was a couch she could rest upon. A damp cloth was laid on her forehead and he silently withdrew, leaving her to struggle with pain and frustration.

The ache did fade, becoming little more than a dull memory, but the disappointment remained. She was stuck with it. Geas, going to Athere. White Snakes.

※

As soon as she was able, Medair left the couch. Sitting around reflecting on the setback would only depress her further. Adept an Selvar was in the next room talking to a pale, exhausted pair of mages. He immediately suggested lunch.

"I'm sorry to have been of so little help to you, Miss ar Corleaux," he said apologetically over a glass of very good ginger wine. "We will, of course, refund your fee."

Medair shook her head, still moving cautiously. "The payment is for the effort, which I'd wager was more than you had bargained for. You may have had a busy morning, but I think I've ruined your afternoon for you."

He nodded in acceptance, since Medair's geas had effectively exhausted the seven best mages in Kyledra's Arcana House. "I am concerned for you – does this geas truly make you travel continuously? What will become of you if it is not broken?"

"It's not so awful as that. The geas wasn't designed to harm me, merely to cater to someone else's convenience. There's a set destination and the geas will leave me when I reach it. It's simply tiresome to be going to a place I hadn't intended to visit. Perhaps, in the next large city I reach, I will be able to try with more mages."

"I would recommend ten." He gave her a delicate look. "In all Farakkan there are perhaps seven people strong enough to have cast that geas, unless I have been giving far less of my attention to such matters than I should. I do not wish to pry, but I would very much like to hear your story."

Toying with her glass, Medair hid a grimace. She liked this man and would be glad to have a long and frank discussion with him about a certain bag of rahlstones and exactly what the Kyledran involvement with the battle for them might be. But she couldn't outright ask strangers about a fortune in rahlstones she'd found in the forest. Not if she wanted to survive the week.

"I'm afraid I've been constrained not to tell people about it," she replied, regretfully, wondering if there was a subtle way to ask questions about rahlstones. "Nor would I be able to enlighten you particularly. I stumbled across a stranger and he put a geas on me to – to deliver a message. I don't even know what his name is. Who are the seven people powerful enough to have created this geas?"

"Was it in Kyledra?" an Selvar asked, then raised his hands in negation. "I'm sorry. I know that if you try to answer against a geas, things could become very unpleasant for you. It's merely that something has been happening in Kyledra which people seem to be trying to hide and I spent half the morning talking myself hoarse at the palace, to no good effect. If you've been caught up in the same business, perhaps you might be able to help me."

"Happening how?"

"I only wish I knew. An associate of mine – an adept of Arcana House – was called on by the Crown almost two weeks ago. They told him very little of what they wanted – something about smugglers, it seemed, or border taxes. A very confused and frankly odd story they gave him. But he went with them, and was overdue back yesterday. Now I can't get a straight word out of the palace, for all it's buzzing like a nest of hornets."

"Well, I haven't been geased to smuggle anything. Was your associate powerful enough to be the adept who geased me, by any chance? I didn't think he was Kyledran."

"No, that could not have been Hendist. He hasn't even sent me a wend-whisper, yet he knows I must arrange for someone to take his classes if he does not return soon."

"It doesn't sound good."

"No."

With just one of the rahlstones, an Selvar might be able to break the geas. But would he feel inclined to keep the stones secret? Even if he knew nothing about them at the moment, his ties to the palace might oblige him to report her. It was too risky to ask.

"Such deep thoughts."

"I was thinking of ways around this geas," Medair replied. "Who are these seven most powerful adepts?"

"It seems we can narrow the field to four, since your adept is, apparently, male. There is Vale an Sensashen, currently in Ashencaere. He is known for an uncertain temper and a delight in meddling with politics. Some Mersian blood. Three who are varying degrees Ibisian. Kemm ar Morgallan, who lives in Westerland and who is a great peacemaker among those fractious lands. Illukar las Cor-Ibis – I would suggest twelve magi, if it were he. And Senegar las Tholmadrae, whom I had heard from rumour was travelling in Farash, very near. There is also the Palladian prince, of course. There is no doubt that he has the power – his mother is one of the seven – but he is young and a geas takes a deal of skill and learning. Does this help you at all?"

Medair nodded, having identified "Lukar". Why the name sounded doubly familiar she was not certain, chasing errant memory. The 'Ibis' in his name indicated that he was, not surprisingly, of the royal bloodline. She had expected that, with the resemblance. He could not be a direct descendant of Ieskar however, for she was certain there was no Farakkian blood in him.

Was that true? If Ieskar's child had bred only with Ibisians, surely the Farakkian blood would be so weak as to be undetectable by now? She shivered, disliking the thought of associating with a descendant of Ieskar. Where had she heard the name Illukar before?

"I know his name, now," she told an Selvar. "I wish I could help you in return, but there is a great deal I think it would not be wise for me to say, even if I were not prevented."

"I'm sorry I cannot help you more."

Collecting her new horse, Medair spent the rest of the day shopping, keeping an ear out for tales of rahlstones with no success. Even the barber had nothing more interesting to talk of than the Spring markets and some upcoming races as he trimmed ragged edges and scraped her hair neatly back into a black riband. Still longer than she was used to, but she did not at the moment want to wear it the way she had during the war. That Medair seemed so young and out of place.

Most of her shopping was for clothes. The richer fashions seemed to be heavily influenced by Ibisian robes; all silks, layers and subtle patterns and nothing Medair wanted to wear. She eventually found a simple dress of dark blue which at least resembled the clothing she was used to wearing on formal occasions. It was easier to replace her everyday garb. Long-sleeved shirts of different colours, close-fitting trousers, jackets which were not too different from those she was comfortable with. They might not proclaim her ancestry, but she no longer looked scruffy and out of place as she rode once more into the yard of the Caraway Seed. Her satchel was all she retained from that morning.

The stable hand was more confused by her change of horse, since her new animal was worth infinitely more than the two sorry nags which had brought her to Thrence. When she walked through the front door, even the innkeep seemed unsure if she was the same person. Then he looked at her with obvious relief. Medair ignored him, but was aware of a small, spiteful pleasure. Illukar las Cor-Ibis must have regained consciousness and asked after her. That possibility had been part of the reason she had spent so long browsing the offerings of Thrence's markets. After yesterday's insults, she was not inclined to make life easier for Ibisians.

Wondering when she had developed this inclination to be vindictive, Medair made her way into the dining room. Thanks to her satchel, she didn't even have to take her shopping upstairs. Most heralds ended up with their entire lives in their satchels, as she had been warned when she was presented with the deceptively simple leather case. Not in itself a bad thing, since she could always cast a trace on the satchel, but there were risks. There had been occasions in the past when satchels had been stolen by those anxious to get at some official document. Thefts usually ended up with the stolen bags and their contents being destroyed in an effort to break them open.

Medair started her meal with a masterpiece of lamb in black nut sauce, which made her sincerely regret living for half a year on her own cooking and scant supplies. She was close to finished when Jedda las Theomain and the two other Ibisian Kerise arrived, las Theomain regal in rose and blue, while dragonflies shimmered in the youth's white silks. The girl was probably of lesser status, her robe muted and not costly. She had been wearing sword, shirt and trousers the previous evening and Medair noticed that this new outfit had been cut to allow easy access to a weapon belted beneath the open front of the robe. The other two were unarmed.

Medair carved a sliver of lamb, savouring the bitter delicacy of the sauce. Then, timing their arrival, she laid her utensils cross-ways on the edge of the plate. "Keris las Theomain. Have you come to join me?"

"No," the Keris replied, indifferent to any slight Medair could offer. "You are required upstairs."

Quite a beautiful woman, with intelligent eyes, but no diplomat. The youth was most likely related to Cor-Ibis, a resemblance Medair had not remarked before became more obvious when he wore the same expression of thoughtful consideration on his more handsome features. The part-Ibisian girl was wary, troubled.

"Whatever for?" Medair asked.

"This is not an occasion for questions. Come with us now."

It had been a long time since Medair had reason or inclination to snub someone, but yesterday had woken pride half-forgotten, and Heralds knew how to be insulting.

"Madam," she said. "I am sure I do not know why I should be obliged to obey your commands. Allow me to inform you that I find you abominably rude."

A spark of sudden delight leapt into the eyes of the Kerin in figured white. He was apparently not a friend to Jedda las Theomain. Medair, reminded that there was a great deal she did not know, made an effort to swallow her anger.

"However," she said, on a slightly less austere note, "if you would care to sit down with me until I am finished, then I may consent to joining you after. As it is, you are keeping me from dinner."

If Keris las Theomain had taken a seat and offered, if not an apology, some acknowledgment that Medair was not a serving-girl, she would certainly have endeared herself more than she did by coldly saying: "Bring her," to the girl before walking away. It was an entirely futile command to give in Kyledra, where an Ibisian trying to force a Farakkian anywhere would create more problems than they solved.

Medair watched Jedda las Theomain's departure, then shifted her attention to the young Keris and Kerin. The youth was still smiling, and the girl had erased any expression, but they could not hide a certain tension. Obviously now aware that Medair was someone to whom they already owed a debt. She wondered if they'd follow Jedda las Theomain's lead and depart from the strict Ibisian codes of courtesy.

"Are you going to drag me upstairs now?" she asked, and felt sorry when the girl flushed: a delicate pink colour which made her seem more Farakkian. "No. Sit down," she said when they would have made denials.

She gestured at chairs and waited while they sat. It gave her a brief sense of being in control, and an opportunity to decide what tack to take. These were people she would be associating with until Athere. She might try to remember that, instead of just damning them as White Snakes.

"I suppose Keris las Theomain is a bad enemy to make?" Medair asked, with less bite.

"She can be inopportune," the youth replied. "Allow me to make introductions, in the hopes that we do not all end up at odds. This is Ileaha Teán las Goranum and I am Avahn Jaruhl las Cor-Ibis."

"Medair ar Corleaux," Medair replied, resigned to the reaction she knew would follow. After a moment of shock, Avahn las Cor-Ibis laughed aloud, while Ileaha las Goranum looked first disconcerted, then disbelieving, then guarded.

"A Medarist!" The Kerin had just wit enough to keep his voice down. "Oh, too rich! A Medarist geased to assist Cor-Ibis! What splendid irony. I am very glad I came now."

More ironic than you could guess, Medair thought, but only waited out his laughter. She had not been fool enough to introduce herself as Medair an Rynstar since that first village, had since used the family name of the father who had never given her the right of claim. But she would not name herself other than Medair.

"I'm glad you enjoy the joke, Kerin las Cor-Ibis," she said, struggling to keep her even tone. "I'm almost sorry to tell you that the name is merely one my mother gave me and no reflection of my political beliefs."

The girl called Ileaha remained doubtful, but Avahn las Cor-Ibis shrugged and made a smiling gesture as if he was disappointed, but did not disbelieve. Medarists, after all, did not deny their cause.

Medair had been annoyed, then angry, when Medarists had been explained to her. It was not so much that a group of loyalists to the old Empire had decided to use her name as some sort of banner. It was that they were such fools.

A little less than five centuries ago, with its heartland conquered by arrogant White Snakes, the shattered Empire had turned the name Medair an Rynstar into a legend, into a myth. It had somehow become widely known that she was questing for the Horn of Farak and, hope of the slimmest sort, the conquered Imperials clung to the belief that she would return and summon an army to drive out the invaders. Her name became a talisman and there were many ballads which depicted her as some sort of sword-wielding hero, or, at least, someone mystically significant. This Medair could shrug off, embarrassed as it made her.

The Medarist movement had begun several centuries into Ibisian rule. Someone had had the bright idea of adding the name Medair to her own, and trying to raise an army. She hadn't succeeded, but she set an example for a stubborn core of resentment in Palladium, struck a chord with those to whom the Ibisians would always be invaders, no matter how many centuries they had dwelled in Farakkan.

The dry facts of the Medarists were something Medair had learned in Athere. It had explained a great deal, for her entire journey from the north had been doubly marred by the reaction to her name. In Morning High, that first village, she'd introduced herself as Medair an Rynstar and been treated as a madwoman. And she *had* been half mad with grief, till they'd tried to lock her up. But it wasn't until the border town of Burradge that she'd discovered why the name 'Medair' alone would provoke such repulsion. It had been incomprehensible to her, the way strangers would stare at her, disbelieving, when she said she was called Medair. Vendors would suddenly refuse to sell to her, and children were hurried out of her way. She'd even been turned out of an inn, before she'd learned to keep her mouth shut.

In Burradge she'd sent a too-persistent admirer on his way by finally answering when he asked what he could call her. He'd let her be, with the alacrity with which she was becoming familiar. And Medair, returning to her inn, had found a young woman blocking her way along an alley.

"Medair?" the woman had said.

"Yes?"

The wary note in Medair's voice must have been expected. The woman had smiled and stepped forward, a hand outstretched.

"Welcome sister," she'd said, gripping Medair's hand firmly. "You come in good time."

"Thank you," Medair had replied, more than a little blankly. She'd become aware that they were not alone in the alley, that another two people stood behind the woman, and more were behind Medair. "In time?"

"Amelda an Vestal, who holds the Braesing Reserve under Empire Right, is planning to wed into the las Dormednar line," the woman had said, to Medair's complete confusion. "We are too readily known in Burradge to venture into the wedding feast, but the cause would be well-served if you would take on the task. We have a charm prepared, which will make the bride's hands run with her own blood, if only it can be got to her at the feast."

The lengthening silence which had followed that little speech was one of those things which would always be imprinted on Medair's memory. It had been a cool night. The wind had whisked at her throat, and she'd heard a dog bark in the distance as she searched her mind vainly for something to say to the woman. And, after weeks fixated on loss and a blind determination to reach Athere, all Medair had managed was: "I think you must think I'm someone else."

"You said you took the name Medair!" the woman had said, recoiling as much in shock as anger.

"My name *is* Medair," she'd protested. "But I don't know what that has to do with this wedding. I've never heard of these people." Memory of the note of pleading in her voice still made her writhe.

"A Hand's heir taking a White Snake and you don't know what that has to do with one named Medair?"

They had pressed forward, but Medair had simply said: "No."

"How *dare* you!" the woman had spat then, only intensifying Medair's confusion. "How *dare* you claim Her name, and turn your back on Her cause. Can you tell me that your name is Medair, and yet you don't yearn to see every White Snake dead and gone?!"

The stupid thing was, Medair's answer to that question would not have been 'no'. They hadn't waited to hear what she would say, had started forward with fists and heavy boots. Medair was a stranger to combat, and without the strength ring she might never have left that alley. She'd been bruised for weeks after.

Quelled. That's what she'd felt when she found an explanation for what had happened. Five hundred years into Ibisian rule there were groups where women called themselves Medair and men Medain. They lived violent and uncomfortable lives, spitting in the faces of White Snakes and letting the world know they thought that all Ibisians should be cast out, that the people – the Farakkian people – should rise up. That none of Ibisian blood should be tolerated to live.

Medarists aped some of the codes of the Heralds and forever spouted their fury in the name of Medair an Rynstar. As if she had somehow founded their order. They usurped both her name and history and talked constantly of the stories of how Medair an Rynstar would be reborn and would lead a war to drive the White Snakes out. And, much as Medair hated Ibisians, the idea revolted her.

Certainly she would have done anything to prevent the invasion, perhaps rebelled against Ibisian rule in those early years, when they had still *been* invaders. But, considering that it was sometimes impossible to tell if a person had Ibisian ancestry or was merely tall and pale, she thought it the height of idiocy to go around saying that all of Ibisian blood were evil and deserved to die, and to beat people in back alleys because their hair was white-blonde. Or because they introduced themselves as Medair. The Medarists were one of the reasons she'd retreated to Bariback.

"You should consider changing your name," Avahn las Cor-Ibis told her, still full of laughter and not in the least off-put by her stiff face and eyes full of painful memories. She blinked away the past and looked at him. How very different from any other White Snake she had met, this youth. How, she wondered, did that flippant attitude go with the remnants of such a strict and formal culture? He was even wearing white, a shade which had been reserved for the Kier alone in her time.

"I'm afraid that I've grown attached to it," she said, managing to shrug. "It's only a bother when I travel, since my home lacks both Medarists and people who don't know me well enough to not know my beliefs."

"You must live in a very small town," Avahn said, dubiously. Medair knew she was behaving in a contradictory manner, sometimes poised and sophisticated, and by the next turn haunted and hostile. She told herself sternly that she would do well not to arouse their suspicions further.

"I settled in a very under populated area," she said, striving for neutrality. Wanting to move the conversation along, she looked at the mix-blood woman. "I can guess where you are supposed to bring me and why," she said, "but perhaps I am wrong?"

Avahn chuckled, returning her attention to him. "You played the innocent well," he commented. "It was something to watch the inimitable Jedda's face when Cor-Ibis told her to fetch you. She dug herself in so nicely too, going on to say you'd been paid off adequately, that she'd made certain you knew nothing of import and that your word had been extracted not to speak of the matter. Neatly trapped. I compliment you."

"I didn't set out to trap Keris las Theomain," Medair replied. "She achieved that on her own. I did abet her, however, and I wonder if that might have been a mistake." Ileaha las Goranum had grown only more subdued during the discussion. "The Keris has no authority over me and I am in no demesne of hers. I will not be the one suffering the consequences of going against her will."

"The Keris can give cause to regret," the girl agreed tonelessly.

"Oh, show some backbone, Ileaha!" Avahn said, impatiently. He obviously knew more about whatever weighed on the girl, but spared it little regard. "The lovely Jedda is hardly of concern now that Cor-Ibis is back with us."

"You think not?"

The girl had the blood to match that ornament of jade, Medair decided. No-one without *some* breeding and background could manage quite that note of contempt. The youth felt it and looked annoyed, then cooled, and began acting a good deal more like a proper Ibisian.

"The matter is of little import," he said, and deliberately turned away from Ileaha. "Kel ar Corleaux," he continued, awarding her the form of address suitable for commoners. "My cousin wishes speech with you. He was asleep when word came of your return, so you need not hurry your meal. Keris las Goranum will, I hope, be capable of escorting you when you have done." He rose and bowed exquisitely to Medair, not at all to Ileaha, and left. Very much on his dignity.

There was a short silence while Medair continued eating and Ileaha played with the edge of the tablecloth. "What is Cor-Ibis' title?" Medair asked when she was finished. She was feeling more in control of herself now, able to think about what to do next.

Ileaha looked at her, not quite startled. "You do not know?"

"He didn't introduce himself," Medair replied. "And Keris las Theomain took pains, last night, to be vague about his identity. A stupid thing, since the stable hands seemed to know who he was and would be happier than I to spread the tale. The way his cousin referred to him made it obvious that he is head of that family."

'las' meant 'of the line' and was only dropped from reference when the person was the active controller of the line, title and fortunes of the family.

"He did not know even your name," Ileaha replied, fencing.

"I didn't introduce myself either. Considering his first words to me consisted of a geas, I can surely be forgiven for feeling less than friendly. Being drawn out of my way for something which, from the body count, looks to be more than dangerous, does little to put me in a good humour. Without even an explanation, which I suppose you would not supply if I asked."

"Better not," Ileaha replied, and allowed the silence to stretch before answering. "He is Illukar Síahn las Cor-Ibis, Keridahl Avec."

High Lord Right of the Cold Blood. Medair had always found Ibisian titles clumsy in translation. Kier was a title which meant Highest 'Ruler' more than High King, since the word was not specific to a gender. Keridahl was High Lord, something similar to a Duke. Avec was an extra title awarded to only one Keridahl at a time. The man was the current Kier's second most favoured lord. She had guessed the Keridahl, from those absent earrings, but not the Avec.

Medair, after a short pause, recited: "Keriel, Kerivor, Kerikath, Kerikal, Keriden, Keridahl, Keridahl Avec, Keridahl Alar, Kierash, Kier."

"And AlKier," Ileaha finished, softly.

"That I've never quite understood, this idea of a Ruler of All. Farak does not rule, she provides, nurtures."

Ileaha shook her head. "Worship of the land. It is –" She paused. "Probably it is best not to become embroiled in a discussion about the AlKier or your land which provides."

"No," Medair agreed, studying the girl. Farakkian and Ibisian both – there had been none of her kind during the war. "Who are you? A name tells so little."

"Your name is one which usually tells everything."

Medair would not be drawn. "My misfortune."

"I am one of Cor-Ibis' wards."

"One? He has many?"

"A half-dozen. He is Cor-Ibis. Dependants are inevitable."

"You don't seem a child. How long do you remain a ward?" This girl was at least twenty, which was the Ibisian majority.

"I am no longer in care," Ileaha replied carefully. "But, being without family, a suitable trade, or sufficient property, I am not quite disposed of."

The traditional poor relation. "So...the Keridahl Avec, Illukar las Cor-Ibis, travels to Kyledra with a cousin, an ex-ward, a singularly impolite woman, a couple of Farakkians and remarkably few servants. He settles them in an inn in Thrence, shape-changes into a Farakkian child and somehow ends up spell shocked at the site of a battle in Bariback Forest, an area essentially underpopulated and dull, too far west of the Lemmek Pass to be of interest even to the merchants who died there, let alone the Kyledran Kingsmen, various mercenaries and oddly dressed Decians. And I see you're not going to tell me what it's all about."

The girl shook her head, mutely.

"Very well, then. Who is this Jedda las Theomain, who seems to be in charge of Cor-Ibis' people? She's an adept, isn't she? Don't tell me she's another ex-ward or cousin? His wife?" No, las Theomain had not had a second piercing in her right ear.

After a pause, the girl replied carefully: "Keris las Theomain is an adept, yes. Her family head is Keriel Theomain. The Keris is strong in arcane power, more so than most, and has made a name for herself acting on the Kier's behalf and as a close friend of the

Kier. She is not in charge of Cor-Ibis' people, but had authority in his absence."

Medair decided to pry. "Over you in particular?"

Ileaha was inspecting the tablecloth again. "I believe Keridahl Cor-Ibis has discussed the possibility of my being given into service to Keris las Theomain as secretary. I have a small amount of mage skill, which would be useful to an adept."

"Someone for her to snap orders at?" Medair interpreted. "Couldn't you serve the Keridahl in that capacity, if you must serve? Or is the carefully dressed cousin already filling the role?"

"Kerin Avahn is Cor-Ibis' heir," Ileaha replied, again startled at Medair's ignorance. A frown came into her eyes and she closed her teeth on whatever she had been about to say. It was apparent she did not approve of Avahn. Something to remember.

Medair drained her glass and stood.

"Well, shall we go and see if your ex-guardian has woken up? I assume Keris las Theomain has not gone to rouse him expressly for the purpose of telling him I have no manners."

"You did not display such self-command yesterday," Ileaha commented.

"I was tired, yesterday, and I knew it was unlikely that Cor-Ibis would be going anywhere immediately. All haste to get here, knowing that he would fall down by journey's end. I suppose he wanted Keris las Theomain to send a wend-whisper, knowing that he could not."

Ileaha did not reply.

Seven

More than a decem passed before Medair was summoned into the presence of Cor-Ibis, and she had to work hard not to stoke her resentment. There was very much an air of a royal audience in the manner in which she was finally conducted, after much to-ing and fro-ing by the attendant Ibisians, into a large, gently lit bedroom which smelled of sandalwood. Jedda las Theomain and Avahn waited until she had stepped past them, then positioned themselves on either side of the door, almost as if they thought she would try to escape.

Illukar las Cor-Ibis had been transformed. Silk-clad, he was propped against a mound of cushions: an impromptu throne of brocade and tassels. His hair flowed in two shining streams, breaking into little rivulets which pooled on the coverlet and came close to dripping off the bed. Single braids before each ear shaded a triple set of tigers-eye, and Medair fixed her eyes on those banded stones, the one thing very different to an image in her past. He was shockingly reminiscent of Ieskar, not as Medair had first seen the Kier, but after the capture of Iskand.

It was all in the skin. Ibisians would at times peel, but never tan, and their skin went through whole ranges of white. Cor-Ibis was at present an unhealthy milky colour, a white-blue shade no Farakkian skin could manage, with the addition of pronounced circles beneath his eyes. And that wonderful black-violet splotch marring his jaw. He appeared alert, but decidedly fragile, as Ieskar had been after Iskand. She'd thought at the time that the Kier had been injured taking the city, and had learned the truth only last year.

He had been dying. All the time, he had been dying.

Resolutely, Medair focused on the present, but it did not help that this shape-changing Keridahl wore the same mask of neutrality which had served Kier Ieskar so faithfully.

"Kel ar Corleaux," Cor-Ibis said, sending a shiver down her spine. "Please be seated."

Medair carefully settled into the chair, a large, wing-backed piece drawn up to the bedside. Determined not to show how unsettled she was, she pushed all shadow of the past at least from her face as he studied her. His pale grey eyes were reflective and silvery in the light of the mageglows, and the effect was enhanced by the blue, green and silver robe he wore. He successfully gave the impression that there was nothing unconventional in receiving visitors while enthroned in bed. The muddy battered creature she'd dropped into a horse trough was a long way in the past.

"I hope you were not too badly punished when Arcana House failed to break my geas, Kel ar Corleaux," he said.

Medair, busy keeping hostility and discomfiture from her face, was nearly overset by this apparent reading of her mind. Surely he could not have had her followed?

"*What is this?*" Keris las Theomain asked in Ibis-laran, her voice sharp. No-one answered her.

"I had been taught that once a geas is cast, the caster has no connection to it," Medair said. "That it becomes a thing entirely unto itself." That was what the Emperor's mages had decided, when they investigated the hold the Ibisians had over their captives.

Cor-Ibis inclined his head, muted light shimmering over his hair and robes. "That is so. But an attempt at geas-breaking announces itself clearly enough. A loud magic, sufficient to wake me, especially in its failure. Arcana House is the only place you could have gone for the attempt."

"*Keridahl?! You did not—*"

"Jedda, be so kind as to use a tongue our guest understands," Cor-Ibis said, not even looking at the woman. Medair decided this was not the point at which to admit to a very reasonable comprehension of Ibis-laran.

"I shall remember that you are sensitive indeed to the arcane, Keridahl," she told him, testing her way across a quagmire. "It was a particularly bad headache, yes, but it passed."

Sensitive and disturbingly intelligent. Certainly the geas-breaking would have been detectable by Thrence's magi, but it would have been felt merely as a surge of power, not as anything specific. Cor-Ibis had linked her day's absence to the surge and correctly deduced the cause. He was proving a little *too* like Ieskar for her comfort.

"It is inconvenient for you, I am sure, but may I suggest that you do not stop at the nearest Arcana House in Ashencaere for another attempt? As matters stand, there no longer exists a desperate need for secrecy, but advertisement is still undesirable. Can I assume that Therin an Selvar does not know the entirety of the tale?"

"The strength of the spell informed on the caster's identity," Medair replied, finding herself falling into the same pattern of speech as Cor-Ibis. "But only as one of four. Adept an Selvar did not question me closely, having received the impression that the geas extended to discussion." She paused, turning over her options. "We did speak of a colleague of the adept – a man called Hendist – who had been called away on duty for the Kyledran Crown. Something about smuggling, or border taxes, they were not at all clear. I was not certain if this man was among all the various charred folk, so I did not mention the matter."

"You gave your word not to speak of it at all," Jedda las Theomain said, cold accusation.

"Even so," Medair replied, remembering abruptly that she hated White Snakes. Did they think that no Farakkian had honour?

Cor-Ibis turned his head, a hint of the invalid in the care he took, and rested his silver-lit eyes on the Ibisian woman for a full ten breaths. He looked patient, an expression which was effective indeed in silencing the female adept. Hostility suddenly thickened the air and Medair was forced to revise her assumptions about Keris las Theomain. She was not, as Medair had assumed, a supporter of Cor-Ibis. Had the ex-ward not said something about being a close friend of the current Kier? Was las Theomain with the party to monitor Cor-Ibis' activities? Did this mean the Keridahl Avec and the Kier were at odds? Politics and intrigues and she had no place in them.

"I hope I am not the reason you purchased that charm, Kel ar Corleaux," Cor-Ibis continued, as if he had never paused.

Medair automatically lifted a hand to touch the necklace, which he could apparently also sense. A formidable mage indeed. She had no intention of trying to explain the Decians, and hid her unease in increasing blandness.

"Not at all, Keridahl. This is more a matter of a person whose horse I...borrowed, who I expect is in an ill-humour. And I don't even have the horse any more – it was that bay which ran off when you so inconsiderately changed shape."

Cor-Ibis inclined his head to one side. "An eventful journey. I am sorry to have caused you such inconvenience, Kel ar Corleaux. Unfortunately, I must continue to do so. Can I hope that Athere is not too far out of your way?"

"A little further east than I was intending." Medair shrugged, inwardly pleased because he had as she wished assumed she'd stolen the horse on his behalf. She also noticed, as the neat braids framing his face swung out of the way, that he only wore a single adept's sigil of silver in his right ear, despite two piercings. It meant his wife was dead, or the marriage bond broken. She ignored the possibility of sympathy and turned to tackle her questions head-on.

"Since it seems I cannot yet leave your company, would it be too great a request, Keridahl, to know the why behind that fight in Bariback Forest? I have thought up an explanation or two and would appreciate knowing whether I had guessed correctly."

White-lashed lids dropped, veiling the silvery eyes. There was a little silence, during which Medair could practically feel Keris las Theomain restraining herself. The woman had not hidden her opinion of Medair, but she had been rebuked twice in a manner so restrained it was crushing, and her rank was very much less than this man's.

Cor-Ibis, Medair decided, was not in the slightest bit surprised by her question. Any sensible person would have been expecting it. It seemed this particular mannerism was a sign of amusement. No. Something else.

"It would be churlish indeed to deny such a request," he said, still without breaking from the mode of polite courtesy. "It appears, from what you have said to Keris las Goranum, that all which remains to be told is what prize was fought over in the Forest."

"Smuggling and border taxes," Medair said, with the tiniest hint of cheer. "Not Koltan brandy, one presumes."

He smiled, a species of open good humour which she again found startling. But a White Snake who smiled was still...no more her enemy than any other. She would be forever having to cut off such thoughts as these, if she was obliged to remain in the company of these people. It would do her no good to gloom and glower and nurse her grievances like a Medarist.

"Not Koltan brandy," Cor-Ibis agreed. "But before I go on, I have a question for you, Kel ar Corleaux. The scene of the battle – you identified those involved readily enough. Did you have any impression as to the victor of that messy little skirmish?"

Medair contrived not to appear concerned by this question. "No," she replied. "It didn't seem as if any care had been taken over the dead. Everyone was where they'd fallen, unless, perhaps, there was yet another party involved and they'd taken off all their dead. Most of the bodies were well-crisped, besides." She shuddered, recalling the scent of cooked meat. "That spell was decems old by the time I reached the site," she added.

"Unfortunate," he said. "I would like very much to know who survived that wholly inadvisable casting. Well, you are aware, I presume, of the situation between Palladium and Decia? This is—" He paused as she shook her head.

"I'm not, no. There was some fuss about Decia encroaching on Ennas Ashra, last time I asked, but that was Autumn."

"Indeed? In précis then, Decia encroached a little too far on Ennas Ashra. Producing some interesting claims about the legitimacy of the Corminevar succession, they made an highly abortive attempt to liberate Ennas Ashra in the name of the true heir to the Silver Throne."

Doubtless those steady silvery eyes caught her sudden stillness, but Medair's voice, Herald-trained, was perfectly calm when she spoke: "How do they base this claim? I had not heard of any who could possibly prove a more direct descent than Kier Inelkar." But she would dearly like to know everything about such a one. Behind her, she heard Avahn las Cor-Ibis shift position, and knew she was not keeping her thoughts well enough hidden.

"A descendant of Prince-Elect Verium, we are told," said the soft voice. "This 'heir' apparently possesses various tokens and documents to indicate a liaison between the Prince-Elect and a woman called Cathale an Sendel. It is difficult to discover the truth of the matter. Extensive research shows us only that Cathale an Sendel was at the Silver Court during the relevant period and gives no indication as to whether she had any association with the Prince-Elect, let alone was carrying his child when the *Niadril* Kier took Athere. Such, however, is the basis of the claim."

Medair was in a dark, distant place, a few nights before she said goodbye to Jorlaise. She had noticed two heads bent towards each other and thought with disgusted amusement that Verium had made yet another conquest. The timing was right. The timing was all too right.

From the vantage of that distant place she looked towards a colourful blur which resolved into dragonflies dancing in the patterns of Illukar las Cor-Ibis' robes. It brought her back to herself.

"If such a child existed, it would not be legitimately heir. Verium died with his father; he could have had no chance to acknowledge a child." Her tone was flat.

"Yes, there are several points of dispute to the claim, whatever the truth," Cor-Ibis agreed, continuing to take note of her reactions. "It is an excuse, not a legal pivot, and serves best as a rallying cry. Perhaps, if the move had not come from Decia, so long an enemy of Ennas Ashra, it would have been more effective. Perhaps not. As it was, the country failed to rise up in support of the so-called heir. Few lives were lost on either side. Something of a non-event, except that it made a true conflict almost inevitable.

"That was just before the snows set in last year. Spring brought renewed political manoeuvring, but only Rilanny and Hibbolt have declared outright with Decia. We wait for more and reinforce the borders. That, then, brings us to the task at hand."

"Preparations for war," Jedda las Theomain said, startling Medair. Cor-Ibis did manage to absorb all a person's attention.

"That is the heart of the matter," the adept agreed, bestowing a glance upon his fellow. "The Kier's defences have ever utilised magic to every possible degree. To this purpose, rahlstones have been collected, hoarded against such exigencies in the vaults of the White Palace. Enter a thief of supernal ability, now a very wealthy thief. I would like to meet this person, but that pleasure is for later days.

"A merchant acquired the rahlstones and let it be known that she was willing to listen to offers. We made our bid, naturally enough, but also put some effort into locating the stones, preferring not to pay a kier's ransom for our own property. The merchant was at least not fool enough to keep them with her, and you can see what happened after that, can you not? Decia attempted a double-cross, there were two different ambushes by third parties. That is always the difficulty with such matters – making the exchange.

"My own presence went, I believe, entirely unremarked. To my regret, I did not anticipate that the merchant would sacrifice her own men and the mercenaries she had hired by using one of the stones. A thing of incredible force – you saw the result of my last-moment protection, and those who were less fortunate. I was concerned with speed in reaching Thrence so that Keris las Theomain could quickly set into motion our resources in attempting to trace whoever has possession of the stones now. Thus, your why."

He made a deprecating gesture with one hand, which Medair, sunk in thought, ignored. First she dealt with the possibility of Verium Corminevar's child. It would not at all surprise her if that oversexed young man had left several children, truth be told. Mistakes were often made with worrynot, at times deliberately. If Verium did acknowledge a child, it would stand as heir. Cathale had been one of the bright lights of Court, but Medair was not at all certain that she would enter into the risky politics such a bid for the throne would entail.

Verium's or not, the child would have been unacknowledged by its father or his family, as Medair was unacknowledged by her own father. Ieskar had firmed the rule of his descendants by wedding the only surviving Corminevar. Under Imperial Law, Alaire's descendants held the Silver Throne by right, unchallenged. But the old Imperial successions mattered not at all, for the Silver Throne had been conquered, not properly inherited.

Thinking of Alaire's marriage always made Medair furious, but anger was immediately followed by hopelessness. This was a cycle she had experienced over and over. Anger, misery, numbing apathy. Even after the marriage, had Medair returned something could have been done. But not now, when half Palladium was in some part White Snake. So wretchedly stupid and pointless to hark back to their arrival. Palladium was their home now. They were Palladian.

This inescapable reasoning had kept her far from the ranks of the Medarists, had driven her to her mountain retreat. Medair had once knelt before the Silver Throne and made an oath. It hadn't been to the Emperor or the Corminevar Family or even primarily the Silver Throne, for all it was called the Oath of the Throne. It had been to Palladium, heart of the Empire, now peopled by those who had destroyed the Empire.

"Oddly, I had thought you had guessed what prize we sought," Illukar las Cor-Ibis said into her silence. That soft, detached voice only served to further lacerate wounds he did not begin to suspect. "The size of the blast would be beyond the ability of most magi not employing a rahlstone."

Their explanation had the ring of truth, and she had said she would return the stones to their owners, but she hadn't wanted to hear that they belonged to Ibisians. Could she really do as she had planned, and give them back? To White Snakes? She looked at the man on the bed, watching her with eyes that cut far too deep. Medair felt so old. There was too much history behind her, issues which had become irrelevant. Simpler just to forget the hate and the loss and all that boundless irony and look merely at the fact of ownership. They belonged to Palladium.

"I did know it was rahlstones, yes," she replied, speaking almost as if someone else had control of her tongue. Hauling her satchel onto her lap, she unsealed it. "As to who had the victory after that wholly inadvisable casting..." There was a swift, indrawn breath behind her as she drew out the anonymous little purse, radiating its distinct aura. With only a small twinge, she tossed it to Cor-Ibis. "I rather think you did, Keridahl."

✿

"AlKier!" breathed Avahn, while Jedda las Theomain made some incoherent noise of disbelief. Cor-Ibis, who had caught the stones neatly, tipped two out onto his palm. Wholly inscrutable. Medair watched him replace the rahlstones, then raise those silver eyes.

"Thank you," he said, for all as if she had just passed him a bowl of sugar over a tea table. "Might I see that satchel, Kel ar Corleaux?"

There was a knot inside Medair's chest, and she knew her face was far too set as she resealed her satchel and handed it over. Even that felt like a betrayal. She wished very much that she could take back the last few moments.

"You defeated a truth-spell," las Theomain said, a thread of confusion in her voice. She moved forward to the opposite side of the bed and stopped, watching as Cor-Ibis ran long, sensitive fingers lightly over the embossed scroll. "No. Your answers were within a very limited scope of the truth." She seemed to look at Medair properly for the first time. "Why did you not produce these before, Kel ar Corleaux?"

"I didn't know they were yours," Medair replied. It was becoming easier to breathe. Thought was gaining control over irrational feeling. The past was dead and the dead did not care and she should not either. But she always would. They were White Snakes! White Snakes.

"Those stones are worth...I would not care to estimate," Avahn las Cor-Ibis said softly, voice suddenly very similar to his cousin's. "I had taken the impression that you were Kyledran. What profit to you to simply return them?"

"I saw what happened to the last woman who tried to profit from them," Medair replied, then turned back to Cor-Ibis, adding in explanation: "The merchant killed herself in the casting. It did not look as if any but you survived."

"That result had not occurred to me," he commented, not taking his eyes from the satchel.

"*Keridahl, what is this woman? Is she, after all, a Medarist? Or an agent of some unknown player?*"

This time Cor-Ibis did not rebuke las Theomain for speaking Ibis-laran. Perhaps he no longer considered Medair a guest.

"This is the truest reproduction I have ever seen of the old Heralds' satchels," he said, voice still conversational. "It must possess near-perfect shielding, since I can only barely sense its emanations, even with it in my hands. Far beyond what we are capable of. I will presume it has also been gifted with the same capacity for self-destruction as the satchels described in the histories." He turned it about in his hands once again. "Only four or five years old." Silvery eyes lifted to Medair. "I would very much like to meet the one who created this."

"She's dead," Medair replied. Her mind was clear, crystalline. It had not been a betrayal, truly it hadn't been. These people were neither enemy nor friend and she had done the right thing to return the rahlstones. And something clawed and bawled inside her chest and called her liar.

"A pity. Did this craftswoman leave behind records of her research? This shielding is one we have sought to recreate for centuries and is worth nearly as much as the rahlstones. As is the dimensional pocket these are rumoured to contain. Can it be that both these things have been found only to be lost once more?"

Medair shrugged, as if it mattered very little to her. It seemed to take a lot of effort. "I wasn't there when she died, but I doubt that her notes still exist."

"It must have the dimensional pocket as well," Avahn interjected. "The hosteller said that she had no gear, only a single shoulder bag. Who are you, Medair ar Corleaux, to not only give away twelve rahlstones as if they were glass, but to own a thing long since become legend?"

"Someone who wouldn't be here if not for this inconvenient geas," she replied, shortly. She turned back to Cor-Ibis. "But the geas could be broken, could it not, if Keris las Theomain employed one of the rahlstones?"

Cor-Ibis handed back her satchel, and she worked to hide the way her fingers tightened on the strap. That had been a calculated risk. She felt as she had in that alley, when the Medarists had decided she did not deserve her name. Even a strength ring would not let her escape, if they chose to mark her as a threat.

"I am thrice in your debt," Cor-Ibis said gravely, face still a mask. "Not a small thing." He sat up a little straighter in the bed, became even more formal, and made the three hand gestures which Ibisians used to signify thanks and the unbalanced scales of debt. It was as clear a way as any to declare that he did not intend to clap her in chains and put her to question. But then, he had the geas to keep her.

"It would be only just to have Keris las Theomain free you," he continued, in that soft, soft voice. "But use a rahlstone? No. It would be an announcement to all who dwell in this city that we possess them, when it is to be hoped that we are thought to have nothing to do with them. You must bide in patience, Kel ar Corleaux, and travel as my guest to Athere. I said that there no longer existed a need for secrecy and could not have been farther from the mark." His eyes shifted to his fellow adept. "We will leave on the dawn, Jedda."

This provoked a spate of protest. The man was Keridahl Avec and these two were obviously not used to going openly against his will, but they voiced their objections strongly enough. He was not recovered from the spell shock. His departure would be looked for. They should split their force, send the rahlstones off while Cor-Ibis remained as a decoy. He could not possibly endure another swift journey so soon. Cor-Ibis listened silently. Finally he picked up the bag of rahlstones once more.

"Are you able to key that satchel to another person?" he asked Medair, who managed not to look wholly incredulous in response.

"No," she replied, firmly. "Surely you had some method of transportation prepared?"

"Nothing so effective." He studied her, but made a small gesture of negation and turned again to Avahn and las Theomain. "It is not a matter for discussion. If you are concerned for my endurance, I suggest you leave me to my rest and prepare for tomorrow's departure. Avahn, will you send Cortis in to me?" An inclination of the head was awarded to Medair. "Kel ar Corleaux, I offer you once more my thanks and my apologies. It is a debt I will not forget."

Medair had expected the refusal, but was angry anyway. She studied the palely shining figure, then deliberately pictured him smeared with mud, being dropped into a horse trough. The incident was amusing in retrospect, but she couldn't smile even inside.

"Your powers of recollection are doubtless refined," she said, only just keeping the edge from her voice as she rose and offered him a very correct half-bow. "Quiet night, Keridahl."

Avahn joined her as she reached the door and paused immediately after closing it behind them. "Are you certain you're not a Medarist?" he asked, with that atypical forthrightness. "Owning a reproduction of a Herald's satchel, along with the name of that most infamous of Heralds, begins to push the bounds of credulity."

"Do Medarists have reproductions of the satchels? They didn't strike me as possessing the organisation or resources."

"They do tend to be aimless hotheads," Avahn agreed. "But that is the most vocal and visible of the group. It's those who do not call themselves after your namesake, but direct their actions, who might just be able to produce such a thing."

"They play a deep game indeed, if they direct me. I would enjoy hearing what explanation you could conjure for my actions, if I were one who hated your race."

Pale eyes studied her. The youth who had chortled at her name over dinner had been replaced by someone who was disturbingly like his cousin. "You don't like us," he said, in judicial pronouncement. "There is none of the irrational hatred of the average Medarist, true, but you have called us 'White Snakes' in your time, I'd wager." He laughed, returning to the Avahn she had first met. "A deep game indeed, but I like puzzles." He turned as one of the servants opened the next door along. "Cortis, the Keridahl wants you. We are to leave on the dawn."

"What game are you playing, I wonder?" Medair asked, as Avahn walked through the connecting door.

"Show me your hand, tell me your secrets; perhaps I will return the favour." He turned a bright eye on her, and grinned when she shook her head. "How unhandsome of you, Kel ar Corleaux, when it's an exchange I might almost be tempted to make. You'll be good company on this journey."

Eight

It was one of those pristine dawns where all the colours are greyer than usual, yet sharply clear. The horses, crowded into the yard, were prick-eared and restive. All but two had their riders waiting by their heads, and Medair kept herself occupied by attempting to pick which unclaimed animal belonged to which absent Ibisian. She decided the gleaming chestnut was las Theomain's taste, which left the dusky grey for Cor-Ibis. Both very fine animals. Avahn rode the one Medair would have chosen out of the nine assembled: an eager black which was pretending to take fright whenever a bird flew overhead.

In due course, Keris las Theomain and Cor-Ibis appeared, dressed elegantly in flowing riding apparel. For travel they wore linen rather than silk, but still made a striking beacon to any thief or less casual predator. Very expensive and very Ibisian. It was the first time Medair had seen Cor-Ibis on his feet, and she noticed with faint surprise that he was not so tall as she'd thought him. An inch or two over six feet, which was no more than average for an Ibisian, but–

Medair shook the thought away and watched Cor-Ibis lift himself into the grey's saddle. He no longer displayed the terrible weakness of spell shock, but his movements were precise, conservative of energy. It was too soon for him to be truly recovered, and Medair wondered what they'd do if he fell over at the end of the day.

With curious stable-hands in attendance, there was no discussion of their route as they turned to leave. The two Farakkian guards led the way out, followed by Cor-Ibis and las Theomain. Medair, beside Avahn, had just cleared the gate when the riders ahead of them stopped.

Avahn muttered something as he saw the men who had blocked the way north. Grey cloth and leather armour, no insignia. Medair kept her face blank as the Decian mage leaned toward the ear of his captain and whispered something. She wondered if the way those dark eyes then fixed on her face, taking in each and every detail, was as obvious to her companions as it was to her.

"Early to rise, Keridahl?" the Decian leader asked, his attention returning to Cor-Ibis.

"Perhaps not early enough this day, Captain Vorclase." Cor-Ibis didn't sound perturbed. How, she wondered, did he know the Decian?

"You cannot always be lucky, Lord High," Vorclase replied, mocking the title. "Your reputation works against you. I don't know how you came to be on this trail, but on learning of your presence in Thrence, tracking down a certain lost prize became simplicity itself. In fact, it becomes apparent that a number of ventures gone awry can be explained by your involvement, and for that I can only offer my respect. And now we dispute possession."

"Pitched battle in the streets of a city fond of neither of us? That is less than I expected of you, Captain."

"Desperate times, desperate men, Lord High. The Kyledrans can be reasoned with."

"Then may I point out that you are outnumbered?"

"I draw your attention to the roof."

Cor-Ibis did not seem to look, but Medair did, and discovered three men with crossbows on the building across the street.

"Why give us warning?" Avahn murmured, so low Medair could barely hear him. She didn't tell him the Decians wanted her alive.

"My compliments," Cor-Ibis said. "Your preparation is exemplary. You would do well, however, to study the schedule of the nearest guard-house."

Following Cor-Ibis' gaze, Vorclase turned in his saddle. Medair couldn't see his face as he realised what was approaching, but only his eyes were angry when he turned back. He promptly signalled his men to withdraw to the alley from which they had emerged.

"Another time, Keridahl. Take care of my prizes; I need them in good order." Then he was gone. A small troop of Kyledran guards marched slowly down the street toward them, looking bored.

"Who is Captain Vorclase?" Medair asked Avahn as they hurried on. He grimaced, and glanced at Ileaha as she drew up alongside them.

"An old foe. He and Cor-Ibis have crossed swords before."

"I gathered that. He's an agent for the Decian crown?"

"*The* agent. He is formidable. Interesting that he was not in the initial squad chasing the rahlstones."

"We have them, don't we?" Ileaha asked, in a flat voice. "The rahlstones?"

"How very quick you are, Ileaha." Avahn's words held cheerful mockery. "Yes, in an effort to prove conclusively that she is not a Medarist, our new friend most kindly presented them to Cor-Ibis. I believe he was surprised," he added. "A rare achievement."

Ileaha compressed her lips and looked forward to where Cor-Ibis rode. His excessive length of hair was restrained in two looped-up braids which swung and jerked in time to his grey's stride. Ileaha then awarded Avahn a fulminating glare, correctly guessing that it was he who had chosen not to reveal this titbit of information. A flush rose beneath her skin, emphasising her Farakkian heritage, but she passed over the matter without comment.

"They knew we were leaving this morning," she said, instead. "It would hardly have been possible for them to spend all day and night waiting in that alley for ambush. Not in this part of Thrence."

"Quite so," Avahn replied, having followed her reaction with an air of malicious interest. "Perhaps you would care to stun us again with your acuity and produce some explanation for how they knew?"

Ileaha continued to glare at him, but replied to the taunt seriously. "There's three obvious choices. The first that one of us told them. That is unlikely." She looked past Avahn to Medair. "Those with Cor-Ibis on this journey he knows well, has worked with before and trusts."

"Do you include las Theomain and her servant in that category?"

"It has never been suggested that Keris las Theomain is disloyal," Ileaha replied, voice dropping a degree as her eyes darted to the beautiful adept. "Nor is she likely to take into service one who would betray her." She dismissed the possibility with a gesture. "There is a chance one of the inn residents, in the pay of the Decians, eavesdropped upon us, but we took adequate precautions against that. Still, the staff of the inn is most likely. We sent down word for our horses to be prepared. If one of the stable boys had been bribed to bring news of such an order and the Decians had established themselves nearby, then that would have given them time enough to ready themselves."

"Why Ileaha, you had best not allow the lovely Jedda to realise that you have a brain as well as a hand with the sword, or she will most certainly take you into her service." Avahn still mocked, but there was a hint of genuine surprise in his eyes.

Ileaha, ignoring Avahn, looked across at Medair once again. "You had the rahlstones all along? I don't see how you could have concealed them, unless you hid them outside the inn. Their aura is distinctive. Cor-Ibis would surely have noticed them on the journey here, even in his condition."

"Ah, Kel ar Corleaux, who is not a Medarist, rather suspiciously possesses a remarkable reconstruction of one of the Empire Herald satchels. A fully working model, whose creator, she claims, is unfortunately dead. If I were less well-mannered I would be tempted to place her under a truth spell and ask her that question again. And yet, since we are so deeply in her debt, perhaps not."

Medair, less than comfortable with Avahn's chatty assumption of friendship, decided to forestall questions with one of her own. "If the Keridahl's reputation is such that these Decians decided that his presence meant he had the rahlstones, won't the Kyledrans make the same assumption? Won't they have left orders at the gate that he not pass unmolested?"

"A possibility," Avahn agreed cheerfully. "They are unlikely to know Cor-Ibis was present for the exchange, but they might well risk an incident on strength of suspicion. We have our stratagems."

The confident words were belied by his watchful expression when they reached the north gate. There did not seem to be an unduly large number of guards, but Medair was not alone in noticing the woman with grey-streaked hair who stood watching them from the guardroom.

"So that's to be the way of it," Avahn murmured, and met Medair's eyes. "What a ride we'll have this day! Decia and Kyledra in hot pursuit, both determined to bring us down in some lonely corner. A fine piece of sport."

"The hunt from the hind's point of view." Ileaha glanced back at the city gate. "We should split into more than one group, send the rahlstones ahead while the rest draw the pursuit."

"It seems only logical, but if you can convince my esteemed cousin of that, you have more influence than I." Avahn shot an assessing glance forward to where Cor-Ibis, head inclined, listened to Jedda las Theomain. "Not a matter for discussion. He does not usually have such difficulty with delegation."

"The Kyledrans have the resources to trail more than one group," Medair offered. "Together you have more chance at defence. With the rahlstones, you have every expectation of survival. Sending people off would not be a decoy, but a sacrifice."

"I can't believe Kyledra would put itself in that position," Ileaha objected. "They don't like us, but such an attack would be a declaration of war."

"War is coming," Avahn replied, shrugging. "A small kingdom like Kyledra would be pleased to take the rahlstones and deal with Decia for its own protection. And our demise would be a bandit attack, or, more likely, we would disappear altogether, with Kyledra able to claim no knowledge, since we left Thrence unmolested. They'd not be able to stop a wend-whisper, but wend-whispers can be faked, and would not be nearly proof enough to suit a Court of Crowns."

This delightful thought was sufficient to keep them silent until Cor-Ibis signalled a halt.

"Some four miles ahead is the township of Macaile. If we had been searched at the gate, and found empty-handed, there would be no objection to passing through it. However, it seems probable that we are to be waylaid. So we will not go through Macaile, will instead pass through the northern corner of Farash on as direct a route to Palladium as we dare. That will not be expected, for they will not know of Liak and Marden's familiarity with the region." The Keridahl nodded towards the two Farakkians, who gazed back impassively.

"Despite precautions, we may have left something at the inn that would provide a trace spell. Nor is it possible to quietly sustain trace-wards for so many." Pale eyes touched on Medair. "We will have hounds on our trail soon enough, whatever the case. Five days to Palladium's border."

This, it seemed, was enough of a speech for the Keridahl. Without another word he turned his horse and gestured for the Farakkian woman called Liak to take the lead.

Farash stood directly between Kyledra and Palladium and the Farashi had no tolerance for Ibisians at all. It was daring of the Ibisians to leave the roads and try and dash through northern Farash, banking on the region's relative emptiness to shield them from interference. Medair rode silently, reflecting on the idea of being pursued out of Kyledra like a common thief. And a Kyledra which would think of waylaying travellers for its own advantage. Duchess Stameron had been so upright, one of the most respected of the Emperor's Hands. She would turn in her grave at this. "Even White Snakes," she had said once, "have honour. Indeed, more honour than we do, if we are to believe their pride. They fight us on what they consider just terms, they do not molest our Heralds, they allow us to collect our injured, do not torture or mistreat captives. When we accord them less than that, merely because we hate them, we truly do become less than them."

<hr />

By nightfall they were in the Wind Forest, which spanned the triple border of Ashencaere, Kyledra and Farash. Sunset proved as beautiful as the dawn. The birds spoke in different, deeper voices and, true to the name, the Wind Forest was rarely without the skirl and hush of a strong breeze. It was chilly, even in late spring.

Liak led them straight to a pool hidden on the crown of one of the rocky little hills. Avahn dismounted first, and let his black suck greedily at the water. He looked about him as the sun-painted hilltops began to shade into dusk.

"*And in the Whistling Hills we hunted death,*" he said,
"*Cold death 'midst rattling black-bone branches,*"
"*Quick death, borne on the wind.*"
"*At nights-fall we paid homage to the grey traveller,*"
"*And left our lives to clatter by a pool of dusk.*"

The young man's gaze was on Cor-Ibis dismounting, whose grip on his stirrup suggested that he was not entirely certain of his legs. Avahn grimaced and added more prosaically: "No fires up here to catch the eye, no spells of warmth to draw our hunters. I wish I'd brought an extra blanket."

Medair was trying to recollect where she had heard those words before: they were familiar, but subtly wrong. Sitting atop her horse, she watched the colour creep out of the south, then slid lightly to the ground.

"That's a version of 'Faron's Lament', isn't it?" she asked, amidst the general stretching and faint groans of people who had ridden too long.

"'Faron's Lament'?" Avahn was still distractedly watching Cor-Ibis. "I don't know that name. That was from 'The Lady of the Hills'. I take it that you're not well-versed in your Telsen?"

"Not to boast of," Medair said, wishing she hadn't asked. He had reworked and renamed the song, but she had recognised the subject. Telsen would be pleased to know that his work hadn't been too complex to achieve popular immortality. This song, at least, had outlasted him.

Wanting to turn the conversation, she opened her satchel and drew out a blanket. Avahn started to refuse when she offered, then caught himself.

"For a moment I forgot," he said. "What else have you got in there, Kel ar Corleaux?"

"Everything but the horse," she replied. "It's a bad habit, but easier than carrying the full weight of everything I own." She was a little amazed at the lightness of her tone, but she was finding it difficult to resist Avahn's ready humour. White Snake or not, he was good company.

"So if you lose this, you have nothing? I see why you call it a bad habit."

"It's difficult to lose," she replied. "And I'd still have the horse."

"Then it's also possible to trace?" he shot back, with a mild grin. "You give yourself away so easily. Little by little I shall have all your secrets from you, Kel Medair ar Corleaux."

"Thank you for warning me," she replied, laughing. He was probably uncertain why she fell so silent afterwards and turned her attention fully to tending her horse, whom she'd decided to name Eidal. Or perhaps he saw her immediate reason well enough, if not the history behind it. White Snakes. She didn't want to befriend this youth, with his glib tongue and whatever secrets he was hiding behind his carefree attitude. Yes, she'd called Ibisians 'White Snakes', and a few things worse than that. A year and five hundred more ago they had been the enemy, the invaders, evil founded on pride. Now they were people.

※

Medair finally ran out of things to do with Eidal, and was forced to join the others. They had settled in the clearest area on the hilltop, where the rocks were few and the grass soft. Stars and a half-moon shimmered in the pool and, beneath the fathomless well of the sky, everyone seemed small and shadowy and not quite real.

"Please be seated, Kel ar Corleaux," Cor-Ibis said, indicating a space to his left, in the shelter of the jagged rock he was resting against. He may well have been watching her all the time, without her realising. Now, he coolly followed her every movement, pale eyes turned silver once more by the uncertain light.

It was stupid to feel uncomfortable sitting close to a man she had bathed, dressed and fed. But he had been less than himself then, not watching her in that horribly incisive way. Settling out of the bite of the wind, she tried not to lean obviously out of his reach.

"*I would ask you of the people of Farakkan,*" said a soft voice out of the past. She closed her mind to the memory, to all thought of blue eyes. But she could not so easily shut away a living voice.

"The capacity of a Herald's satchel is rumoured to have been enormous," Cor-Ibis said. "Do you have some estimate of how much can be contained within your own?" He paused, perhaps because she was staring at the stars like they were escape just out of reach, then continued. "Forgive my curiosity, Kel ar Corleaux. It is apparent that there is a great deal you do not wish to discuss and it would be impolite to try and force the issue, but the legends of the past have their fascinations."

"That can be taken as a warning not to leave it lying about open anywhere," Avahn put in. "Or you will most certainly find us trying to discover how it works. How many blankets do you have in there? More importantly, how many will you give to me?"

His words earned him an admonitory frown from Keris las Theomain. Medair wondered if Cor-Ibis found his heir unsatisfactory. But then, she doubted he would be fooled by the pose.

"Twelve, I think," she replied, knowing that it was pointless to wish them all dead so that she could shut out their voices as well. "It's very easy to lose track." She looked back to Cor-Ibis, patient and silent in the twilight. "You're correct, Keridahl. I have no wish to discuss my satchel, its creator, its contents, my destination or any organisations I may or may not be affiliated with. If I had thought it likely that I could have travelled to Athere without my satchel's qualities becoming obvious, I would not have revealed it."

"We cannot in honour press you," said Jedda las Theomain, unexpectedly. "But your silence rouses suspicion."

"The Silence of Medair," Avahn said, expelling his breath in a soft laugh. The others seemed to comprehend his inexplicable amusement, but did not share it. Medair looked at him blankly through the gloom, trying to weigh the strength of Ibisian honour, which at least was more clear-cut than Ibisian humour.

The two servants chose this fortuitous moment to start passing around the beginnings of the meal: crusty rolls, fruit, pieces of cold roast chicken and slices of lamb.

"We should have thought to consult you about transporting supplies," Avahn said as he accepted the double-folded cloth which held his portion. "We will not be eating this well again until we are over Palladium's borders."

Medair shrugged, deciding there was no point in offering the supply of dry food she had stocked in Thrence. "It's not the most stable storage," she said, not wanting to encourage him. "If it were, it would have been merchants, not Heralds, who had used it."

Avahn was inclined to discuss the difficulties of creating dimensional pockets and the many failed experiments to recreate the method used by the Empire, but Medair simply ignored him. They did not press her.

Cor-Ibis had acknowledged debt, a triple debt. He, and those who obeyed his commands, would accord her guest rights until the debt was paid or she did something which broke the Ibisian codes applying to guests. She was not in the slightest way obliged to answer their questions and though they might surmise all manner of things from what she did and did not say, might suspect her even of being allied to an enemy, they would not offer her anything but courtesy and questions while she behaved as a guest. Once in Athere, she should be able to leave without hindrance.

Guests, however, had their obligations as well, and she was wondering if she should tell Cor-Ibis that the Decians had a trace on her. It took until the end of the meal for her to reason that since they were operating under the possibility that a trace might be set on one of the Ibisian party, it made little difference knowing for certain there was one on her.

Depending on the power of the Decian mage, the trace would slip in a week or two and with the charm she wore they would be unable to establish another. The charm also lessened the danger of the current trace, dispersing it over a large area. But the Decians would know that she was heading into Farash.

There didn't seem to be a way to fix the situation.

Nine

The city called Finrathlar hadn't existed in Medair's time. Her recollection of the area just south of the triple border of Palladium, Ashencaere and Farash was of ruins: an ancient and decaying fortress at the entrance of a large valley sheltered by a ring of hills. There'd been a small but useful Imperial base hidden in caves among the western hills, but most only knew Vatch Fort as an abandoned outpost.

No more. Unlike Athere, the Ibisians had not converted the existing structures to their own use. The decaying fortress had been razed to the ground, and the stone employed in the construction of a thing part wall and part castle which had withstood the test of several centuries of intermittent aggression from Farash. Huge vaulted arches led to a city covering half the valley.

They rode between houses which were alien to Medair's eye. Most were multiple stories with a great deal of glass shining from too many windows. For some reason, each building had two stairways curving up to a balcony-like entrance. Within the shelter of these stairways there were tiny gardens, statues, crests, even fountains. It gave Medair a glimpse of what Sar-Ibis must have been like.

During the past few days it had been decided that Keris las Theomain would take the rahlstones with a suitable guard on to Athere. Cor-Ibis would remain in Finrathlar until he had recovered from a journey whose only drama had proved to be his declining condition. They had spoken of staying at The Avenue, which Medair had assumed would be another expensive inn, but at the end of a street lined with tall flame trees they stopped at the bronzed double gates of a large private residence surrounded by a high wall. A dragonfly motif decorated both gates and pillars, and Medair had seen enough dragonflies worked into Avahn and Cor-Ibis' clothing to guess it was the family symbol. 'The Avenue' must be part of the Keridahl's holdings.

Through the gate she found an airy grove where shafts of sunlight shone on soft hillocks and small ornamental pools. Clover and verbena covered the ground with a riot of tiny white blossom. A drive of dark, broken rock made a question mark from the gate to the front of the house, and was mirrored by a curving wall of rockery terraces dripping with greenery. Both stone crescents were backed by an honour guard of flame trees fluttering with fresh Spring leaves. In Autumn, when the small leaves turned dark red against the pale branches, they would become walls of fire.

The house was built against a small hill and rose to three levels. It seemed all balconies and windows to Medair. The obligatory twin stairs curved so drastically that they almost joined together again, like arms cradling a precisely perfect garden, exquisite in blues and whites with undertones of maroon. A weathered statue of a woman – Ibisian tall, of course – held central prominence in the middle of a stand of lavender, one hand held out from her side as if she moved to touch the purple-grey tips.

Ignoring the main entrance, they rode around one end of the house to a double row of stables incorporated into the side of the hill. Stable hands, alerted by the crunch of hooves on the drive, hurried to take hold of bridles. Medair thought this would be a suitably dramatic moment for Cor-Ibis to collapse, but he didn't even deign to stumble as he slid from his horse and surveyed his tranquil estate.

"It never changes," Avahn said, with satisfaction. "It's just like it was when I first came here."

Cor-Ibis glanced at him, but made no comment before turning to Medair. "Welcome to The Avenue, Kel ar Corleaux," he said.

"Thank you," she replied, though she felt impatient with the need to delay in this small city and then travel to Athere. "I've been wondering what reason you'll give me now, not to free me from this geas."

She had managed to conjure that rare smile. An acknowledgment that the rahlstones would be whisked off, probably gone in the morning, and she would be hanging about this manicured cage until they could move on, 'as quickly as convenient'.

"Perhaps it would be best not to offer you that reason," he said. Jedda las Theomain seemed inclined to add something, but he forestalled her with a glance, before returning to meet Medair's gaze with unimpaired serenity. "I would be grateful if you would remain my guest, Kel. Until Athere. You have my word I will not keep you longer."

There was nothing to do but allow herself to be escorted inside. The house was uncomfortably like the spare, graceful palace-tent where the Ibisians had declared war five hundred years ago. Every line looked carefully drawn, every object judicially placed. In the bedroom she was given, windows made up of many squares of excessively clear glass overlooked the avenue of trees, and Medair stared out over the alien city to the familiar hills beyond.

Sighing, she sat down on the bed. There didn't seem to be any way to force the issue, so she could only resign herself to making the room hers for the next few days. They were suspicious of her, curious about her satchel and her origins, and had no intention of letting her go without prying further. But the debt Cor-Ibis had acknowledged should tie his hands. He owed her for his life, his return, and the rahlstones. And had given his word. She could not imagine Cor-Ibis as *valask*, an oath-breaker.

She prowled about the room, trying not to look at the view or the graceful lines of the furniture, both of which threatened to overwhelm her with memories of the past. It was true that Athere was in the general direction she wanted, if several days off course. And, having spent five days in their company, she couldn't honestly claim to find these Ibisians unbearable. The adept and his entourage were useful protection from the Decians, who might very well have followed across the border, "if she was as valuable as it seemed". Weighing against that was the delay, giving those same Decians a chance to plan any further attempts on her. Which did nothing to alter the fact of the geas. She was stuck.

At sunset Medair dressed in clothing marginally less casual than the kit she'd worn on the road and went downstairs. The outfit became barely passable when she saw the finery of Avahn and las Theomain. Even Ileaha had found a robe of patterned silk.

Avahn was playing host, in this place which would one day be his. He divided his energies between amiably showering Medair with trivialities she knew little about, being graciously polite to las Theomain, and insulting Ileaha. Since she wasn't in the mood to make conversation, the only part of the meal which interested Medair was when Avahn questioned las Theomain about plans for the transportation of the rahlstones. It appeared that an entire detachment of troops was escorting the Keris to Athere.

"The Keridahl suggested you travel with me, Ileaha," las Theomain concluded. "Be sure to have your baggage prepared in time. We leave soon after dawn."

"Yes, Keris," Ileaha responded, only the way her eyes found her lap revealing any opinion of this arrangement. Avahn watched her a moment, then shook his head in disgust.

After dinner, Ileaha was given the task of showing Medair about the house, which Medair thought a good opportunity to satisfy her own curiosity.

"Is Avahn a first cousin of the Keridahl?" she asked. "A child of an aunt or uncle?"

"No," Ileaha replied, after a short pause. "They are all descended from the same great-grandmother, but none are first cousins."

Medair raised her eyebrows. "Who are 'they all'?"

Ileaha glanced toward the centre of the house before she answered. "The Keridahl's heirs. Or, to be more correct, the Keridahl's potential heirs."

"Avahn is not heir outright, then?"

"He is now that the Keridahl has declared him so," Ileaha replied and, although she obviously tried to suppress it, her voice and face revealed that she could not at all understand what had possessed Cor-Ibis to take such a rash step.

"All children of the same line?" Medair mused. "The Keridahl's mother was eldest, obviously. How many others are we speaking of?"

"Three," Ileaha replied, after an unnecessarily long pause. "But Kerin Mylar is usually not counted," she added, "since his blood is not pure."

Medair was genuinely surprised. Was this, then, the source of any supposed difficulty between the Keridahl and his mix-blood Kier? "That rather puts him on par with the Medarists, doesn't it? Another century or two and the line will be inbred, for lack of 'pure' partners. Does the Keridahl have some solution to this problem?"

"I don't believe I have ever heard the Keridahl mention the subject," Ileaha replied, face very blank. "To be completely clear, I cannot say that I know of him expressing an opinion on the future of his bloodline, or if he believes the tradition of purity should be maintained. The Cor-Ibis line has, of course, never declared open allegiance with the purists." She looked down at her hands, while Medair tried to work out the implications of 'the purists', then said, "I offer you the use of my name, Kel ar Corleaux. Might I have yours?"

The first exchange of friendship was not what Medair had been expecting from this woman, who obviously set more store by the formality than Avahn. "By all means," she replied, managing to hide her sudden confusion. She had no reason to refuse what Ileaha offered.

"Thank you, Medair." Ileaha read her face easily enough. "You wonder why, don't you? It's not that you are easy to talk to – you listen well, but I can feel the weight of your secrets. Perhaps it is that you are an outsider, even though we suspect you are aligned to the Hold or to something even worse. When I talk to you, I listen to myself. Already I have discovered from your questions how much I reveal which I should not. You find it very strange that I think poorly of Avahn."

"Does that make you reconsider your opinion?" Medair asked, as she rapidly revised her own.

"Not really. He pretends to be less than what he is. I always thought it was from laziness, a love of pleasure over industry. He has ever played this game, chased the moment. Despite a formidable ability, he turned his back on his studies once he had reached the point where continuing meant true effort. He talks of nothing but racing and the bards and all that is enjoyable but of little use; Avahn who will one day be Cor-Ibis. None expected the Keridahl to choose him as heir and when he did, most believed that the Keridahl had discovered grievous faults in the competitors. This past week, I asked myself again why the Keridahl named Kerin Avahn over Keris Surreive and Kerin Adlenkar. How much of this display of feckless frivolity is act and how much is nature?"

The tone was analytic, but Ileaha was looking carefully away from Medair. Avahn's attitude, particularly toward Ileaha herself, obviously cut deep. "Why do you let yourself be bullied into Keris las Theomain's employ?" Medair asked, impulsively. "It's clear that it's not what you want."

"Clear to whom?" Ileaha said, a little bitterly. "Avahn sees that because he dislikes her also. Despite first appearances, you, Medair, have obviously never been without money."

Medair shrugged. "True."

"You see without really understanding. I have lived all but the first few years of my life on charity. Now, when I have been properly schooled in all that I would need for employment chosen for me long ago, a suitable prospect has been selected and offered a chance to look me over. And if I object to an excellent opportunity to work for a powerful woman who pays those in her employ very well indeed, merely because I find her tongue too sharp and her beliefs not mine, who would be wrong in calling me ungrateful, nothing more than a burden who will not be shifted?"

"Couldn't you find someone you liked better? Surely they wouldn't object? Do you want to be a secretary?"

Ileaha lost her air of cold self-dissection. "It becomes a trap, status," she sighed. "I was Cor-Ibis' ward, which strengthens my tenuous link to the family. It limits my choices, for a lesser position than the chosen one would reflect badly on the Keridahl and the former Keridahl's guardianship. It could bring shame on this family which has clothed and fed me if I fell to a position of common

101

servitude. A ward of Cor-Ibis in the scullery? That would not be well done."

"That's your ambition? The scullery?"

A shadow of a smile appeared on Ileaha's face. "A noble profession," she said. "No, if I were free of ties, I would pursue the path of Kel ar Haedrin and Kerin las Lorednor. My strength is with the sword, and they are trusted, and not expected to blindly follow orders."

Medair had gathered during the past week that the two Farakkian members of Cor-Ibis' entourage were rather more than simple arms-men. Spies. Agents of the Palladian Crown.

"But isn't that a suitable profession? Hardly common servitude."

"It is the appearance of the thing. In the eyes of the world Kel ar Haedrin and Kerin las Lorednor are bodyguards. Kerin las Lorednor is thought to have come down greatly since he entered the Kier's service, for such as they do not win public acclaim, or even acknowledged promotion. Nor, were their roles clear, would they be thought admirable."

Medair understood. The intelligence agents of her Emperor had been feared or despised, no matter their value. "I set my goals very young," she said, considering the woman beside her. "In some ways I didn't have a choice. My sister was possessive of what would one day be hers and I knew I would have to make my own place. But I was fortunate to want, oh, something which let me preen and think well of myself and not have people think badly of me. My mother encouraged me to it. I don't know how she would have reacted if I'd announced a desire to be a shadow-lurker."

"Velvet Swords, they call them," Ileaha murmured. "The best of them, at least. Kel ar Haedrin tells me much of her world is dull and there are times when it is necessary to debate honour. But I am sure that I would prefer it to the well-paid and unrewarding role of Keris las Theomain's secretary."

They drifted on in silence and Medair was left to think about the stark contrast between Avahn, Ileaha and the first Ibisian she had known. Selai Attau las Dona, adept, Kerikath. Assigned to teach the Imperial Heralds the Ibisian tongue. An eternally formal woman, she had spent many months in their company and never let her reserve slip. Except for that first time, before their Kier had even declared war, when Kedy had asked their new teacher about the disaster which had destroyed Sar-Ibis. It had been so unnerving, listening to the Ibisian woman describe the destruction of her home without so much as a quaver. Medair had been almost relieved when the mask had cracked, if only for an instant.

They had just delivered the Emperor's message and been sent away to wait. A simply amazing meal had been brought to them: fruits, cheese, miniature pastries and tiny bowls of sauces, all arranged into a complex flower pattern. Scarcely believable in the wilds of Kormettersland.

"There is a great deal for us to discover today, Kerikath," Kedy had said. His hair had been as white as the Ibisians', but the craggy, generous lines of his face were never so cold. "I fear at least half these fruits are new to me."

"Some will never be seen again," the Kerikath had replied. "We carried away seeds and seedlings, even uprooted established plants, but it was impossible to take everything in time." She reached out and selected from the arrangement a fruit which resembled a large cherry, darker and firmer. "A black denan takes ten years to grow to maturity and bear. In the best conditions they are a challenge for any who nurtures the AlKier's gifts, prone to failure outside their ideal environment. We have seedlings, but they may not fruit here."

"Farak's blessing on your planting, then," Kedy had murmured. "I must admit, I am overwhelmed by what you have brought with you. We have always been told that the misuse of wild magic could spark an uncontrollable fire which would consume the whole of Farakkan. If that is what your people faced, and still you had time to think of black denans and seed-stock, then it is a simply amazing achievement."

The Kerikath had selected a diamond of pale cheese from the array, face solemn as she considered Kedy's unspoken question. "We did not face fire, only a crawling black roil of power which transmuted everything it touched to water."

"An opposite," Kedy had said. "If you are able, can I prevail upon you to tell us what happened? I know our adepts wish to

The Silence of Medair

discuss this in detail, that you will be asked more often than kindness and forbearance should allow, but you understand our need to know?"

"Of course. I have been commanded to assist you in all you must discover." There had been no feeling at all in the woman's voice, and Medair had begun to think the Ibisians completely inhuman.

"One whose name will never again be uttered called on wild magic to resurrect her dead child," the Kerikath had said. "She knew well the ban against her actions, and removed herself to Myridar, an empty region on the northern shores of Sar-Ibis to make her desperate gamble, outside the reach of those who would stop her summoning.

"We do not know if she succeeded, whether the child returned to life. If he did, it was only to die again as the power summoned by his mother cascaded out of control. It takes flesh more quickly than earth. I saw once, towards the end, a man consumed by the Blight. He misjudged his step making a precarious crossing, dipped the edge of his foot into the Blight and literally dissolved as we watched, falling away beneath himself. Four breaths. That is all, from turning to see his son safely following, to liquid indistinguishable to that all around, his clothes and belongings marking the spot for only moments after, until they too were gone, and then the stones he had been standing upon."

Medair had only been able to stare. Kedy, better able to command himself, murmured: "Was there nothing to be done?"

"Nothing which worked." The Kerikath had taken a tiny sip of water, replacing the glass on the table with an excruciatingly controlled click. "All Sar-Ibis knew, almost immediately, that we faced disaster. Wild magic screams aloud its strength, and we could hear and read the danger of that cry, though we could not see what made it.

"It had spread only the smallest distance by the time the first *lok-shi* reached the Blight, had consumed only the lonely house where the one had wrought her misdeed. All that was be found was a pool of water, so lividly powerful it was painful to approach, yet to the eyes wholly innocuous, dark and peaceful, with a rim of black about the edge. And, just perceptibly, growing larger.

"At first, we believed we could stop it. Spells of nullification, containment, cancellation. We plumbed the depths of our knowledge, and it was not enough. The Blight transmuted every container, even those constructed of raw force, and it fed on everything we tried to use to neutralise it. Soon, Myridar was a bay, a bite gnawed out of the north. Every animal, bird, and insect of the region had fled south and the Myridans with them, and we turned to solutions born of desperation.

"Sar-Ibis is – was – a long, narrow island, at one point only half a day's journey across. We resolved that this would be the place to stop the Blight. The entire north was evacuated: cities, towns, the cottages of wood-cutters. Even those places which would not be reached by the Blight for weeks were emptied, taken south.

"Then, gathering together all the *lok-shi* able to contribute to the casting, we shattered Sar-Ibis, sheared off a third of our island and cast it, and the Blight, into the sea."

The Ibisian woman had paused then, taken a deep breath and looked down. Her face remained expressionless, but for the first time the effort in the telling of her tale had been palpable. It had been the only time, in the months that Kerikath las Dona had taught her, that Medair had been certain her teacher felt the horror and sorrow that such disaster should inspire. And, after a moment, that loss of control had been mastered and she'd gone on.

"We could feel the power of it still, somewhat muffled. We believed the Blight to be eating away the remnant of the north beneath the water, and kept close watch while we organised those who had been displaced. The breaking of Sar-Ibis had roused the earth, and it trembled constantly. We had known that we would suffer for our deed, and did what little we could to soothe the land, thinking the worst was over. Then Tenrathlar, one of our most beautiful cities, fell into the sea.

"Forty thousand people, gone in the blink of an eye. And Tenrathlar was in what had been the most stable region. We could feel the power of the Blight expand, though it was no longer visible to us, and realised our peril. Wild magic now ate away the foundations of Sar-Ibis. The breaking of Sar-Ibis, that unspeakable sacrifice, had made matters worse. Those who knew well the land's humours made their judgment. Even if we could eradicate the Blight that very moment, Sar-Ibis was beyond saving. We must leave or fall with it into the waves.

"Even with the enhancement of every rahlstone in the *kiereddas*, a gate such as we used would not ordinarily be within our power. Not one we could hold open long enough for every Ibis-lar to travel through. But with wild magic loose, our reserves replenished almost as quickly as we could cast, so it was possible, though a massive undertaking.

"What we have brought with us is far outweighed by what was impossible to shift, what we could not reach, and what was forgotten. And there was a difficulty which overwhelmed all other considerations: the Blight. If it had spread to the foundations of our island, it could travel across the ocean floor. If it travelled beneath the ocean, then there would be no point in fleeing to another land only to watch it also be consumed."

"Is Farakkan in danger?" Kedy had asked immediately, as was his duty. The Kerikath had shaken her head.

"No. The Kierash-that-was made a final attempt to stop the Blight. A desperate gamble. Even as the last few thousands were hurrying through the gates, he went to Desana, a mountain rapidly becoming an island, and attempted a great conjuration. He drew all that was power to himself." Selai had looked down. "Such a thing would kill any mage, and we could see the pyre of his destruction even as we struggled to maintain gates which were no longer fuelled by wild magic. He succeeded. The last few of us, escaping through gates originating from this land, witnessed the final wreck of Sar-Ibis, and there was nothing of wild magic in that devastation, only the trembling of rootless earth."

Medair had felt impossibly sorry for the Ibisians, as their new teacher had finished her tale. Then they had been summoned back to the throne room, and Kier Ieskar had declared war. It was little comfort for Medair to reflect that black denans had not survived. That they, unlike the Ibis-lar, had not taken root in Farak's breast.

Ten

A fort on a hostile border would always be a place of precautions and watches, but the current situation called for more. Avahn, taking Medair about Finrathlar's valley, trailed her past numerous drills of militia. Preparations for war. She had thought their entry into the city had gone unremarked, but watching other travellers challenged made her realise that Cor-Ibis' party had been recognised and allowed through unhindered. He was, after all, its Lord.

Everyone Avahn met asked after Cor-Ibis' health, for the adept had finally given into dramatic necessity and developed a fever. Although only mild, it had kept him to his rooms for the past five days and convinced all Finrathlar he was at death's door. Avahn obviously relished the poorly concealed dismay of the Finrathe dignitaries who came to pay their respects to him as Cor-Ibis' proxy. His appointment as the Keridahl's heir was truly not popular, and with rumours about his cousin's health running riot many were finally considering the prospect of Keridahl Avahn las Cor-Ibis seriously.

Avahn made sure they went away with their preconceptions confirmed. His pose of feckless disinterest in anything resembling a solemn issue by turns infuriated and shocked them, though none ventured to criticise him to his face.

"Did you grow up here?" Medair asked, as he took her out of the city to show her some of the look-out points among the circling hills. The way he talked about Finrathlar revealed a deep-seated affection for the place.

"As good as," Avahn replied. "Yearly visits when I was very young, and after Amaret we were practically shackled to my esteemed cousin."

"We?"

"Oh, all the potential heirs. Our doting parents weren't about to risk another twig of the great family gaining prominence in Cor-Ibis' eyes. Excuses were found for all of us to spend much of the year thrusting ourselves in his way. My parents took a house..." He stopped, turned in the saddle and indicated an area of Finrathlar a short distance from The Avenue. "We wintered here, dined with him as often as permitted." Avahn's mouth compressed, then he shrugged. "There isn't a place like Finrathlar anywhere else in the world," he continued, stroking his gelding's neck. "Maybe it's the size, or the Cor-Ibis presence, as folk say. Whatever the cause, Finrathlar's clean and beautiful and safe, with adventure just beyond the hills. Probably it is just that I did, as you say, grow up here, but despite being a fortress on a border, this is still the most peaceful place I know. This is Sar-Ibis, remade."

Medair considered him: precisely dressed, handsome. A White Snake who loved a Palladium made to resemble Sar-Ibis. "When did you decide to stop competing?"

Avahn flashed her a sharp, amused look. "You've been talking to Ileaha. Be assured that my true nature was revealed early. Surreive was always thought to hold his favour. The jewel of the family, truly the ideal heir."

Smiling, he took her up to the crest of the hill to show her the walls which stretched around the outer slopes of the valley. It had always been a very defensible area, but the Ibisians had reinforced the natural features to make it near-impregnable. Avahn pointed out a squat barracks building incorporated into the wall.

"I won't say it's impossible to get a force into Finrathlar without the entire valley rushing to the defence, but an invader would need to know a few well-guarded secrets to manage to take us by surprise."

Nodding, Medair glanced back across the valley to where the Imperial base had been. Damp and unpleasant, but a haven when those bandits had made such pests of themselves. Belatedly, she noticed Avahn's stillness. He was staring at her with wide, disbelieving eyes, swiftly veiled when she turned. The base could only be one of those well-guarded secrets and now he was suspicious and alert. She had hoped this ride would allow her to gently pursue such interesting topics as "the Hold" and "the purists", and she'd just made the task doubly difficult.

Cursing herself, Medair ignored his sudden withdrawal as if she had no comprehension of what she or he may well have revealed. "'After Amaret'," she repeated, blandly. "What was Amaret? Some sort of battle?"

He laughed, startled, and shook his head. The smile returned to his lips, but the watchfulness did not leave his eyes. "It's sometimes difficult to remember that you claim only the vaguest knowledge of society. Keris Amaret was Cor-Ibis' wife."

So Medair had guessed. "She died then? I don't understand why he would need to take an heir from his cousins. Did he swear undying loyalty to her memory or something?"

"Not many people would be able to say that with a straight face, unless they truly were ignorant of the truth. No, Keris Amaret left him, and he certainly didn't regret her going. I was young when they wed and don't know if they ever even liked each other. It was only a *sha-leon* marriage after all. A political alliance. But the end was enough to put anyone off marriage in general."

"I must be misremembering what I know of Ibisian society. I thought marriage was no more required for the getting of heirs than it is in any other land."

Avahn shrugged and nudged his gelding to a few slow steps. "What do you know of the previous Keridahl Cor-Ibis?" he asked.

"She was this one's mother," Medair replied, promptly.

He waited until it was obvious that she wasn't going to continue, then looked as if he suspected she was being deliberately obtuse. "Very well. Yes, Keridahl Galen was my esteemed cousin's mother. She was Keridahl Alar, Regent when the Kier was too young to rule, an adept of such strength that only her son is known to have surpassed her. 'Galen Never-Wrong'. That was meant to be an insult, but as my father says, it was too close to true to sting. A frightening reputation, a formidable woman. I remember the first time we came to The Avenue, just before the Kier was crowned. My parents had lectured me for days about how to behave, how to not offend. I was eight and terrified and when I saw her she was this quiet, rather plain woman and she had the rarest, most lovely smile. She could charm the birds from the trees just by listening to them, and she saw nothing unusual in spending her afternoon indulging a child's desire to be introduced to every beast in her stable. By the end of the day I had asked her if she could be my mother." He met Medair's eyes and shrugged. "My own mother hates horses. Keridahl Galen seemed like perfection to me. I envied my esteemed cousin her above all else."

Avahn stopped speaking, and sent his gelding into a trot. Medair matched him easily, waiting until he had slowed.

"So you didn't want to admire him, didn't want to perform to win his approval, but you couldn't help yourself at times."

His eyes narrowed and he deliberately looked her up and down, an expressionless blonde woman on a chestnut horse, who knew Finrathlar's secrets when she should not. But then he smiled, regaining at least the appearance of a light heart. "You remind me of Cor-Ibis, actually, but you're more talkative. Now what was it I was saying? Ah, yes. My cousin and his need for heirs. He married Keris Amaret when he was only twenty, at his mother's recommendation. Even after Kierash Inelkar contracted a child with Kerikath las Reive, many thought that Keridahl Cor-Ibis would arrange things between her son and the Kierash, that there would be a final rejoining of the lines after all these centuries. But they were wrong, as usual, when it came to dealing with her. A marriage, even *sha-leon*, put an end to any speculation that Kerin Illukar would marry Kierash Inelkar."

Avahn hesitated. "When it was announced, it was thought confirmation that Keridahl Galen objected to the Farak-lar strain of blood in the Saral-Ibis line. The purists make a great deal of it still."

Somehow, Medair didn't have it in her to be pleased that Cor-Ibis' mother had been as arrogantly superior as any other White Snake. "Are they right to do so?"

"I don't know. It can't be escaped that the Kier's blood, the entire Saral-Ibis line, is not pure. The Cor-Ibis line is loyal to a fault, and I've heard no suggestion that Keridahl Galen dealt with pure-blood differently from Farak-lar or those who are both. Yet no Keridahl Cor-Ibis has ever mixed blood with Farak-lar.

Keridahl Galen chose a pure-blood to father her son and a pure-blood to marry that son. Of course the purists think it significant."

This was more complex than Medair had realised. "Does anyone actually admit to being a purist?"

"Oh, yes." He looked at her again, and she could see him assessing whether she was offended by the topic. "There are those who keep their opinions to themselves, but it's not impossible to walk a fine line between expressing a wish to keep the blood cold – even you must know what that means – and failing to point out that the Saral-Ibis line no longer has that purity."

Cold blood. Nothing to do with temperature or emotion, and everything to do with self-control. The Ibisian idea of nobility. "Mixed blood is considered less...disciplined?"

Avahn nodded. "I don't even know if it's true there's a difference," he said, baldly. "Mylar – one of my cousins – is the best of men. Powerful in magic, already adept, never unjust or out of sorts. I've not once seen him angered, unlike Surreive. Unlike me. And his mother is fully Farak-lar – it was a great scandal long ago. Some of the family will never forgive it."

"Does Cor-Ibis?"

"I doubt Mylar complains of his treatment at my esteemed cousin's hands." Avahn's fine mouth twisted into bitter lines. "I don't know, Medair. I'm his heir, but I haven't graduated to the level of confidant. No-one has *that* honour. He agreed to a *sha-leon* marriage with a pure-blood woman, but why is something no-one would be so crude as to ask him. Whether because purity matters to him or simply because his mother suggested it. Or if he didn't care who he married, or briefly did want Amaret – who knows? Not, at least, because he was under his mother's thumb. My father loved their occasional disagreements. Winter at The Avenue." He reined in his black, and glanced down into the valley, the frown smoothing from his face. "I can scarcely believe I'm talking about purists with a woman named Medair. Let alone Amaret. Do you know, I've never discussed her before? Something everyone knows, except you."

"You've not often travelled outside Palladium, have you?"

"Not extensively. It's interesting to have our famed egocentrism demonstrated. Let me summarise the rest of their relationship. During the first year of the marriage, Keris Amaret conceived twice and lost the babe practically as soon as it was confirmed she was pregnant. The third pregnancy proved more lasting. Then Keridahl Galen died and Keris Amaret left my cousin before the tomb was set. She was four or five months pregnant at the time, and rather gleefully announced it wasn't his. She really hated him, towards the end. The marriage lasted less than two years."

"You talk about her in the past tense."

"She died giving birth, the child stillborn. Wasn't his, either; she was telling the truth about that. Mixed-blood. Cor-Ibis made no move to get another heir, after, but it was the fact that Amaret had carried someone else's child almost to term which brought the Family out. It was taken as an indication that he could not father a viable child. His mother had miscarried three times before he was born. So the various branches of the family moved in to secure their positions." Avahn's voice was full of disgust, but Medair was remembering the familiar contempt with which he treated Ileaha. To her, it sounded like the Cor-Ibis family were purists who were not willing to admit the fact.

Stray memories chose their moment to lock into place and she exclaimed softly. Avahn looked to her in enquiry and she lifted a shoulder.

"I just remembered that Illukar was the name of the Ibisian who died with Sar-Ibis, getting rid of the wild magic. Kier Ieskar's brother. I knew I'd heard the name in connection to the invasion. What a thing to call a child."

Laughing, Avahn nudged his gelding closer so he could reach across to pat her arm. "Yes, Medair, parents are unaccountable when they are faced with offspring in need of a name. Have you only just realised that the family descends from the brother of the *Niadril* Kier? There have been four named Illukar las Cor-Ibis. The first used the strength of his blood to destroy wild magic, when the Blight overwhelmed Sar-Ibis. Before that he was Illukar las Saral-Ibis, since he was the *Niadril* Kier's brother, but according to the histories he declared himself Cor-Ibis before going to his death, because he was to be the end, not the heart of the land."

"The *Cuor*." It was an instrument of execution and Medair was not altogether surprised that no Ibisian of her time had explained the name Illukar las Cor-Ibis to her. She belatedly remembered that she wasn't supposed to understand Ibis-laran, but Avahn didn't seem to have noticed. He nodded once and continued.

"The tradition carried on. The second Illukar las Cor-Ibis killed a dragon which came down from the frozen north, much to the surprise of everyone who thought them extinct. And died in the process. The third gave his life to turn the tide of a battle which threatened to bring down the Silver Throne. It is a fated name."

Kier Ieskar had only once mentioned his brother to her, and that when a small child, a girl of three or so years, had slipped into the room where they had been playing marrat. She'd climbed into his lap, fretful over nightmares and wanting the only family she had left. He had held the child, whispered to her. That had been the last time she'd played marrat with him. The very next day she had asked the leave of her Emperor to find the Horn.

Medair closed her eyes. They called him the *Niadril* Kier now. It was a confusing word, a mixture of 'great', 'eternal' and 'doomed'. He was dead within six months of that night. He had known he was dying when Adestan climbed into his lap, had known that she would be left to face the overwhelming strictures placed on the Saral-Ibis family alone.

"My brother's daughter, Adestan Shen las Cor-Ibis," he'd said, making formal introduction only when the girl had quieted. He'd stood with the child in his arms, his face as blankly unemotional as it always and ever was. "We will continue this game another day, Keris an Rynstar. Your pardon." And he'd carried Adestan away. Medair, stricken by things she couldn't put into words, had left and never gone back.

Looking up, she saw echoes of him in Avahn's face. He wore that same mask, and was taking in her every reaction in much the same way his cousin had when they were speaking of the possibility of a Corminevar heir. Doubtless he was misunderstanding just as much.

"Cor-Ibis, whom you admired and envied, who frightened you and attracted you," she said, in hopes of pushing the past away. "He would have been, what? Twenty-three or four when he became Keridahl and your parents were encouraging you to try and become his heir. The idea sickened you and you retreated into Avahn the Irresponsible, who loves only pleasure, thinking less of your parents and your rivals for their behaviour, and resenting Cor-Ibis as its source. Ileaha thought you were just lazy when you turned away from studies and responsibility. I would not be at all surprised if you learned in private what you publicly rejected. How long before you realised that Cor-Ibis saw through you? Or were you completely surprised when he chose you as his heir?"

Avahn blinked twice, then sat forward in his saddle, the leather creaking. "Why do you carry a replica of a herald satchel?" he asked, voice low. "Can a woman called Medair be believed when she claims not to be a Medarist? Especially one so patently unhappy to be in the company of Ibis-lar? How did you come to be in Bariback Forest at just the right moment to recover the rahlstones? Who pipes your tune, Medair ar Corleaux? The Hold, if not Medarists?"

Medair had no idea what this Hold was, and didn't dare ask in case it revealed too great a gap in her knowledge. With a prodigious effort she pushed away her ill-humour.

"The difference in our attacks being that I made a series of statements and you asked only questions," she pointed out, hoping to make peace. Avahn looked briefly exasperated, then relaxed his angry pose.

"I don't trust you, Medair," he said. "But I am glad to know you. Trying to trap you into revealing yourself will make the journey back to Athere more entertaining."

"Or frustrating," she replied. "We should probably head back."

※

"Have you been to Athere before?" Avahn asked, as they turned their horses towards the outskirts of Finrathlar.

"I was there last year."

"You obviously travel a good deal," he said, eyes crinkling as he returned to blatantly fishing for information.

"I've been over most of Farakkan," Medair replied. "Not much in the south."

They began a rambling conversation on the comparative merits of various cities, which was a far more dangerous conversation for Medair than Avahn realised. Fortunately, he had not travelled very often outside Palladium and she was able to keep the discussion from cities she had not seen for over five hundred years.

"Kerin? Keris?"

They reined in, having seen the young woman before she called to them. Mid-twenties, about Medair's age. Her hair was a fine floating blonde, currently mussed and falling about her face. The dust on her loose white riding pants and tight-fitting dark blue jacket told her story even as she rose from the rock on which she had been sitting and came limping toward them.

"I am sorry to intrude, Kerali," she apologised. "My mare shied and I made poor work of handling her."

"You've hurt your ankle." Avahn slid from his saddle to lend the woman a hand.

"Has your horse gone far?" Medair asked, scanning the area carefully.

"Straight back to her stall, no doubt," the woman sighed, leaning on Avahn gratefully. "I don't want to spoil your day, and I know well enough that it will be out of your way, but–"

"It would be mannerless indeed if we didn't take you home," Avahn interrupted. "Do you think you can ride pillion with me?"

Smiling her gratitude, the young woman professed her willingness to try, and Avahn carefully lifted her up behind his saddle. Medair had been thinking that he was not immune to a pretty face, and so was surprised when he shot a frowning glance of warning in her direction, necessarily brief because his passenger was in a position to notice. Not certain what had made him wary, Medair again searched the hillside, seeing no sign of lurkers.

The woman, whose name was Melani, directed them to an outlying farming settlement among the northern hills. Not knowing what else to do, Medair took the precaution of sliding her satchel off her back to where she could more easily reach its contents.

Melani continued to apologise prettily. It seemed to Medair that the encounter had been arranged so the woman could have an opportunity to flirt with the heir to the Dahlein. Certainly the way Melani pressed against Avahn, arms wrapped firmly about his waist, suggested only a bedroom ambush. But, Medair told herself, if that was so Melani would surely have tried to separate Avahn from Medair.

They rode along the edge of the eastern hills of Finrathlar, then followed a winding stream, glittering in the Summer sun between two of the massed hills to the north. Medair noted deep ruts in the road, and the hoof-prints of a number of horses. Recent, but hardly unusual. The north of the valley was given over to farmland.

She felt a trickle of magic escaping nearby, and looked at Avahn, who inclined his head a fraction in return. He had been the caster then. A defensive spell or perhaps a wend-whisper, sending a message on the wind? It had not been anything which released a huge amount of power. She slipped a hand into her satchel, pulling out a ring to slide into her pocket.

A solid farmhouse came into view. "My mother should be home by now," Melani said, smiling with apparent relief. Medair began to wonder if they had been altogether too suspicious as a grey-haired woman lifted her head from where she toiled among rows of vegetables. She gave a soft cry of distress and hurried over.

"Oh, Melani! Whatever have you done to yourself?"

"Thrammit tossed me, Mama. Has she come back?"

"That cursed mare! Too skittish for her own good." The woman drew Melani down into her supporting arms, made a practiced inspection, then smiled up at Avahn. "Kerin, how can I thank you?"

"We did very little, Kel," Avahn replied as he dismounted. "The mare has not returned?"

Shaking her head, the woman steadied her daughter as she took a limping step. "No, I've not seen her." She looked distractedly at Medair, then returned to Avahn. "My other daughter will be back in a decem. If the mare hasn't returned by then, she'll collect the herders together and mount a search. Likely the creature's gone back to the stables where she was bred." She turned pleading eyes on the handsome heir to the Dahlein. "Kerin, if it's not too much trouble..."

Avahn obligingly scooped Melani into his arms, hefting her with an ease only an Ibisian could manage. Medair wondered if he would drop her at the first sign of danger. Gathering the reins of their horses, she looped them around the posts of the garden fence. It gave her a chance to stare into the hills for any sign of movement. Nothing. With a final glance about, she followed the other three inside.

Melani was directing Avahn upstairs, and her mother ushered Medair left into a kitchen. "How can I thank you and the Kerin for going so far out of your way for my daughter, Keris?" she asked. "All because she's overfond of that pretty mare's looks, no matter the creature's temperament. I hope she's not inconvenienced you too greatly?"

"She has given us a chance to see another part of Finrathlar, Kel–"

"–las Raithen," the woman continued, smiling. "It is very good of you."

"Do you live here alone, Kel las Raithen?" Medair asked, since she saw no sign of any others, though the house was large enough.

The woman laughed. "AlKier, no! Besides my daughters, we've Miasa in the main building, and a half-dozen herders crowding out the back house. Babies the lot of them. They call this Orphans' Farm because I've taken so many in, but they make good herders if you start them young enough. Some say I'm a fool to trust urchins, but with fair treatment, I get fair workers. Keridahl Galen's wisdom."

Medair asked for clarification and was treated to an enthusiastic account of certain laws Keridahl Galen had put into effect concerning homeless children.

"But I'm running on. My other daughter has taken Miasa into Finrathlar for supplies and the herders are out chasing the Spring lambs over the hills. And Melani..." The woman shook her head, but smiled fondly at the same time. Medair, who thought Avahn had been upstairs for too long a time, relaxed on seeing him appear at the top of the stairs.

"She asked for water, Kel," Avahn said, looking amused.

"Oh, and where are my manners, keeping you standing about without even offering you something to take the dust off?" Kel las Raithen turned, after a slight curtsy to Avahn, and took a cloth off a jug standing on a sideboard. Setting out two pottery cups for Avahn and Medair, she filled another for her daughter. Begging them to make free of her kitchen, she went upstairs.

Avahn shook his head, looking wry. He held up one hand and sketched a series of figures in the air, then closed his eyes and cocked his head to one side as if listening.

"I was convinced it was an ambush," he said, after a few moments. "But there's no-one else in the house and I can't detect any enchantment threatening. Over-caution. We spent too long in Kyledra waiting for my cousin to send word, convinced that every second person was a spy."

"What made you suspicious of her?" Medair asked, pouring out the water.

"Her ankle's not at all swollen, and she looked too...picturesque, as if she'd set herself up as maiden in distress."

"Hadn't she?" Medair asked. "My concern was for your breathing, she was holding on so tight."

"Yes, a different sort of trap to what I assumed. Never bend over a woman on a bed if she has designs," he advised. "You would be amazed how often such things have happened to me in the last six months – since my cousin finally chose his heir. Surreive, who is due a considerable fortune, even without the possibility of succeeding Cor-Ibis, complains about having to constantly foil marriage plots. I didn't believe her once." He straightened his riding coat. "Well, I learned something about you, at least. We weren't certain if you were a mage, but you gave yourself away when I released the wend-whisper."

Medair shrugged, handing him a cup. "What would you do, Avahn, if you discovered that the only secret I had was where I picked up a handy satchel? Will you be terribly disappointed to learn I'm not involved in some complicated plot?"

"I think that you are a wild piece on the marrat board," Avahn replied. "I have yet to think of a reasonable explanation why someone working actively against us would return the rahlstones, and I prefer to believe that you've simply been drawn in, away from whatever nefarious activity in which you were previously engaged." He shrugged. "At least, that's my esteemed cousin's opinion, but I agree and so make it my own. I'm not sure what amount of duplicity will be required to find out exactly what, but, just so you know, we're lulling you into a false sense of security before we pounce."

Medair, who had been raising her cup to her lips, paused, brows drawing together. She swirled the clear liquid, and shrugged when Avahn held up the cup he had drained.

"Did it taste strange or anything?" she asked.

"Stale water. There's no enchantment on it. I would have detected that."

Frowning, she put her cup down.

"If you're trying to make me nervous, you are succeeding, Medair ar Corleaux." Then he swayed, and went the strange colour of an Ibisian who had paled even further. "Damn," he muttered, as the sound of approaching horses became audible. "Medair, you'd better run while you can. You might be able to make it out the back way."

"I expect they've covered any escape routes." Angry that she hadn't stopped him drinking, her mind skipped through alternatives. "Who did you send the wend-whisper to?"

"Cor-Ibis. One of his rules: sending a message if something unusual happens, especially keeping him informed of alterations in plans for wandering. I have to send another a decem afterwards or..."

With a speed which suggested magic had been involved after all, Avahn collapsed and she caught hold of him, a double armful of warm flesh scented with sandalwood. Surprised by the strength of her concern, she lowered his limp form to the wooden floor. Detouring her mind away from the concept of genuinely caring for a White Snake, she looked wildly around the room. The only thing in her satchel that would protect them both needed a little more space.

Hoping Avahn had been about to say "...or he will raise the alarm," not "...or he'll lecture me when I return," Medair pushed chairs out of the way. Heart pounding, she positioned Avahn in a clear corner of the kitchen, then put a chair carefully over the top of him. The jingle of stirrup and bridle told her the riders were dismounting and it was tempting to just turn invisible and run. But she couldn't leave him. And here she'd been planning for the Ibisians to protect her, not the other way around.

Her hand darted into her satchel, selecting a long silvery cord. Measuring it doubtfully, she repositioned Avahn on his side, drawing his knees up and tucking his arms in. Then, with frantic haste, she lay the cord out in a circle around her, the chair and Avahn. The metal locking mechanism slid together with a firm click and she was rewarded with a surge of power, both visible and tangible. A shield-wall, much like the one Cor-Ibis had almost killed himself summoning, but hers was far more enduring. Safe.

She let her breath out as a voice outside called caution. And so they should. The contents of her satchel might not be able to give her what she wanted, but they made her dangerous. After checking Avahn again, she planted herself firmly on the chair, folded her arms and waited, listening to their progress. They wouldn't know that the source of the power surge was defensive magic, or that Avahn was unconscious. They would come in expecting every kind of attack.

She wondered what arcane weapons Avahn could produce at need, what set-spells he would have drawn upon if only he hadn't been unconscious. It had been an elegant little trap. If the woman had pressed the water on them, if she had stayed to watch them drink, had not offered it as a carefully orchestrated afterthought, they would have been more suspicious. Medair sighed, feeling terribly vulnerable despite her resources. If, if, if.

A door at the back of the house burst open and something bounced across the floor, exploding with a dull blue flash. Behind her shield-wall, Medair couldn't sense the power which might be involved. Presuming they still wanted her alive, it was probably some sort of sleep. She watched it dissipate, wishing she'd run.

Flanked by two stocky female warriors, the mage she had first seen on Bariback Mountain trailed the tossed spell into the room. The sight of her, leaning back on her chair in a half-globe of glimmering power, stopped them short. The women looked to the mage, who gestured them into a guard position. Then the front door was opened less violently and the rest of the Decians entered the room, weapons at ready.

"A spell shield, Captain," the mage said, moving towards them.

"So I see, Cerden," Captain Vorclase replied. He looked from Medair to Avahn, curled at her feet. "Can you break it?"

"I can try..." The mage hesitated, then met his Captain's flat black eyes. "But you can feel its strength as well as I. Farak's Teeth, they can probably feel it in the centre of Finrathlar! We could chip at that for a year without making a dint."

"Well, well." Vorclase didn't seem particularly perturbed. He circled around Medair, then tested the shield with the back of his fingers. There was a faint hiss, and he jerked away quickly. 'Kel las Raithen' and her daughter emerged from upstairs and his eyes flicked toward them, then back to Medair.

"Introductions are in order, I think," he said and bowed, short and sharp. "I am Captain Jan Vorclase, of His Majesty King Xarus Estarion's armies. May I have the honour of your name?"

"Medair ar Corleaux," she replied, uncrossing and recrossing her arms. The posture helped to hide her trembling.

"Truly a great pleasure to catch up with you at last, Miss ar Corleaux. It has been quite a chase."

"I would be very glad to know why you take such an interest." She was pleased there was no quaver in her voice. Calm and in control: it was important to make them believe it.

"Would you? Speaking of assuaging curiosity, tell me, Miss ar Corleaux, what is a Medarist doing travelling in the company of White Snakes?"

"Getting away from you, for a start."

"I'm sorry to have driven you to such an association. Has it occurred to you that we need only wait until you are driven to us by hunger and thirst?"

"What, in a decem?" She smiled at him unpleasantly. "This spell-shield would be enough to attract the Keridahl's attention, even if Avahn had not sent a wend-whisper. I can't see any troops he sends taking more than a decem to get here." She cocked her head toward Melani. "If you are going to pretend to twist your ankle, you might consider some visible swelling."

"She's bluffing," said the Mersian, coming forward to glower at Medair. He seemed to have recovered from being hit on the head.

"What if she's not?" Kel las Raithen asked, matronly calm gone in favour of tense nerves. "I didn't contract for a battle with White Snake guards, Vorclase. This has gone bad. Face it and let's get out of here."

"Don't rush off just yet, Fariti," Vorclase said. He selected a chair and placed it opposite Medair. "I had assumed Cor-Ibis didn't know what he had," he said, conversationally. "But if he has provided you with protection of this order, he obviously has some inkling. Well, Medair – may I call you Medair? I shall share the history behind this chase, if that will make you more reasonable. You cannot want to continue in the company of Ibisians, surely? I admit we handled our first encounter badly, but there is time to make amends. A decem or so."

Medair, nothing loath to hear an explanation, merely raised her eyebrows and leaned back more comfortably on the chair.

"A captive audience, in a way," the Decian said. "Well, you must know that we grind slowly towards war. King Xarus has made solemn vow to set the rightful ruler of Palladium on the Silver Throne. Tarsus, the Emperor-in-Exile, descends from Prince-Elect Verium, son of the great Grevain Corminevar."

"I assume that there's proof of this?" Medair asked, her interest showing in her voice. She had heard the Ibisian side of this story. She would listen to the Decian version.

"Of course. The Prince-Elect died before his daughter was born, but he sent the child's mother out of Athere with written acknowledgment of paternity." He paused, dark eyes narrowing.

"Sealed with the Imperial Ring, so none might gainsay the girl's parentage."

Medair stiffened, and saw his satisfaction at her response. The impression of the Imperial Ring was impossible to forge. Constructed to prevent the falsifying of documents in the Corminevar name, it had descended into the hands of Kier Inelkar. Inelkar was unlikely to go forging documents to end her own rule. So Verium truly had–

"These are only your words," she said, stiffly. "Nor does it at all explain why you pursue me from Kyledra into Palladium itself. What am I to kings and emperors? I assure you I have no Imperial blood."

"Perhaps not. But, as I said, war darkens the horizon. We skirmish for possession of the best weapons. Collections of rahlstones, mercenaries, women who live on mountains. My King would see that this battle is won with the least bloodshed possible, and he turned to military advisers, histories, even seers to ensure this end. Most seers are charlatans, but one, one had a reputation earned with true power, and he spoke these words to my King: *'When the thrones of all Farakkan hang in the balance, control of the one who dwells on Bariback Mountain will decide the future.'* Exactly how and why we would have asked him, but the True Seeing cost him his life's breath. Inconvenient."

"I don't intend to take sides in the coming battle," she replied, forcing her voice to remain even.

"Everyone must take sides, Medair ar Corleaux. I don't know what it is that you can do, but I can see that you are Farakkian, hear the message of your name. Yet you travel with White Snakes. Why? Out of fear of us? Then I give you my word and my oath – in the name of Xarus Estarion, on the blood of my ancestors, to the peril of my soul, I swear you will not be threatened in any way if you come with us. Every honour we can extend will be yours." Hawk face sincere, he leaned forward on his chair. "You know it's the right thing to do. Too long has the usurper race sat upon the Silver Throne, while the true Corminevar heirs have lived in hiding. Can you truly say 'this battle does not concern me'? Live up to the promise you made when taking the name of an honourable and loyal woman. Be true to her memory, to the Empire she served, and help us drive the White Snake invaders out."

Medair looked down, unable to meet his eyes any longer. His words would not draw her out of the spell-shield. Her understanding of the current political situation was shaky, but she'd readily gathered that Xarus Estarion sought to expand his own borders and was using this Tarsus as a stalking horse. But what if there truly was a Corminevar heir, duly acknowledged? Instead of returning to the northern mountains, should she find Tarsus, offer him support not connected to the ambitions of the Decian throne?

Medair looked down at Avahn, his face obscured by a braid of silky white hair. Finrathlar was his home, Palladium was the land to which he had been born and raised. She didn't know what to do, didn't know how to interpret her oath, or if it was even valid any more. She didn't want to be part of this and Vorclase read that in her face as she raised her eyes to his again.

"There will come a time when you will have to stand forward," he said, firmly. "No-one lives outside this war, not even on Bariback Mountain. I add this. My king searches for a way to victory. Failing you, and without the rahlstones, he will tread a more dangerous path to cleansing Palladium. Think on that."

"She's not budging, Sir," the Mersian said, tersely. "If there're troops coming, we've got to make tracks soon."

"Then answer me, Medair ar Corleaux. Will you stand with the White Snakes or your own kind? Are you loyal to the blood of Corminevar?"

"I stand with neither," she replied, without hesitation. "I will not win this war for you."

Vorclase let his breath out in a short, angry exclamation. "So be it. But I cannot, you realise, leave you in the hands of White Snakes." He turned to the Mersian. "We'll burn her out."

Medair didn't protest or visibly react to the words. She sat and watched as his men set about dousing the kitchen and other rooms with lamp oil. Under Vorclase's instructions, they left a clear passage to the front door.

"If you change your mind and move quickly enough, you should be able to make your way clear. Oh, and don't expect that invisibility trick to work twice. We'll be waiting for it."

"Thanks for the warning," she replied, curling one corner of her mouth up, though she was more than a little worried. The spell-shield would keep out conjured effects, people, missiles, but she wasn't sure it would be effective against natural heat and smoke.

The mage paused at the door and looked at her, sitting in her circle of safety. He smiled, and clicked his fingers, producing a tiny spurt of flame.

The farmhouse burned.

Eleven

It would have been possible to run for the door if she had gone immediately, but Medair waited. Soon droplets of oil on the 'pathway' had ignited and it was passable only to salamanders. Tasting the acrid smoke, feeling the heat through the shield, she knew she couldn't stay.

Kneeling, she unlinked the spell-shield and tucked it safely away. The Decians would be able to sense the abrupt disappearance of its power emissions just as they would feel but not comprehend what she planned to use next. Avahn groaned, but showed no signs of recovering as she levered him precariously over one shoulder, one arm wrapped firmly across his thighs. His hair flicked the back of her knees as she rose with difficulty to her feet. Smoke stung her eyes, tore at her throat.

It was a moment to make Medair regret her decision to stop investigating Kersym Bleak's hoard, since there could very well be something in her satchel which would protect her from the flames, if only she knew what it was and how to use it. Struggling to keep Avahn slung across her shoulder, she fished into her satchel and produced the very ring which had prompted her decision to give up experimenting with artefacts. Managing to cram it onto the middle finger of her left hand, she closed her eyes. When Medair had first tried on the ring, a simple circle of silver, it had not activated. She could only be sure that it possessed some strong magic, but could make nothing of the engraving inside the band. Six hundred feet of what? The next time, she'd found out. She'd put it on, seen no response, heard a noise and stared toward a nearby stand of trees. And from the ring, as happened now, a circle of light expanded. It had spread along her arm, stretching to cover her entire body. Then she had been in the trees. About twenty feet off the ground, sharing a branch with the squirrel whose nut-gathering attempts had attracted her attention. But only long enough to fall off.

Teleport spells were something only a very powerful adept would dare attempt, and most would prefer to use a gate instead. It was necessary to very precisely picture a destination within the spell's range. Those who did not visualise their target clearly might never arrive, or even appear within an object. Or twenty feet above the ground.

Medair pictured the low, sheltering hill which curved around to hide the farmhouse from those travelling north from Finrathlar. She'd had a nice long look at that when she was tying up the horses, scanning for men with crossbows waiting in ambush. The light crawled up her neck and face, covered her eyes with a glimmering haze and she concentrated with all her strength on every detail she could remember of the very crest of the hill, of just exactly how and where she wanted to be. Inches above it, not in it. Her arm tightened on Avahn's legs as the light grew brighter, blocking out roiling black smoke and dancing flames. Above it, not in it.

She hadn't realised how hot the room had become until she fell into the wind, tumbling to the ground in a tangle with long Ibisian limbs. She righted herself, then hastily flattened to the ground. Spiky tufts of grass pricked her flesh as she stared down at the burning farmhouse, but no-one was looking up at her.

Grabbing Avahn beneath the arms, she dragged him further up the slope. The flames were only now becoming visible, though the inside of the building must be a furnace. She had positioned herself in the elbow of the hill's sheltering arm, and was able to see the rear of the farmhouse and other smaller buildings behind it. Two of the Decians were stationed there, to prevent any suicidal dashes through fiery and unfamiliar rooms. Vorclase and his mage were in close conversation at the front. She wondered what they had made of the surge of power which would have announced her teleportation. They did not so much as glance towards her hill.

It was a warm, sunny day, heading into late afternoon, but her teeth chattered and she was shivering uncontrollably. Now that she was out of immediate danger, reaction was setting in. Medair was a Herald, not a hero. She barely knew how to swing a sword, and would always prefer to run than fight. She could smell smoke in her hair, her clothing, and was amazed that she hadn't faltered when the blaze pressed upon her. But she'd been told she was cool under pressure. And jelly after, it seemed.

The Decians were not quick to leave. Medair wondered if the trace which was set upon her had anything to do with their delay. She didn't know if a trace lapsed after the death of the subject, and breathed a sigh of relief when her pursuers finally mounted and galloped off. South towards Finrathlar, though they'd doubtless detour away from the road as soon as they could. After the hoof-beats had faded, she rolled over onto her back and stared up at the blue summer sky, thinking about heirs and Ibisians and oaths until it all whirled about in her head.

Even if this Tarsus was rightfully Emperor, it did not change the fact that the Ibisians weren't invaders, not after five hundred years. The parentage of all but these purists could be traced to the noble families of the Empire as well as Sar-Ibis. She had sworn oath to Grevain Corminevar in his capacity as Palladium's ruler, not to him as an individual, not to his bloodline.

What was *wrong* with her?! How could she even suggest an Ibisian had more right to sit on the Silver Throne than an acknowledged child of the Corminevar line, one who was not tainted with White Snake blood and values? But attempting to 'cleanse' Palladium would involve killing a huge portion of its inhabitants, including descendants of Empire nobility. Merely because an Ibisian had climbed into their family tree.

Her conviction that it was not her war remained unshaken. She was out of her time, her moment had passed. The Horn of Farak could not be used against the Ibisians now and she would return it to its resting place. She might feel wretched about her own inescapable logic, might dream of her Emperor turning his face from her, but she could not act against the Ibisians. Self-justification took her around the circle again and again and only succeeded in making her unhappier.

Eventually she sat up, fairly certain that any lingering Decians would have given up, if they had indeed stayed to spy. The farmhouse was burning merrily, sending up a black gout of smoke. It would be an admirable beacon for anyone Cor-Ibis might have sent to investigate Avahn's wend-whisper.

She examined Avahn more closely, wondering what the drug had been. He was looking a little battered, his face scraped some time during the escape. She brushed a wandering ant from his cheek and analysed her emotions warily. A friend who was an Ibisian. She couldn't imagine using the Horn of Farak to kill him, or Ileaha. Or Cor-Ibis, no matter *who* he reminded her of.

On the slope of the hill opposite she saw Avahn's horse peacefully cropping grass. Catching horses seemed a better pursuit than her current thoughts, so she shifted Avahn onto his side so his face was out of the sun and set off to round up their mounts. With the help of the silver ring, she had collected them both and even brought Avahn down off the hill by the time the rescue party finally showed up.

The farmhouse was still blazing merrily, though parts of it had begun to collapse into embers and char. Medair was out back investigating some strange thumping noises, audible over the crackle of flames and the hysterics of a coop of chickens, when approaching hoof-beats took precedence.

She headed back to Avahn, and found him surrounded by horses. Cor-Ibis, worlds better for five days' rest, had already dismounted. He bent to check his heir for signs of life.

"Just drugged," she informed him. "He said he would have known if it was enchanted. Though it did take hold very quickly."

The Keridahl ignored her words, satisfying himself over Avahn's condition before rising. He gestured for two of the arms-men he had brought with him to attend to the youth. Then he turned his attention fully on to Medair, studying her almost as if he hadn't seen her before. She noted that he was as perfectly groomed as if he had just stepped away from the mirror, his muted finery pristine, his hair unruffled by the ride. Truly a far cry from the mud and ash-grimed man she had first seen. Keridahl Avec.

"What of those who dwell here?" he asked, turning his attention to the fire without immediately delving into the how and why.

She shrugged. "I haven't seen anyone, but I suspect that a search among the buildings out back might prove fruitful. Someone's certainly banging on something around there."

Another pair of guards were dispatched and then Cor-Ibis turned to the fire. Speaking softly beneath his breath, he watched impassively as the flames flickered and died away. Medair suspected that he was annoyed, whether with her or over the fact that his demesne had been invaded she was not certain. The remains of the roof caved in, as if the fire had been the only thing holding it up, and Medair winced at the cloud of ash and tiny cinders which billowed out.

"Tell me what happened here, Kel ar Corleaux."

They walked around to the back of the house as Medair, carefully choosing her words, told him of the well-played trap. It was difficult to decide exactly what line to take.

"Avahn drank first," she said. "It only took, oh, not very long for it to effect him." She paused, because the two guards sent to investigate the thumping had opened the doors of what looked to be a root cellar and several distressed and angry women tumbled into the light. "Melani or her mother must have signalled from an upstairs window, because the rest arrived at just the right moment, moving in ready to fight if we hadn't helpfully drugged ourselves into unconsciousness." She considered his fine-boned profile. He was following her story without any change of expression, watching the women.

"It seemed that their plan, at the outset, was to take us alive, but I barricaded us out of their reach and their solution was to set the building on fire." She paused again. "I suppose I shouldn't have told them that Avahn had sent a wend-whisper, or they'd still be here, trying to get us out of the barricade. With time a pressing factor, they chose to cut their losses."

Working on the theory that it was safest to say as little as possible, Medair stopped speaking, and listened in silence as Kerin las Lorednor skilfully extracted the tales of the angry women. The Decians had descended on them at midday, as they sat down for a meal. One woman held her arm to her chest, having made an attempt to fight against their attackers. Her name was Melani.

Cor-Ibis spoke briefly to the elderly woman who seemed to be their leader. Arrangements would be made for temporary shelter until the farmhouse was rebuilt. He did not speak again until they were on the outskirts of Finrathlar.

"Tell me, Kel ar Corleaux," he said. "Was it Avahn or yourself who was the target of this raid?"

Medair lifted one shoulder. "Both, I should think."

"You have a trace fixed upon you."

"I know."

His face was a mask, neither cold nor forthcoming. "The trace could not have been set after you obtained that charm."

"No, it was before," she agreed. "It's been very inconvenient. I was hoping it had worn off, by now."

Cor-Ibis gazed at her. "I owe you life-debt, Kel ar Corleaux. And the rahlstones weigh the scales further. To continue to question where you choose not to answer is difficult, but I cannot ignore this attack. Vorclase is not fool enough to have failed to ascertain that the rahlstones have been sent on with Jedda. To make such an elaborate attempt in the heart of my Dahlein speaks of a strong motivation beyond the stones." He turned his head slightly to consider the cluster of guards to whom he had entrusted his heir. "Avahn has not such intrinsic value."

"Does a trace dissipate when the subject dies?" Medair asked.

Pale grey eyes were briefly veiled. "No," he replied. "Since the link is to the shell rather than what dwells within." He raised one long hand in a languid gesture. "In a fire, with the complete destruction of the traced...object, then yes, it would be possible."

"But not guaranteed," Medair verified, pleased. She gave Cor-Ibis an apologetic glance. "I do think they came for me, for reasons other than the rahlstones. I didn't expect them to follow into Palladium, and certainly don't suppose they will continue this chase, especially if they leave Finrathlar before learning that Avahn and I still live."

"Your escape surprises me," he remarked.

"Luck." She was certainly not going to go into detail. She could only hope his debt would outweigh his no doubt strong wish to compel a few straight answers out of her. "I was close to joining Avahn and then they would have only been faced with the task of smuggling us out. You seem fully recovered Keridahl. Can we hope to resume our journey tomorrow?"

The grey eyes searched her face dispassionately, then Cor-Ibis inclined his head.

"Presuming Avahn is unharmed, we will travel on, Kel ar Corleaux."

Twelve

"How did the rahlstones come to be stolen in the first place?" Medair asked, resisting the temptation to look self-consciously away at green, sprawling Pelamath, their journey's halfway point. They were resting a day in the city, a major trade junction sitting squarely on the border of the massive Cor-Ibis Dahlein. Only a week's ride from Athere, it had once been a herding town called Pelladon.

Cor-Ibis' eyelids dropped a fraction, a mannerism she still suspected betrayed otherwise hidden amusement. Conversation with the man was like walking through a forest full of snares, with the trapper following behind to study her fumbles. She kept falling over questions like the one he had just asked — what she thought of the Simonacy — and having to abruptly change the subject to hide her complete ignorance of who or what he was talking about.

Was the Simonacy some dreadfully obscure topic he had dredged up from the far reaches of his memory, just to see whether she would weasel out of answering? Or the equivalent of the Western Kingdoms, or the Korgan Lands, or Farak herself? The sort of thing about which no normal person would not have some opinion. Even ambiguous answers could be treacherous, so she had to resort to a transparent change of subject.

"It is not a story which depicts Palladian security in any favourable light," Cor-Ibis said now, accepting the shift from Simonacy to rahlstones without demur. He never challenged her when she squirmed from one topic to another, just made her feel hopelessly clumsy in the light of his eternal courtesy. She wished Avahn had breakfasted with them, instead of deserting her to Cor-Ibis on the balcony of yet another ducal mansion while he gallivanted off to visit friends.

"As is boasted, the vaults of the White Palace are protected by gates, guards and glamour," Cor-Ibis continued. "Gates are the easiest to circumvent, and do not even require magic for the feat. The guards themselves are *kel-sa* rank mages, and suffer the usual scrutiny levelled at such sentinels."

"Geases and truth spells," Medair murmured. If it weren't for Cor-Ibis' unwavering scrutiny, this would be a pleasant place to breakfast. The Pelamath residence was less secluded than The Avenue, and this balcony offered a view over a public park with a small lake and, distantly, the surge and bustle of a busy marketplace.

"Even so, Kel. The guards were not suspect. A thief aspiring to the vaults must overcome the physical impediments, along with several layers of detection and reinforcement spells. Without alerting guards sensitive to magical interference."

"As well shoot the moon. Yet it was done?"

"It was done. And I cannot tell you how, because I still do not know. A routine inventory revealed the rahlstones' loss something on the order of two months ago. Nothing else was missing, the wards and trips were all in place, and the guards had not reported a single unusual occurrence. A remarkable thief."

"Who was not, I take it, among the victims of that blast?"

"Not from my observation. But Thern Mara – the merchant attempting to sell the stones on – kept secrets close to her chest. Since nothing else was taken, I can only presume the thief was hired specifically for the task."

"Quite a commission." Medair toyed with the slices of apple and cheese she had so busily carved while avoiding his gaze.

"Have you been to Pelamath before, Kel?"

"No." She didn't imagine that the dozen times she'd passed through Pelladon counted.

"Then I will show you the city." His eyes were veiled when she looked up. "It is a place of many moods, Pelamath, and I rarely have a chance to see them. Ever a crossroads."

That didn't sound like an attractive prospect for a number of reasons. "I–" Medair began.

"You would rather not traipse about Pelamath in my wake," Cor-Ibis said, and a corner of his mouth curled up. She looked away, for she found these rare, wry smiles highly distracting.

Medair had no doubt about his motives for playing the courteous host. Avahn had quite certainly told Cor-Ibis what he had learned on their outing in Finrathlar and so both Cor-Ibis and his heir were more intent than ever on prying loose her secrets. She supposed she should be grateful that they chose to do this by trying to lure her into betraying herself in conversation, but keeping her wits about her through every minor exchange was truly wearying. She wished more than anything for an end to this sojourn among White Snakes.

Taking her silence as acquiescence, Cor-Ibis arranged for their excursion and Medair found herself at least not refusing. She didn't change to go out, only washed her hands after breakfast and went to wait at the front door. It was not too long before he appeared, walking down the stair of the main hall.

Cor-Ibis had found the time to exchange outfits and no doubt this affair of shot silk beneath a fine linen demi-robe was the precise thing for a quick tour. He hadn't spent the time for travelling braids, merely clasped a band of black and silver above the last foot or so of that extravagant fall of hair. Its pendulum weight swayed with each graceful step, as mesmerising as a cobra.

She thought he looked at her rather strangely as she stared up at him, so she pretended interest in the arrangement of magelights suspended from the ceiling until he reached the foot of the stair. After constructing some excessively civil apology for keeping her waiting, Cor-Ibis ushered her out the main door. It seemed only Liak ar Haedrin and a single guardsman were to accompany them. And the Keridahl proposed to go without horses.

For someone of his rank and wealth, Cor-Ibis exhibited an extreme lack of pomp. They had travelled to Pelamath with only four guards and three servants to see to the needs of Cor-Ibis, his heir and his 'guest'. Since they were no longer attempting to keep a low profile in enemy territory, Medair could only presume subdued was to his taste.

It occurred to her that Cor-Ibis must not be in any way concerned about attacks against his person, here in Pelamath. To wander through a once-conquered city on foot, with only a pair of attendants, spoke of a certainty that only the most-loved of the

Emperor's Hands had enjoyed. Or the most feared. Few dukes of her time had been adepts.

They crossed the small formal garden to the gates and were duly released into the tree-studded park. "Ourvette's Lake," Cor-Ibis said, as they followed a flagstone path around the northern bank. The lake was a featureless circle, dully reflecting high grey clouds. "Ourvette," her guide continued, "was a Mersian mage of considerable ability, if chancy temper. And a would-be suitor to the youngest nephew of Keridahl Tanikar las Cor-Ibis. She was not favoured by the family and was given to understand this in no uncertain terms."

"How did the youngest nephew feel about her?" Medair asked, curious.

"Less unfavourably than many, I would presume, since he abandoned Pelamath to travel in Ourvette's company."

Medair glanced at him and saw only that tranquil mask. "How does the lake come into it?"

Cor-Ibis paused and turned to look out over the water. "Ourvette had a certain artistry. And a desire to make a point. This parkland was once the site of the Spring Fair, and the elopement took place the night before. She left a casting which triggered with the dawn, cutting down to the bedrock. A large portion of the result was Ourvette's family crest, and the rest – stories range from the salacious to the seditious, but details have remained uncertain since it was not yet full light before Tanikar las Cor-Ibis had covered the entire thing with water. The pattern remains there to this day, beneath the lake." Which was as unreadable as Cor-Ibis' eyes as he watched the wind make ripples across the surface. "It was not long after the creation of Ourvette's Lake that Finrathlar became the central seat of the Dahlein," he added, and Medair decided that he simply couldn't be telling her this as a homily on the Cor-Ibis family's ability to come out on top. She was almost certain he was thoroughly amused.

"A very Mersian revenge," Medair said, and all he did was incline his head in agreement and stroll on toward the market.

Pelamath, or at least the copious portion currently visiting market, proved to be very Farakkian. There were a great many blonde people who showed some portion of Ibisian ancestry, but more than half of those they passed were the same range of sandy and freckled or copper-brown and creamy as she'd encountered when the place was called Pelladon. And they seemed utterly delighted to see Cor-Ibis.

Not that everyone would mean it, Medair thought sourly, watching people turn and smile and bow a very formal and correct Ibisian observance to their lord. Searching the crowds, Medair saw a man who turned abruptly away, and a woman who bowed prettily enough, but wore a frown when she busied herself over a stall of fine-worked leather. No-one was universally popular.

Somehow, it didn't please her to see those shadowed faces among the mix of the curious and admiring. It turned her thoughts to the Medarists, the most vocal and violent of those who did not care for Ibisians. A movement like that didn't grow out of nothing. It was fuelled by never-ending skirmishes and long-standing injustices. The south-west of Palladium had been Earl Vergreen's lands. The Vergreens and the Corminevars and too many others had been displaced by the invasion, had lost their lands and their fortunes along with those who fell in battle. And though the Ibisians did not seem to have proven tyrannical rulers, the initial blow was not balmed by subsequent fair dealing.

Medair looked around at smiling faces and wondered who was wrong. Those who plotted a revenge less amusing than the slighted Ourvette's, or the ones who accepted the present without care for the distant past? Medair could hardly blame those who could not forget, when she was unable to do so herself.

※

A familiar rattling clatter sent icy fingers of recognition skittering beneath her skin. She turned, searching among the stalls until she found a sturdy table wedged between a milken vendor and a display of early harvest. Two women, their dark hair streaked with grey, were just sitting down, sipping bowls of steaming milken as a young girl finished turning a cloth bag the ritual three times and up-ended the contents into a specially indented section of the table.

Dozens of flat black disks cascaded out and the girl nimbly began sorting them into piles, turning them so that they would all be face down. It was a scene achingly familiar and jarringly wrong. It was marrat.

Medair had been in Sevesta the first time she had spoken to Kier Ieskar outside an official audience. It was after Kedy's death, and the fall of Holt Harra. She'd been sent to winter at Holt Harra's ducal seat, newly conquered by Ibisians. Sevesta had put up a better fight than Mishannon, and there had been captives on both sides to exchange, interminable negotiations, and Medair had almost become used to standing before the Ibis Throne and speaking the Emperor's words.

The audiences had been so formalised that the evening summons had taken her completely off-guard. Imagining all kind of disasters, she'd stared at the white-clad boy who waited to escort her, then hurriedly snatched up her cloak and satchel. The room he'd led her to was not the starkly bare chamber which housed the Ibis Throne, but a sitting room with a single shuttered window and warm braziers burning in the corners, each with an attendant child wearing the black-trimmed white uniform of the Kier's household.

Her escort had whisked away while she wasn't looking and Medair had known better than to try and question the attendants, who were always so careful not to even raise their eyes from their appointed task. She'd stepped forward to inspect the table which took pride of place in the centre of the room. Old, dark wood, inlaid on one side with a square of slightly paler material, and on the other a neat depression almost large enough to rest her satchel in.

"Please sit down, Keris."

How hard it had been not to jump, when she'd heard Kier Ieskar's sublimely even voice directly behind her. She knew she'd stiffened and, because the idea of him standing behind her had made her skin crawl, she'd crossed to the far side of the strange table. Only then had she turned to look at him.

"*Ekarrel?*" she'd asked, her throat dry. The word meant 'most cold', and was used the way the Empire employed 'Your Majesty'. He had certainly looked like ice, standing in the doorway in a robe of colourless silk with all that white hair neatly arranged across his shoulders, and those pale blue eyes looking straight through her assumption of calm. She'd never even seen him standing before, had only ever seen him seated on the Ibis Throne during formal audience. She remembered being shocked by the very fact that he walked, as he crossed the short distance to the table and drew out the chair opposite her, then inclined his head in patient courtesy, waiting for her to take her seat.

The attendants came forward as she settled into the chair, pouring out bowls of the sweet, herbed drink Ibisians called *vahl*. It gave her a moment to collect, to remind herself that she was an Imperial Herald, that she represented her Emperor among the enemy.

"How can I assist you, *Ekarrel?*"

"I would ask you of the people of Farakkan, Keris." His voice had been as expressionless as ever and his eyes had looked straight through her Herald's formality to the frantic suspicions this unexpected audience had roused. "For I must know those whom I would rule."

The feeling of being backed into a corner was still strong, years – centuries – later. She had wished desperately for Kedy's advice, convinced that the Kier intended to trick Palladium's secrets from her. The thought of her mentor had at least given her the strength to lift her chin and say: "I can only tell you what my Emperor disposes, *Ekarrel*."

He had inclined his head, just the tiniest amount, as if that had been the answer he was expecting. "Then I request of Grevain, Emperor, that his Herald be given dispensation to speak," he'd replied. "I will await his answer."

And then, to confuse her further, the Kier had gestured to one of his attendants. The boy had carried a heavy velvet purse to the table, turned it over three times while what sounded like a thousand tiny rocks clattered inside, and then emptied it into the table's depression. Coin-like disks of dark stone had poured out, each marked on one side with complex symbols in gold, red, silver and blue. The attendant's fingers had darted over the stones, turning all face-down, then arranged them into piles of ten. Rows and rows of disks.

Then, for the rest of the evening, Kier Ieskar had lectured her on marrat. He had not asked one single question about Farakkan. He had not asked any questions at all, merely began a week-long explanation of the fiendishly complex game.

The questions had come eventually, of course. Medair had sent a wend-whisper to her Emperor and Grevain had obliged his enemy. It had been a precarious position for a Herald, and she had been relieved when the questions had focused on customs and traditions which could only be remotely useful in a tactical sense. Death rituals and marriage laws, harvest festivals and the worship of Farak: she'd explained them all over innumerable games. So he could 'know whom he would rule'. She wondered if he'd found any use for it all, in the short time before his death.

Feeling old and out of place, Medair watched the two women laugh as one placed a stone, changed her mind, and shuffled it to a diffcrent part of the table with careless indecision. That was not marrat. Marrat was ceremony, and questions after long silences, and the constant sick dread which Kier Ieskar had always seemed to inspire in her. He'd had a way of not moving at all while she drew her stones and tried to decide what use to make of them. Then he would reach out without even seeming to look at the table and pick up one of the stones between his thumb and the third finger of his hand. As he placed it delicately in his chosen pattern, he would turn it over twice. There had been a thin scar across the back of his fingers and, countless times, she had thought of beheading snakes as she watched him make that precise movement.

It had been Kerikath las Dona who explained the gesture, during one of Medair's own lessons on the language and customs and binding laws of the Ibisian invaders. That had been the first time Medair had really taken in the significance of the ceremony which surrounded Kier Ieskar's every act. She had been told during her first lesson that it was against custom for the Kier to do things like speak in the Palladian language, as he had when he declared war. Over the months, the Kerikath had provided Medair with an increasing list of things which were against custom. And things which were against law. When Medair had questioned the Kerikath about marrat, she had been warned not to turn the stones in the same way, for it was against custom for any but the Kier to do so. For the Kier not to do so was against law.

Faintly disbelieving, for she had long since formed the opinion that the Ibisian Kier's will was absolute among his people, Medair had pressed her tutor for detail and been treated to a list of restrictions which only scratched the surface of what was forbidden the Kier.

"There is only one person the Kier is permitted to touch," the Kerikath had said in the measured voice which had described so much of the Ibisian world to Medair. "Since his brother's death, the Kierash Adestan is the only other of the direct Saral-Ibis line. The Kier is forbidden contact with any outside that line."

The Kerikath had calmly described the difficulties posed by a childless Kier, and the good fortune that his brother had left an heir to ensure the succession. Otherwise, the Kier would be obliged to arrange a conception by magic alone, forbidden from touching any woman he married. Kerikath las Dona had only broken off her description of the purification rituals anyone who would bear such a child would have to endure when she noticed Medair's disbelieving face.

"But *why?!*" Medair had asked, incredulously. "Why these rules? What purpose can they possibly serve?" It had perplexed Medair that for all his power, the Ibisian Kier would live such a rigidly ascetic life, following laws which dictated the games he could play, the food he ate, the very dishes and cups he ate from.

The pause which had followed was one Medair had come to recognise as her tutor adjusting her mind to her pupil's immense ignorance.

"The Kier is more than merely one who rules," Selai las Dona had explained, as if trying to put into words what rarely needed clarification. "The Kier is the focus of the land's protections, the convergence of all enchantments to ensure health and fruitfulness. The Kier is the focus of the AlKier's regard. If the Kier ails, the land ails, and so the Kier's life is paramount. To do anything which would threaten that life would be to betray the trust of the *kiereddas*."

"But why the turning of the stones?" Medair had asked, confusedly. "How could that possibly serve any purpose?"

"Marrat stones are onyx," Kerikath las Dona had replied. "They possess a capacity for becoming imbued with the essence of those who handle them, particularly one who is a powerful *lok-shi*. By turning the stone, the Kier prevents any accumulation of resonance, which could lead to a dilution of his essence."

"Why not just make a marrat set out of something other than onyx?" Medair had asked, reasonably, but the Kerikath had only looked at her blankly and repeated that marrat stones are onyx.

The dissonance between a people who could efficiently handle such a massive upset as the destruction and complete evacuation of their homeland, yet would not make marrat stones out of anything but onyx because "marrat stones are onyx" had made Medair dizzy. She had asked only a few questions as the Kerikath had told of the Kierash Adestan's circumscribed but less enduringly restricted life. Until she ascended the Ibis Throne, the Kierash was permitted to touch any who had undergone the appropriate purifications, although custom again restricted that number to a select few. The rules were without end.

Much as Medair had hated the White Snakes, it had felt senselessly cruel to prod at the wound of their loss, so she had forborne to point out that, given the destruction of Sar-Ibis, it was surely futile to continue to enforce laws born out of the Kier's 'protections' of that land. She was not altogether certain it would make any difference to them. Tradition was not something the Ibisians seemed anxious to question.

"Kel?"

She had by now learned to distinguish between their voices. Cor-Ibis' was a trifle lighter, and he accented words differently. And, though many would find it hard to believe, he was infinitely more expressive than Kier Ieskar. But his eyes cut through her the same way, stripping away shields and lies until she was naked and squirming. He was looking at her now, watching her stare at the two women. Farakkian women, playing with stones too light to be onyx.

"Do you play marrat, Keridahl?" she asked, clutching at her bystander guise rather than betray the tidal wave of her past.

"At times," he replied, after a tiny pause to underline what wasn't said. "It is a useful aid to thought, once the patterns become second nature. I do not compete."

"Compete?" she asked, blankly, and immediately knew she'd blundered.

His lids dropped, then he inclined his head. His voice struck that particular cool note which she interpreted as Cor-Ibis at his most dangerous. "I imagine the Tournament will be missing a few of the major players this year," he said, watching her. "Given the hostility between Palladium and Decia. But it will certainly continue in the Western Kingdoms. 'Sooner hold back the sea than keep Seochians from the marrat tables.'"

The idea of the Seochians, the people of Western Farakkan, being proverbially linked to marrat made Medair blink. She had no doubt Cor-Ibis was adding her reaction, her ignorance of marrat tournaments, to his list of strange things about Medair ar Corleaux. And there was nothing she could do but ask some question about a thing wholly inconsequential and walk on.

He did not object, or even pursue the subject of marrat. Instead he launched into a story about the trees of Pelamath, which were covered in purple flowers in spring. "They are *calias*," he said, indicating the nearest bushy, pale green tree. "A native of Sar-Ibis, brought out during the exodus. Pelamath is one of the few places where they have flourished, and for a short space each year it is clothed in scent and blossom. The young girls of the city make coronets of fallen petals and one is chosen as the Land's Maiden."

"Farak's Daughter," Medair murmured. It was a Spring game she had played when she was a child, though there had been no *calias*. A celebration of the end of Winter, with Farak's Daughter decked out in the green of Farak's gifts and paid a day's courtesy in thanks for the land's bounty.

Cor-Ibis glanced at her; mirror-grey eyes. "A cloak is constructed of the blossoms, a bruised and fragile thing which rarely lasts the morning. While the Land's Daughter is robed, the children hide in the park, and one is given the AlKier's cup. Before midday, the Land's Daughter must capture that child, wrest away the cup, or the year is not thought blessed."

He was testing her again, Medair realised, and kept her face relaxed and mildly interested. A tale like this, which mixed one of Farak's customs with the White Snake god, was a distortion which would surely infuriate the Medarist they thought she might be.

"So many variations," Medair said, with just enough of a dry edge to her voice to show she thought he was fencing. This time his faint smile was appreciative, and he did not press the point further.

How different they all were! And so the same. Avahn behaved like no Ibisian she had ever imagined, and still she saw in him a core of tradition which had barely altered since the invasion. Even Cor-Ibis managed to somehow be unutterably like the White Snake she had hated the most, and yet Farakkian at the same time.

Medair could only count the hours till Athere.

Thirteen

Palladium's capital, the innermost sanctums of the palace, had been Medair's home for a large portion of her adult life. She had first come to Athere full of excited expectation, then, a year ago, trembling to see how it had changed. This time she felt divorced from her surroundings. She was concentrating on a time past now, on her return to the north, and oblivion.

The land around the city was flat, the fields interrupted only by breaks of trees. Those who approached enjoyed an uninterrupted view of concentric rings of pale grey stone climbing to the massive fort: a blockish collection of squat towers on a tall, table-top hill. It was an excellent site. Easy to reach for trade, amidst fertile farming land, with a protected water supply from springs buried deep within the hill and the Tarental River curving toward the steep eastern slope. Medair had first known a city of four walls. Arren Wall had fallen five hundred years ago, but the Ibisians had rebuilt it, and erased the scars on the Cantry wall, whose gates had not held. Centuries without peace had added two others: Ariensel and Ahrenrhen. Ibisian names, Ibisian design. Ahrenrhen crossed the river, which showed how far the city had expanded.

Athere's architecture had never been harmonious. It was cramped, full of conflicting styles, but the city possessed a majesty all its own thanks to its size and variety and the sheer weight of ages. Athere had been old when Medair had first visited it. Five hundred years later, it was ancient.

"Home," Avahn murmured, and Medair looked at him.

"Not Finrathlar?" she asked.

He glanced briefly toward his cousin, then raised one shoulder. "Perhaps they both are. Like two parents or two siblings. Both bind me with ties of affection and familiarity. Two loves, who enchant me for different reasons. I don't think I could give up either."

"Two worlds become one."

She said it thoughtfully. The previous year she had seen the Ibisian alterations as a blow against all she held dear, a distortion of the Athere of old. She had told herself she would rather see Athere razed by the Conflagration than inhabited by White Snakes.

No doubt the way she looked away from him and the city confused and intrigued Avahn, but Medair did not care. She stared at her hands, longing to be past Athere, to be able to abandon this time altogether. The need to seek oblivion grew the closer she came to the city. It was the focus of too much, had meant too much to her.

Cor-Ibis, who had a knack of approaching without drawing attention to himself, said: "You will stay as my guest while you are in Athere, Kel ar Corleaux."

"I will not be in Athere long, Keridahl."

"We will try not to detain you unreasonably. The Kier will wish to consider you."

Consider, study, interrogate. Medair was not certain the debts owed to her would afford her complete protection against the suspicion that she might be an operative of 'the Hold' or something equally doubtful. Not in the climate of approaching war. The Ibisians had rigidly followed their codes of honour in the past. Could she be sure expediency would not overwhelm obligation? Cor-Ibis named her guest, had acknowledged triple-debt. He would be in a dangerous position if his Kier was one to place Palladium above personal honour. And Jedda las Theomain would have had first word to the Kier about the woman called Medair, who denied the politics of that name and yet carried a symbol of its past.

Medair was wholly oppressed by the mere idea of seeing the Ibisian Corminevar. She remained silent and distant as they passed farmland townlets, crossed the Lapring Bridge and approached Athere. Only a small part of her mind was free to catalogue the wide gates, the guards who watched but did not interfere, the passers-by who halted in their day's tasks to follow the progress of a Keridahl and his company. Athere was more crowded than it had been, but cleaner, for Ibisians were fastidious beasts. And it was very blonde.

Medair tried to ignore it all, her mind wavering between taking in her surroundings and memories of previous journeys through the great city. Ahrenrhen. Ariensel. Remembrance, once called Arren. Cantry. Shield. Patrin.

The nature of the city changed beyond Patrin Wall. The hill sloped steeply. The houses were fewer, terraced, some with towers to mimic those which crowned the hill. There were five main roads, spokes with the palace as hub, but the rest of Patrin was a tangle of winding, secluded streets. Entire blocks were sectioned off by their own gates, exclusive domains of wealthy families.

They'd called this the Shadowland in Medair's day, eclipsed as it was by the palace. The middle and upper rungs of the aristocracy dwelled here, the most exalted also claiming apartments within the palace itself. Now, she saw Ibisians everywhere, and fewer of darker complexion. Athere might be home to both races, but she would do well not to forget that it was the White Snakes who held the reins.

There. She had been trying not to think of them by that name, but it was a difficult habit to break. Parts of her were too obstinate to accept that these were not invaders, but inhabitants of this land. Born and bred here, knowing no other home. Was it self-indulgent to stoke her resentment by thinking that to be a full Farakkian in Athere could be a disadvantage? Or only too reasonable? Was anger not preferable to loss and hurt? Medair tried to empty her mind, to be detached and analytical, to feel nothing as the pale grey stone of the palace loomed ever larger. Last year she had avoided the palace. She had known she would not be able to bear all which should have been.

She swallowed, keeping her eyes resolutely on her hands, refusing to look at the gates they approached. Guards in uniforms she didn't recognise stood beneath the south portcullis, which was still surmounted by an ancient carving of the Corminevar Crown. She had ridden this way in a dream, a fantasy of victory and acclamation. She had been astride a foam-flecked horse whose heart was near to bursting. Clad in her Herald's uniform, with the thunder of an approaching army dinning in her ears and a thick, tasselled cord of silk wrapped around one hand. Athere's defenders had felt the power of the Horn, and were gathered to wait. They had raised a cry of exultation at the sight of her, toiling up the last rise to this stone archway with the crown of the Corminevars carved above. In a dream.

Five hundred years too late, Medair an Rynstar finally crossed into the fastness of the White Palace. Her face was as pale and weary as the stone which mocked her loyalties and the company she kept. She took a harsh breath, like a swimmer coming up for air, and her chestnut tossed his head, for her grip on the reins was too tight. Aware of the gaze of fellow travellers and palace guards alike, she clenched jaw and hands and willed a blankness to her mind. How to survive this last distance?

Riders, coming the other way, scattered in the face of a party of higher rank. A cluster of men and women gathered around a hay wagon stopped unloading and stared. The horses' hooves set up an echo in the bailey yard. It was too much like coming home.

Telsen had taken her on a tour of the palace, when she'd first arrived in Athere. He'd been starting to gain respect for his work then, and she'd been flattered and suspicious, forewarned of his reputation and disarmed by his fascination with the past and his love of the palace. He'd known everything about the city, and he would probably be capable of loving even the changes the Ibisians had made. He had flirted and charmed and bedded and moved on from her, all in quick and easy succession.

Somehow, that old, lesser pain was enough to muffle the moment. Medair had tried to consider Telsen a youthful folly, but had never been able to genuinely dismiss love and loss and treat him as a friend. The never quite forgiven hurt of seeing that he was bored with her, the anger this realisation had roused, served now to straighten her back and ease the constriction in her throat.

They passed through a series of small courtyards to the stables, and Medair overcame her tendency to dwell on every change by noting instead the interest the Keridahl Avec's return provoked in all who saw him. She began to dredge up her lessons on Ibisian court custom and attempted to apply them to what she now faced.

It no longer seemed to be considered poor manners to stare at a person one was not conversing with, unless everyone here was deliberately being rude. The White Snake habit of "not looking" at the Imperial Heralds had been difficult to take in Medair's time, but it was disconcerting to see the custom so altered. Since the focus of attention was shared between her and Cor-Ibis, Medair could only assume that her actions in Kyledra had not been kept entirely secret.

The stables of the White Palace had grown. They extended into what had been an exercise yard and a wall had been taken down to allow access into former gardens, now converted into open space for working the animals. It was all continually disorienting for Medair, whose memory latched onto anything familiar while her eyes found strangeness around every second corner. She wanted so much not to be here.

"You will be tired after the journey, Kel ar Corleaux," Cor-Ibis said, though it was only mid-afternoon and they had not set a difficult pace. "Avahn will show you to your room." Then he was gone and she had only Avahn to deal with.

After disposing of an errant retainer with a soft word, Avahn indicated a direction. "Would you prefer we pretend not to have noticed how the palace effected you?" he asked, voice muted as he escorted her through the maze of corridors, annexes, halls, courtyards, galleries, winding stairs, dead-ends and other sundry features which made up the White Palace.

She raised a shoulder, struggling for calm. "It makes little difference, Avahn. I made no secret of not wanting to come to Athere."

"You said Athere was out of your way, Medair. Not that it would pain you to be here." He paused, weighing his words. "You have been here before."

She wished he would leave it be. "I told you that as well. Why question me, Avahn? You know I don't want to speak of my past."

"Or your future. Or anything, in fact. You've grown even more close-mouthed, these past days. Because of Athere, because of the palace." He reached out to touch her arm, swiftly and briefly. "I think I want to apologise. I've been treating you as a game, your secrets as a challenge. My cousin was right again – I had mistaken you. You have been rational and resigned and I didn't realise that we dealt with something which could make you look so...lost." He offered her a smile, young and genuine. "If you are to leave soon, then I would have you remember me as a friend, not one who made what is apparently an ordeal even more difficult for you."

Medair was touched. "Your questions haven't hurt me, Avahn," she said, truthfully. "I won't remember you harshly."

He smiled, then was mercifully silent as he led her to the section of the palace which Medair recalled as being haunted by the ambassadors and Dukes of the Western lands. The apartments of the Keridahl Avec, Medair judged, stretched over at least half of the fourth level of the massive Lothra Tower. Only the Fasthold, the main donjon of the palace, was larger than Lothra. It was a most desirable section of the palace.

The rooms given over to the Cor-Ibis family were decorated in a markedly Ibisian manner, with iridescent screens, ornaments of opaque crystal, and furniture of spare and elegant line. In the blunt solidity of Lothra Tower the kind of furnishings which had so perfectly suited The Avenue in Finrathlar looked out of place. As Avahn opened the door to her room, she reflected that she had fallen in with perhaps the most traditional of the Ibisians in this time. The Cor-Ibis family had succeeded in retaining purity of blood and obviously revered the customs and trappings of their lost homeland. She could not decide if this made it easier or more difficult for her to deal with them.

"I'm not certain if we will eat here or in the Vestan Hall," Avahn informed her. "Whatever the case, we dine at sun-down." He gestured with one hand, down the hallway to where the sky shone blue through an archway leading onto a balcony. "My cousin has gone, you understand, to report on the events in Kyledra. The Kier may wish to speak with you and..." He shrugged. "I am not one to guess at the Kier's wishes."

"So cautious Avahn? That's unlike you."

"Not really," he replied, bowed with graceful formality, and left her alone.

After she'd washed, and drunk a little of the water left for her, Medair found herself worrying about clothes of all things. She drew the blue and black dress from her satchel. Although the cut and cloth were unadorned, simplistic by Court standards, it did give her the air of having 'dressed up'. At least her appearance could not be deemed an insult, lacking the proper respect for the Kier. The ward against traces was a touch of decoration above the bodice.

Rejecting a second enquiry after her needs from the Keridahl's too-efficient servants, Medair retreated to the balcony at the southern end of the hall outside her room. She enjoyed the cool breeze as she gazed out over this city which could no longer be thought of as home.

"How different you look from when I first saw you," Avahn said, appearing almost a decem after he had left. Medair turned away from her contemplation of the view to consider him instead.

"You, however, have merely exchanged finery for finery," she said. "Perhaps a little more costly than before."

Avahn shrugged minutely, causing the muted greens and blues of his demi-robe to shimmer. Dragonflies danced. "The Kier summons you to her presence," he said. "I make a fitting escort." He paused a beat, then added: "The Kier has expressed a wish to examine both yourself and your satchel."

"Has she?" Medair turned again towards the shadows and reflections of a late afternoon sun. "I am no longer geased," she observed, voice as distant as the jagged horizon. "Would you stop me, if I tried to leave?"

"I believe I owe you my life, Medair," Avahn replied, after a significant pause. "But there are a great many in the White Palace who have no such debt."

"And they are between me and the door." She sighed. "I don't want to meet your Kier, Avahn, but then, I did not wish to do any of this. We had best go and get it over with."

He accepted this with an ambiguous nod, and led her on a path which he could not know was very familiar to her. Down the central stairs of Lothra Tower, through the Rumbling Tunnel to the second floor of Fasthold. Then along the Great Hall, with its ten sets of huge oaken doors, to detour at the last moment, in the very face of the silver-embossed ebony slabs which led to the Throne Room.

The private audience chamber had changed so greatly that Medair, after so much familiarity, was again disoriented. Ibisian ritual did not bend to allowing lesser beings to be seated in the presence of the Kier during any official audience, and the oak table of Corminevar times had been swept away, leaving a room which was larger for its lack of furniture. A single dark throne had replaced the Emperor's table, and Medair felt a pang for the comfortable chairs which had once made speaking to the most powerful person in all Farakkan a little easier.

Eight pairs of eyes watched her arrival. Medair, the extreme emotions of her entry into the White Palace well suppressed, breathed deeply as she walked towards the shimmering cluster of nobility. All so very Ibisian, only a hint of Farakkian blood detectable among these tall men and women in their robes of silk, polished stones glinting through the fine, white veils of their hair. Cor-Ibis was there, and las Theomain. Medair's eyes flicked over their formally expressionless faces, past the other three women and two men to the descendent of Kier Ieskar and a child of the Corminevar line.

Kier Inelkar Var Corminevar las Saral-Ibis resembled neither the ruler nor invader of the Palladian Empire. There were certain features which were apparent traits of the Ibisian royal line – small nose, slightly pointed face – but there was not the marked similarity to Ieskar Medair had found in Cor-Ibis' features. Nor was there any hint of Farakkian blood. The woman was as pale and remote as any of the White Snakes, without even the Corminevar jaw which had kept so many women of that line from being named true beauties. It made it better, that Inelkar did not look like either of the men Medair had known. Her nervously clenched stomach relaxed and she felt more in command of herself.

Avahn stopped some ten feet from the group gathered around the throne, and folded into a bow full of subtle complexities. Medair recognised it and decided to offer Kier Inelkar the same obeisance she had been trained to give the woman's forebear, so long ago. The depth to indicate Medair was someone of much lower, but still courtly rank. The touches to either shoulder, but not to the heart, for Inelkar could surely not count as Medair's sovereign and thus was owed no indication of loyalty. Avahn took himself off to one side of the chamber, leaving Medair alone before the throne.

"Medair ar Corleaux." The Kier's voice was thin and precise and, though she was self-contained, there was nothing of Ieskar's statue-like immobility in her manner. She wasn't even wearing white, which had been the only colour permitted to the Kier who had ruled Saral-Ibis. "You have performed a signal service for us, Kel," Kier Inelkar said, surveying Medair's close-fitting dress, tanned skin and streaked hair. "And raised many questions. An interesting problem, with debt owed and suspicions which cannot be ignored." A brief pause, then: "You are not a Medarist."

It hadn't been a question, but Medair shook her head anyway, and the Kier continued.

"No. For a Medarist who denies her cause is a contradiction beyond resolving. But the name Medair is significant to more than that band of angry children. You bear not only the name of an Imperial Herald: there is also a tool of that dead office."

The interest in Medair's satchel had been marked since her entry: an elderly female Keridahl and a middle-aged man with the single jade of an unranked Kerin appeared to be the most interested. They had both been studying the leather bag from their places on the Kier's left since Medair had entered the room. The man shifted, then restrained himself, drawing the Kier's attention to the degree of a brief, disinterested glance.

"The Empire's Heralds were a stubborn breed. Those who did not perish in the conflict of our arrival departed Palladium. The mage who created the satchels died in her workroom, which was unfortunately placed near Arran Wall. None could reproduce her work, although there have been many attempts over the centuries. Now, it seems, someone has succeeded." She considered Medair's impassive face. "A woman named Medair carrying a functioning Herald's satchel is hardly a coincidence."

Since it seemed to be her cue, Medair said briefly: "The satchel was not given to me for my name, *Ekarrel*."

"Perhaps not. Still, you have both satchel and name, and conflict clouds the horizon. I will not pretend it is not tempting to take satchel and secrets from you, but I do not see that such an act is justified. We owe you a debt, Medair ar Corleaux, and one not to be lightly ignored in the face of what is to come." The middle-aged man on the Kier's left made a hastily stifled sound and she again turned to look at him. Medair had guessed that the elderly woman was Keridahl Alar – perhaps this was a relative or supporter. Foolish, whoever he was, to reveal any sign of dissent to the Kier's decision. But the Kier was forbearing, and merely looked at him until he was still and stiff with contrition. Jedda las Theomain, at the man's side, was looking past the Kier to Cor-Ibis, who was in turn watching Medair, waiting for her to betray herself. Tension snarled the air, but the Kier possessed at least the self-command of her ancestor.

"However," she said, her light, cool voice perfectly emotionless, "I cannot ignore the security of Palladium altogether, and the chance of examining a functioning satchel is difficult to pass by without any attempt to expand our knowledge. Will you consent, Kel, to satisfy our curiosity on one or two questions, and to allow us to study your satchel for a short period – until after the evening meal? We will undertake, most faithfully, not to attempt to open it."

Another resemblance to Kier Ieskar, in the concession which merely paved the road for the polite demand. Medair fingered the strap of her satchel, wondering if she dared to trust not only the Kier, but those who would attempt to discover the crafting of the satchel. An impatient hand could destroy it, and all it–

"By all means," Medair replied, feeling just a little giddy. She lowered the satchel from her shoulder. They wouldn't be able to open it, but Medair did not object to the possibility that they might do by accident what she could not contemplate deliberately. The over-anxious Kerin immediately came forward and took her satchel, and she watched his retreat with only the faintest pang, aware of Cor-Ibis' narrowed eyes and sharpened attention. He had probably expected her eventual consent, but not this abrupt, almost cheerful capitulation. She turned enquiring eyes to the Kier, and found that she, also, watched intently.

"We are obliged, Kel," Kier Inelkar said. "Tell me, what was your purpose in coming to Athere, a year ago?"

Medair had not expected this, and chided herself for underestimating the woman as she cast about for a suitable reply. No doubt she looked entirely guilt-ridden while she sought a relatively innocuous answer. What had happened to her much-vaunted Herald's training?

"It had been a long time since I had been to Athere, *Ekarrel*," she said, eventually. "I wanted to see how much it had changed." The truth, sounding like a lie.

"You had been here before?"

"Some time ago."

"From your voice, I would name you Kyledran. There are few in Kyledra so familiar with the customs and traditions of my people as you appear to be."

"Perhaps they have not had the opportunity to visit Athere."

"Very likely," the Kier replied, one of her pale eyebrows quirking faintly. "It was fortunate for Keridahl las Cor-Ibis that you happened past. For what reason were you in Bariback Forest?"

"I live there, *Ekarrel*."

"Ah. Who was it gave you the satchel?"

Medair considered that one. There was no way she could tell them the truth. Desy an Kerrat's name was well known, and five hundred years in the past. "It would be easier if you didn't ask me questions I am obliged to lie to answer, *Ekarrel*," she pointed out.

"You believe me capable of discerning your position on a question, before I ask it?" The Kier's tone was tolerant, but the expression shared by several of her silent court suggested Medair take care.

"Yes," Medair replied, a simple, serious estimation of this woman's abilities.

"Unfortunate. For it is the questions you do not care to answer, which I wish to ask."

"Yes, *Ekarrel*. That is unfortunate."

They looked at each other, Kier of conquered Palladium and Medair an Rynstar, whose very name was a secret brandished openly. The implacable gaze was Kier Ieskar's. But there was no reason to declare enmity and Kier Inelkar eventually inclined her head.

"Perhaps you are wise enough to know that your lies would have told me almost as much as your truths. We will settle for what we can glean from your satchel, and give you our thanks, Medair ar Corleaux. Our debt will not be forgotten."

It was a dismissal. Avahn promptly came forward to lead Medair away and she went without a word. She had placed everything which was Medair an Rynstar, Herald of the Palladian Empire, into the hands of Ibisians. Everything but the truth.

Fourteen

A hall of light, heat, heady scents and noise. Muted conversation punctuated with soft laughter, the clatter of cutlery and ting of glasses. Unexpected gaiety for Ibisians. The old formalities seemed to have eroded severely in this particular facet of life. Only the sweet, sharp notes of a triband and certain spicy scents served to remind Medair of her Herald's guesting among the enemy. That and all the pale, shining hair, of course.

At least half the hall was blonde and the majority of the rest white, but Medair was surprised to see a goodly scattering of darker shades. Farakkians, dressed as Ibisians, with jade and bloodstone and even tiger's eye in their ears. Their presence made Medair feel queasy.

"Lathan's here!" Avahn hissed, sounding genuinely excited as he guided her toward a table where two empty seats waited. Kept for them, Medair realised, seeing Ileaha watching them approach. Nor was Ileaha the only interested observer – all around the room pale eyes fixed on Medair and voices hushed momentarily, before returning to a more ordinary volume.

"I'll be back in a moment," Avahn said, politely drawing out a chair before absconding. Off to talk to the triband player, whom Medair was able to glimpse in pale profile as she sat down.

"Hello Ileaha," Medair said, with a faint approximation of a smile. She didn't quite feel any of this was real. She had given her satchel to Ibisians, and at the next table she could see a woman the very image of Jorlaise an Vedlar, her left ear studded with bloodstone.

"Kel ar Corleaux." Despite their exchange of name-gift in Finrathlar, Ileaha greeted her with formal circumspection. "How are you?"

"Much the same." Positioning her chair a little more conveniently, Medair tried to concentrate on the collection of Ibisian nobility ornamenting her end of their table. All were young, with jade in their left ears. Only one other showed the marked 'taint' of Farakkian blood visible in Ileaha's colouring. Their silent interest left Medair casting about for some innocuous subject, but she was saved the trouble by the young man on her left. He was a pale blond, with serious grey eyes, serene and intelligent.

"Will you not introduce us, Ileaha?" he asked.

"Of course," Ileaha replied, colourlessly. "Kerin Mylar Vehl las Cor-Ibis, Keris Surreive Alai las Varentar, Keris Estal Jhet las Estasas, Kerin Adlenkar Tiend las Cor-Ibis, this is Kel Medair ar Corleaux."

"*So it's true!*" This soft, delighted exclamation broke from the lips of the handsome man directly across from Medair. "*Cor-Ibis shelters a Medarist. What a magnificent joke!*"

This was substantially the same reaction as Avahn's, back in Thrence, but tonight it rankled, perhaps because he used a language she was not expected to understand. Medair had to bite back the words which rose to her lips.

"Don't gloat, Adlenkar," the one called Surreive said, her voice weary and derisive. Her eyes were distinctively heavy-lidded. "It's not becoming."

"*I detect deep manoeuvres,*" said the woman introduced as Estal las Estasas, ignoring Surreive's hint to keep the conversation in Parlance, not Ibis-laran. "*You've been holding back on us, Ileaha.*"

Ileaha looked down at her hands. Then, pointedly ignoring the woman's comment, she said: "Your arrival is fortuitous, Medair. Lathan is always travelling, and it seems he has hardly been in Athere these past few years."

Thinking that the musician's playing was so obscured by the hum of conversation that he might as well not be present, Medair smiled politely and glanced in the man's direction. She was in time to meet Avahn's speculative gaze as he headed back towards them. He immediately replaced it with a more frivolous expression, but it served to further upset Medair's calm. She smelled plots, and she no longer had the resources of her satchel, of all those trinkets and toys that could solve every problem but not give her a single thing she wanted. Just a woman on her own, among all these White Snakes.

A spate of greetings across the table kept the air busy as Avahn took his place at Medair's right. The hint of tension did not surprise her. She had recognised the names of those Ileaha had mentioned as Cor-Ibis' potential heirs. This group did not gather by chance. Long years of being thrown together in the Keridahl's entourage would have formed strong bonds of both habit and rivalry. She imagined it had been a closely-matched contest. Only Avahn and Ileaha did not wear a sigil of attainment in their right ears. Kerin Mylar had already reached the second rank of adept, which was quite an achievement for one who could not yet have twenty-five years. Medair was not familiar enough with the sigils to understand the exact ranks of the others, but she knew they were only worn by those who had reached a certain high standard.

Listening to their chatter, Medair selected a few morsels from the ravaged platter weighing their end of the table. It didn't take long for the polite exchanges to give way to the topic of such apparent interest to all Athere.

"*You must tell us, Avahn,*" said Estal las Estasas, "*whether travelling with a Medarist affords more entertainment or irritation. It amazes me that Cor-Ibis would tolerate such company.*"

Avahn looked across the table amiably and answered in Farrakian: "Our esteemed cousin is often a cause for amazement, Estal. And I believe he finds Medair exceedingly entertaining, since he is so rarely posed such an opaque puzzle. Irritated, however? No, it has been my observation that only a crass lack of manners or stupidity in one capable of more is likely to irritate him. The combination of those two faults, now that is something he would not be alone in finding intolerable."

The Keris turned a pretty shade of pale violet. "Well said, Avahn," Surreive complimented, as if she were an exacting judge of scathing remarks.

"Wholly uncalled for," said Adlenkar, with just a hint of a snap.

"Too mild," Avahn returned, voice as milk-like as his complexion.

"And now, perhaps, we might consider not talking about Avahn's guest as if she were not present?" Mylar said, his voice cutting effortlessly into the brewing dispute. He smiled at Medair as she turned toward him. "A name is a powerful thing, Kel ar Corleaux. I don't believe I've ever met one who shares yours, for all its notoriety. I'm glad to see that today's bearers do not always dishonour the legends of the past."

"Kind words," Medair replied. She didn't like being called a legend of the past.

"I asked Lathan to play 'Lady of the Hills' for you, Medair," Avahn said, abandoning more provoking topics. "It's very bad form not to know your Telsen."

"*I can think of a more appropriate song*," Adlenkar said in an audible undertone to Surreive. The Keris smiled thinly.

Restraining any number of statements regarding her familiarity with Telsen, Medair wondered if she had the patience to sit at this table of White Snakes. She was in no mood to make polite conversation or parry questions and incomprehensible insults. She no longer wore the uniform and obligations of a Herald. Her actions were her own and reflected on no-one. She could choose to offend whomever she liked.

The attractive prospect of a quiet meal alone in her room receded as the man who had been plucking aimlessly at the triband produced a more focused sequence of notes. A murmur of recognition ran through the dining hall, followed by an obedient hush. Then Lathan began to sing, sweet and grave.

It was "Faran's Lament". Telsen had never been satisfied with the melody and had forever been making alterations. Medair hadn't quite understood what he found to be lacking, and listened as raptly as the rest of the diners. Lathan's sombre voice transformed the melancholy ballad into something sublimely haunting. The triband was an Ibisian instrument, but could have been designed for Telsen's intricate style. He would have been pleased.

A soft storm of Ibisian "applause" rose as the final notes died away. Ibis-lar did not clap their hands, but would instead say "*ahlau*" as a mark of approval, several times if truly impressed. It did, as Jorlaise had once said, sound a little like they were all sneezing.

Avahn looked to her for approval, as if Lathan were a favoured protégé. "He's remarkable," Medair said, sincerely.

"A true child of Telsen," Avahn agreed, unwittingly replacing Medair's pleasure with a whole host of ambiguous and conflicting feelings. Did Avahn mean that the Ibisian musician was literally a descendent of Telsen, or merely following his artistic lead? She speculated on the identity of the possible mother of Telsen's child while Lathan continued to play. The music was more cheerful, wholly unfamiliar, and she did not pay it a great deal of attention. Avahn was probably disappointed to find her not captivated, but he made no attempt to coax her out of her distraction. Servitors came from table to table during the short pauses between each piece, and there would be a brief clatter of noise before Lathan launched into another song.

A difference, a marked tension in the hush which greeted the fourth song, woke Medair from thoughts of paternity. She looked up, and discovered the trio of Kerine on the other side of the table were all watching her with an air of...expectation. A glance at Avahn found him troubled, clear gaze also fixed on her.

She shifted her attention to the rest of the room, and saw that the High Table was still empty of royal presence. Then she focused on the words now being woven into the complex melody. It was another Telsen – she recognised his style from long familiarity, though the piece was new to her. A ballad of unrequited love, it seemed, poignant and starkly beautiful. Quite possibly one of his best, a masterwork, but she could not see–

They were all watching, and so all had the pleasure of observing the sudden stillness, the widened eyes, disbelief, chagrin, dismay and anger which marched in careless progression across her face. When she reached the point of fury, she remembered herself enough to shut down all expression.

A song of unrequited love. A tale of a man in pursuit of an elusive woman, as unforgettable as the song with which he had immortalised her.

I found the words, laid bare my soul.
To the lady fair.
Now I stumble lost, heart echoing,
In the Silence of Medair.

That Telsen had taken her name and rewritten their brief relationship, Medair might have eventually been able to forgive. But he had not stopped there. Instead, he had used his talent as a song-smith to depict a time of war, where 'Medair' seemed to be enacting a role far more risky than what she knew personally of Heralds. The song made Telsen out to be constantly worrying about Medair's safety, not to mention jealously convinced that she'd started a romance with someone else.

The refrain altered slightly with each repetition, but always closed with the phrase 'the Silence of Medair'. The final line saw the singer standing on the walls of a besieged city, staring vainly south, waiting for a woman who had become the only hope of victory. This was truly Telsen's masterwork. She could almost see him, on Shield Wall perhaps, gazing towards distant mountains, straining to catch some glimpse of a lone woman returning from a quest of endless peril, to hear the voice of the Horn of Farak lifted in triumph, but hearing only...

"The Silence of Medair," Surreive said. Medair was staring blindly at her plate. "Undying hope. I believe that song might well have become an anthem for those who take her name, if only it had been set to a simpler tune."

"A little too melancholy, surely," murmured Mylar.

"A little too close to the bone, you mean," put in Adlenkar. "It hints too broadly at the truth."

"What truth is that?" Medair asked, around the hurt and anger in her throat.

The Ibisian lordling looked surprised. "Why, that they were lovers of course."

Medair shook her head, uncomprehending. "Telsen had many lovers. What does that matter?"

"Not Telsen." Adlenkar's eyes were wide and curious. "The Herald and the *Niadril* Kier."

Medair stopped breathing, sat helplessly as the words forced themselves upon her consciousness. Herald. Kier. But it wasn't just the words, it was the tone, it was the 'of course'.

"You truly believe that, don't you?" she managed, her voice a strangled whisper. "You're not even trying to be provoking. You speak as if repeating established fact."

"And so I do," Adlenkar said, eyeing her now as if he suspected some infirmity of the mind.

"A theory, Adlenkar," admonished Mylar. "One of many. No proof at all, no way to judge."

"A popular theory," Surreive offered, in an idle, dangerous voice. "Tell me something, Medair ar Corleaux. Ileaha has assured me, in one of her futile attempts at peacemaking, that you have repudiated any association with Medarists, that you have not taken your name as a banner of war. Why, then, does this old, tired saga cost you so much? Why do you look at me with hate in your eyes?"

"Is that what you see?" Medair asked, in a too-high voice, knowing herself to be on the edge of hysteria. "Hate?"

"Medair?" Avahn, fatally, reached a hand to touch her arm and she jerked from his fingers. Her chair clattered backwards onto the floor and the hall fell into interested silence. Dozens of White Snakes were watching the scene play out, enjoying this Farakkian interloper being overset in their conquered domain. Medair gulped back a harsh breath, and closed her hands into fists, not allowing them to send her scurrying wholly defeated from the hall.

"That is," she said, slowly, "the first time anyone has suggested to me that your *Niadril* Kier was without honour. It is a point I believe I shall have to ponder further."

Medair took another heavy breath, in the shocked hush which followed this piece of heresy. Then, head held high, she walked with a ragged assumption of calm from the hall, through the tower, all the way back to the room which had been given to her. She locked the door firmly behind her, lay down on the bed, and allowed herself to weep.

The view of the city from the balcony had eventually proven more of an attraction than snuffling into her pillow. She stood leaning on the cool stone, sheltered by night, thinking about everything but the distant past. Everything but—

Biting her lip, she shied away from the thought, but there was no escaping what she had heard that evening. Stupid over-reaction on her part, really. It was not as if it had never been suggested before. Two years of war, endless games of marrat with Kier Ieskar. More than one person among the beleaguered defenders, not knowing of constant attendants, not knowing the laws which governed the Kier, had made suggestions. But none of them had actually believed it!

To question a Herald's honour was no small thing. To suggest–! Jennet had knocked down that fool Soven, when he had asked Medair if it were true that Ibisians had blue spines, and even that had only been provocation, not accusation. Medair was an Imperial Herald. One of the Emperor's Mouths, as the Dukes had been his Hands. A Herald spoke the Emperor's words, acted as the Emperor's ears, was unmolested even in the midst of battle. A position of great trust, attained by a rare few. Medair had served Palladium with all her heart, and now, it seemed, people believed she had gone to the enemy's bed. 'A popular theory', even among Ibisians.

Ieskar had been compelling. Brilliant. Frighteningly observant. An attractive, willowy young man whose pale eyes could cut you to the core. Medair had hated him. Loathed him for destroying her world. She had no idea how she would have felt, if she had known him as other than invader. It was impossible to divorce the person from his deeds.

It was probable, she supposed, that he had liked her. He had after all commanded her company. She had long refused to think of it that way, to think of him as a man at all. Had he known of that 'popular theory', or had it only grown in force after his death? Had he ever heard that song? She could not understand how it was that the Ibisians tolerated its subject. Not only did it depict them as the enemy, and close on the hope of rescue, but it suggested that their revered *Niadril* Kier had done something which broke their precious laws and was also incredibly dishonourable. Seduce the

Herald of the enemy? Had they *forgotten* that he was forbidden any touch?

But what Adlenkar had claimed might not have been how the song was regarded at the time. She could not imagine any of the Ibisians who had fled Sar-Ibis even momentarily believing that Kier Ieskar would cast off the restrictions which bound him, however obsolete those laws had become with the destruction of Sar-Ibis.

Today – it was only a song, and a 'popular theory', established by long centuries of speculation by people who no longer lived to the strictest rule of Ibisian culture. Who laughed over their meals, and said pettish things and looked directly at strangers. Did Surreive and Adlenkar even understand what they had suggested?

And, she had to remember, the Heraldic tradition of the Palladian Empire had died after the invasion, its codes superseded by Ibisian practices. A Herald whose actions among the enemy were anything but formal and correct was behaving unprofessionally. A Herald who went to the bed of the enemy's leader might as well fight at his side. Treason. Did time really obscure the situation that greatly? Could they not see what they had been suggesting, what reflection this would be on the morals of both involved? How utterly impossible it would have been?

"Kel."

Medair turned her head to consider Cor-Ibis. The light of the mageglow which had been set in the hallway limned him with a faint blue aura. An outline of a man with a soft, cool voice.

"Keridahl."

Joining her in shadow, he handed her the satchel.

"I give to you my thanks, Kel, and those of my Kier," he said formally.

Medair ran her hands briefly over the familiar leather. Did she regret that the Ibisians had not inadvertently destroyed it? Probably not. It was hers, after all. All that she had left.

"It would be a kindness, Kel, if you did not leave Athere without speaking to Avahn. He believes he has wronged you."

"He did ask Lathan to play it, then."

"At my instigation."

So calmly said. She responded in kind. "Were you pleased with the result, Keridahl?"

"A miscalculation on my part. I had assumed that the song was so famed that no-one could have escaped hearing it."

"Infamous," Medair muttered.

"Even so. Although it is not without merit to have Surreive forced to regret one of her games, I cannot say I am pleased with the results of our experiment. It has merely raised more questions, with no prospect of answers."

"You have my sympathy, Keridahl." Medair shook her head, wishing he would go, then straightened, and looked at the milk and midnight face inclined courteously towards her. "I pose no threat to Palladium, am in league with none of her enemies. I will take no part in the coming war and, leaving with the dawn, will never see any of you again. You have a love of mystery, it seems, for you continue to attempt to solve mine. I will not tell you my past and I doubt your current theories tally at all closely with the truth. Leave it be, Keridahl."

That silenced him, at least momentarily, and he turned to study the jagged horizon, where Farak's Girdle separated Palladium and Decia.

"My current theories, Kel," he said, eventually, "have the virtue of fitting the facts, the flaw of lack of proof, and the fatal weakness of not convincing me with their arguments."

"And you would like to tell them to me, to see what you can glean from my reactions," she observed, weary.

He did not deny it, quite possibly smiled in the darkness. "Would you object, Kel?"

"I am no longer certain I care, Keridahl."

He paused again, out of guilt she hoped, before beginning.

"The name Medair is never given or taken lightly," he told her. "Combined with your satchel, it is obviously more significant in your case than 'a name your mother gave you'. But you are not a Medarist. No Medarist would deny her cause, or aid Ibis-lar. Are you familiar, Kel, with the belief that Medair an Rynstar will be reborn, to rid Farak of the 'scourge' which descended upon it five hundred years ago?"

"I am not Medair an Rynstar reborn," Medair told him, an edge to her voice.

"I do not suggest it. But it is a legend of great strength, and the appearance of a convincing pretender has been used as a weapon on two occasions in the past. The deceits were uncovered, but the belief in her return remains, unwavering. Consider for a moment, Kel, in this time of approaching war, what the effect would be of a woman who was not pretending to be Medair an Rynstar reborn, but who was raised to believe that she was in truth legend given new life, whose entire existence had been carefully orchestrated to give foundation to the lie."

Medair stared at his shadowed face. "That's your theory? You think that fits what facts you have about me?"

"Not quite. But picture this woman, who has been told all her life that she is Medair an Rynstar reborn, who has witnessed various events which make her believe this. She is trained as a Herald, her hatred of Ibis-lar instilled from birth. She has been given a satchel in honour of her supposed past, possibly been told that it is the original satchel carried by her namesake. Perhaps she has been subjected to arcane manipulation. She might even remember events of the distant past. For a skilled adept of sufficient imagination, it is not too difficult to plant images in a sleeping mind. Memories real enough to her to convince any spell of her veracity. Picture her discovering the truth."

It was a compelling image. Medair considered it until the Keridahl spoke again.

"Such a woman could be expected to flee from those who had manipulated her. And be pursued."

Medair made a sharp movement with her head, and he nodded. "A woman such as this might even be worth the risk Vorclase took venturing into Finrathlar. Avahn is certainly not worth so much to the South."

"You're right, Keridahl," Medair announced. "It does fit what facts you know, if somewhat imaginatively."

"And is not correct," he concluded.

"Not at all."

"A pity. I do, as you say, have a fondness for mysteries, but I can see no way to pursue this one. You leave on the morrow, Kel?"

"At dawn." Her tone warned him not to argue, but he made no attempt. Of course, she had little doubt that someone would be set to follow her, once she'd left Athere. But with her ward against traces and her ring of invisibility, she refused to be concerned.

"I still owe you a great debt," Cor-Ibis said.

"I sorrow for you."

She thought he smiled, and found that she wished she could see his expression. It was suddenly hard to believe that she would never see him again. She had saved his life, and he had – what?

"Is there anything I can do to help, Kel?" he asked. His voice was grave, genuinely concerned. Strangely young. "Captain Vorclase is a formidable man, and I cannot like leaving you undefended."

"He'd have to find me first," Medair said, off-balance. This didn't feel like another ploy to extract her secrets.

"I fear he is quite capable of that. At the very least, do not forget the debts owed to you. Call on Palladium's protection, if there is need."

"I will remember, Keridahl. But I don't think there'll be a need."

And still he didn't go, just stood there in the dark looking at her. The hesitation was so out of character, she wondered if he were debating keeping her prisoner. But then he said: "As you wish, Kel."

His voice was oddly constrained, and he took a sudden step back, glancing at Athere's lights. "You will speak to Avahn?" he asked, sounding more like himself.

Medair's turn to hesitate. Then she shook her head. "Avahn is correct. He has wronged me. Perhaps in future he'll be able to distinguish a person from a puzzle. But you may tell him that I lay the blame firmly at your door, if you wish."

"I will do that."

The Keridahl inclined his head in a gesture of sincere respect.

"Goodbye, Medair," he said, and walked away without a backward glance, leaving her staring in confusion after him. The ineffably correct Illukar las Cor-Ibis, using someone's personal name without formally asking for it? She would sooner expect Jedda las Theomain to kiss her good morning.

It was a long time before Medair left the balcony, and half the night was gone before she succeeded in capturing sleep.

Fifteen

An oppressive, insubstantial weight pressed down on Medair's chest, but was not there at all. Confused by dreams of a bellowing ocean, she blinked at the edge of light outlining the door to her room, trying to understand what she was feeling.

Magic. Someone, somewhere, was casting a spell of such immensity that it had woken her from sleep. She struggled from the tangle of sheets, and uncovered the mageglow. A few moments to dress, then she opened the door to her room.

Light blazed in the Cor-Ibis apartments, and Medair could see knots of people in various states of undress gathered together in the large area beyond the empty sitting room adjoining her hallway. She ignored them, turning left to her balcony once again. South. It was in the south.

Sensing magic was like smelling colour. Indefinable and impossible to adequately explain. It came in pulses, flashes, waves and, as with her charm against traces, steady hums. Like noise, it grew fainter the further it travelled. What Medair felt was distant, impossibly distant. Her limited abilities would allow her to sense a truly strong spell within Athere's limits, but not much more. An adept such as Cor-Ibis would be able to sense powerful magic a dozen miles away. Without being able to say why, Medair knew that what she sensed originated at a much greater distance than that.

"Impossibly strong," said a soft, awed voice. Ileaha joined Medair, her eyes fixed on the southern horizon. "It's been building for half a decem, according to Avahn. The entire city's awake. Even those with no trace of mage gift know something's wrong."

"I've never felt anything like it. Not even rahlstone enhanced spells have this effect."

Ileaha shifted restlessly. "They're attempting to scry," she said. "Cor-Ibis, the Kier, Keridahl Antellar. No-one's willing to guess what they'll see, if they manage it. It's as if the AlKier has descended upon Farakkan."

"Beyond the scope of mortals."

"Yes. I can't imagine anyone, not Cor-Ibis, not every adept in the city, casting this. Beyond the scope of mortals."

There wasn't anything else to say. Neither woman was inclined to useless speculation, and could only stare out at the stars and the line of darkness where the sky met the earth. The weight of power increased slowly and steadily, crushing in its intensity, and Medair imagined that she could see a faint glow limning the jagged southern mountains.

"Dawn," Ileaha whispered, as if the sun would rise somewhere other than the east.

The words broke some of the hypnotic fascination which kept their eyes drawn south. Medair looked down at the city, which was ablaze with restless light, and Ileaha turned her eyes to where the sun should truly rise.

As if taking advantage of their distraction, a slight wind tugged at Medair's hair. With the soughing of an indrawn breath, the force of magic which had woken Athere contracted and fled from their senses, leaving them chilled and shaken in the pre-dawn blackness.

There followed a moment of complete silence, and Medair caught her breath in unison with Ileaha. Across the city, she imagined, every eye would be widening, every face turning towards the south.

"AlKier!" Ileaha gasped, flinching as a lance of golden flame shot up from beyond the far-distant mountains to pierce the sky. The power of it was a typhoon, an earthquake which did not stop as the line of fire thickened and steadied, became a column to the stars. It had to be huge beyond reckoning to be visible over so many miles. At the apex, the golden fire spread and dispersed, like smoke which has reached the ceiling of a cave. It wavered, too, a swaying snake of light. The threat was unmistakable. The menace of a giant, so large that injury need not spring from malice, only ignorance. All were ants in the face of this power, insignificance to be crushed underfoot.

And then Medair knew what it must be. The Conflagration. It was the end.

⁂

She registered, but did not properly recognise, the sound of someone wailing around the curve of the tower. All she could do was watch, stunned into nothingness, as that pillar of gold began to expand.

"It is wild magic," Ileaha said. "It has to be."

"Yes."

"As Sar-Ibis was consumed, so shall we be."

"Yes."

"How can you be so calm, Medair?" Ileaha asked, fear turning to anger in her voice.

Medair had to drag her eyes away from the flames. It was as if she was looking down a tunnel, with Ileaha at the end. Nothing seemed real. It couldn't be real.

"With what would you have me greet the Conflagration?" she asked, lips numb. "Anger? Despair? The question of whether this would be happening, if I had given Captain Vorclase the rahlstones instead of your cousin?"

Ileaha made a tiny noise of protest.

"He warned me," Medair said, following a line of reasoning too dreadful to contemplate. "Asked me to consider what his king would do, if the prizes he sought in Kyledra slipped beyond his reach. I never thought that it would come to this." She turned her back on the column of fire. "This is the last in a long series of disasters for me, Ileaha. Perhaps, even a single day ago, I would have railed against it, wept, but just now..." She shook her head. "I'm tired of caring. I have cared too much, lost so much, that it seems only natural that I should lose what little is left." She smiled bitterly. "Think of it as escaping a lifetime's service to las Theomain, Ileaha. Goodbye."

Medair left Ileaha to stare after her and returned to her room, which would serve as well as any as a place to die. But, once there, she found her detachment slipping away, and she sagged against the door, shaking. It couldn't be. The Conflagration, the complete destruction of Farakkan. And she could have prevented it.

The Decian King had to be the summoner. What had Vorclase said? "Failing you, and without the rahlstones, he will tread a more dangerous path to cleansing Palladium. Think on that." Medair had given the rahlstones back to the Ibisians. Medair had chosen not to side with the Decians and their putative heir. Medair had blocked Decian ambitions.

She made a keening noise, thrusting her hand in front of her face as if to push away what followed. She had not forced the Decian King to break the laws against summoning wild magic. She had not led him to discover a means to do so. She was not responsible for this. She was not.

Someone tried to open the door. It jarred Medair from the blank, empty place she had gone, and she blinked dry, burning eyes. Whoever it was pushed the door again, knocking her shoulder and the side of her head, but then they gave up. She could hear their footsteps recede down the corridor.

How long had it been? Forever or a moment. The flames had not yet come. She was still on the floor in her room, satchel clutched against her chest and the world burning outside. The smothering force of power hadn't gone away. It was still happening.

She couldn't stay here. She needed to see. Levering herself to her feet, Medair opened the door onto hot scorching wind. Her ears thrummed with a distant, bellowing roar which could only be the Conflagration and she found herself staring over the balcony at a storm of flame. Fully half the southern horizon was burning, bringing day as would a foundering sun.

Gripping the stone of the balcony, Medair could only stare. She had not done this, but she was indirectly responsible. Her decisions had led to this. Her choices. The thought made her angry. She had had no way of knowing. Estarion of Decia had gambled and the whole of Farakkan would pay. He was culpable, not Medair.

Blame seemed such a pointless concern when the fire continued to advance. She couldn't make out the distant peaks of Farak's Girdle, which meant the flames were already over the border. She thought they were almost near enough to have covered Finrathlar. The flame trees would burn in truth. Then it would be Pelamath. Then Athere.

A desire to do something, anything, sent Medair back into her room. She hefted her open satchel, thinking of the artefacts she'd brought from the Hoard, but at the same time aware that it was a futile hope. Powerful as they were, they could not stop the Conflagration. Useless as ever.

She left her room and looked around. There was not a soul in sight, only sharp-relief shadows cutting into the edges of walls made golden by fire. The noise of the Conflagration filled all the empty spaces, muffling what would otherwise be abandoned silence. It made Medair feel like she was the only one left alive in all the world.

Waiting for death in the palace suddenly seemed insupportable. Not in this Ibisian cage. She didn't have friends to seek out and make her goodbyes to, but if this was the end, she would say farewell to the city which was still in some way her home.

※

The guard who had been at the entrance to the Cor-Ibis apartments was gone, but Medair had not taken two steps out the door when a cold voice said: "Kel ar Corleaux."

Startled, Medair turned. Jedda las Theomain had followed her out of the Cor-Ibis apartments. The adept's face was set into the mask of an Ibisian exercising careful control, and she carried a thick, heavy book in her arms.

"Keris las Theomain?" Medair's confusion showed, and tight lines of strain briefly made the woman look older.

"Keridahl Cor-Ibis requested that I caution you against leaving the city, Kel," las Theomain said, flatly. "There is to be an attempt made to shield Athere, and he wished to be certain you were warned not to pursue your intention to depart."

Without another word, las Theomain turned and walked away, leaving Medair to stare after her. The message had been stiff and awkwardly phrased, the tone no more or less precisely cold than anything else las Theomain had said to her. Yet, of a sudden, Medair felt Jedda las Theomain bore her active ill-will.

Disconcerted, Medair tried to shrug off the entire incident. It wasn't as if her plans to leave Athere were relevant any longer. The Conflagration wasn't something you could begin to run from. But what did it mean, they were going to attempt to shield Athere? How could that be possible?

Thrusting confusion to the back of her mind, Medair pressed on. She hesitated only briefly near the stables before deciding that her horse would probably not benefit from a better view of the flames. Simpler to just get out of the palace, to walk instead of thinking or feeling.

In the half-decem it took her to pass Cantry Wall, Medair found herself caught up, not in her own reflections, but Athere's reaction to the end. People gathered at windows and on the streets; friends, families and strangers facing the fire together. Some wept and some held each other and a few muttered in angry whispers. Most just stared, eyes wide and despairing, reflecting the ever-approaching blaze. Medair could understand that response, for there was no mistaking the futility of action.

"Clear the way!" called a voice from her left and Medair barely ducked aside as a man in a cart drove past, his wild-eyed horses surging frantically in the traces. A pair of frightened children clung to a mound of baggage spilling out of the back of the cart. Trying to outrun the blaze, though any fool could see it was moving faster than a horse ever would. Medair stood watching until he was hidden by the curve of the street. Contagious fear gibbered at the back of her mind, but the numbness kept it at bay. There was nowhere to run to. Nowhere to go. Everyone in Farakkan would soon be dead.

Beyond Shield Wall, Medair walked into a riot.

She heard the babble first but was not quick enough to resist the tide of people flowing through the gate. Before she realised her danger, she was in the fringes of a crowd pressed up against the very wall. People were all around her, shouting, pushing, trying to go in all directions at once.

Most were surging towards an unlucky building, their eyes scared and angry and determined. Medair almost fell as they pushed forward and then eased backwards, jostling bystanders. She caught herself and automatically steadied a young boy losing his own battle to stay upright. Shock broke through the numbness, and she clutched at him.

"Thank you, Kel," he said, gripping her arm. Never mind the Conflagration: they were in immediate danger of being crushed against the wall.

"What's going on?" she asked, keeping hold of his sleeve as she tried to squeeze sideways. She couldn't make out individual words in the roaring gabble which was assaulting her ears. Something about burning.

"Southerners, Kel," the boy replied, then gasped as the surge reversed abruptly, swallowing them both. The boy staggered and Medair received an elbow in the ribs. An arm supported her for a moment, then a shoulder spun her around and she staggered, almost lost her satchel at the same time as her hold on the boy's arm.

"Let *them* burn first!" someone yelled, and the crowd roared. It brought Medair straight back to the alley in Burradge, but without the will to fight as the surge overwhelmed her.

Then her elbow was caught and she found herself being hauled unceremoniously out of the crush by a man of wholly disreputable appearance. Farakkian, round face liberally stubbled, clothes half rags and blond hair matted beneath a greasy kerchief. The Ibisian boy was tucked beneath his shoulder, and his expression was abstractly businesslike as he searched for a safe eddy in which to deposit them.

The crowd worked against him and he lost Medair's elbow and stopped to try and reach her again. Medair was already being carried in the opposite direction. She resisted for a moment, then turned and pushed with the flow, was buffeted this way and that until, abruptly, she was free of the smothering press.

Her breath in her throat, she looked back and caught sight of the pair. The man gave her a brief nod of approval before hoisting the Ibisian boy so he could climb on to the nearest roof. Then he returned to the crowd, heading toward another hapless passer-by. With certain death on the horizon it seemed a futile gesture, but it made Medair wish she could do better than her own useless paralysis.

The bay of the crowd faltered as four riders on blinkered geldings had forced their way to the front of the mass, blocking the entrance of the small inn unfortunate enough to be hosting southerners. The leaders of the mob argued the case for a burning with a woman dressed in the uniform of the City Watch, making little headway. But the crowd was growing, pressing forward again. The confused babble grew and one of the horses tossed its head, plainly tried beyond its training. They would not be able to hold long.

The shouting died. The crowd began to break apart, and Medair found the cause at the Shield Wall gate. Mounted soldiers from the palace, thrusting their way through the northern edge of the crowd, which had been blocking the road almost completely. Eight rows, four abreast, and at the centre – Medair blinked at that clutch of shimmering robes, saw a pale head incline towards another. The Kier.

Even though most of this crowd were Farakkian, goaded by terror and fury, they still moved aside with the instinctive, absolute deference of Ibisians for their Kier. It was like marketplace marrat and the fashion for demi-robes. Not only had Ibisians become Palladian, but Palladians had become Ibisian.

As soon as a way was clear, Kier Inelkar rode on, eyes fixed on the fire in the southern sky. Medair was startled to see that Avahn was with her, as well as the Keridahl Alar. They disappeared in the direction of the South Cantry Gate, trailing a little buzz of magic

The Silence of Medair

which could only be spells used to control the horses in the face of fire.

Curious, lacking any other direction, Medair followed.

❧

She was almost at Ahrenrhen Wall when it began. A counter-note to the ceaseless roar of the Conflagration, a complex thread of rhythm which seemed to come from several directions at once. Some kind of spell-casting, terribly strong.

Rahlstones. It had to be rahlstones, in the hands of the most powerful of the Ibisian mages. But what could they be hoping to cast? Cor-Ibis' message had spoken of a shield, but did they really imagine they could construct one sufficient to cover all Athere? For nothing would turn back that fire, no null-spell or magically-summoned storm would even give it a moment's pause. It was the Conflagration.

Impossible not to try and find out what was happening, but Medair was hardly the only person with that idea. She was soon lost in a river of the curious streaming toward Ahrenrhen Wall, and when she finally saw the ramps and long stairways to the battlements, they were a solid mass of people.

It took considerable determination on Medair's part to work her way along one of the crowded ramps. The walkway up top was packed so tightly that she couldn't slip forward far enough to even glimpse the ground beyond the city walls, where she could sense one of the sources of arcane casting.

Explanations at least were easily had from others in her predicament. The nearest caster was the Kier, flanked by six of her guards. The Keridahl Alar and Avahn had left the Kier and headed around the curve of the wall. They would be two of those many sources of power Medair could sense. They were trying to create a shield, the same kind of shield Medair had used in Finrathlar, but on an improbably large scale. Impossible to save Farakkan, but they would do all they could to keep Athere from the flames.

"But how will they link across the city?" Medair asked.

The short, dark woman who seemed to know most about the casting lifted her hands. "Without line of sight or a graven star? Who knows? Athere's too big and there's not enough rahlstones or adepts of that strength to really circle it. I've never heard of a massed spell where the casters didn't have line of sight."

"Doesn't matter," said a spindly Ibisian girl. "Even if they get this shield up, what do they hope to achieve? The Blight ate through shielding as quickly as it did flesh. It's pointless."

"You'd have them do nothing?" asked a pale boy, hotly.

"That was the Blight," the short woman put in, with a shrug. "This is the Conflagration. Who's to know how it'll react to shielding? Wild magic's unpredictable in every way." She clenched her hands into fists. "What I'd give to have Estarion here, to make him suffer. He'd have been the first to go, quick and easy. Doesn't seem right."

Wanting a better view, Medair worked her way back to the inner railing. She thrust a hand into her satchel and startled those nearest to her by disappearing. Then she climbed onto the parapet and walked swiftly and precariously along its flat surface, cursing Ibisian ideas of decoration each time she had to work her way around a large stone urn filled with too-healthy plant life. Her goal was a watchtower some four hundred feet along the wall, where guards kept the pressing crowd back from the entrance stairs.

When she left the parapet, her progress through the crowd was marked by a series of surprised and annoyed looks, as innocents were blamed for her determined shouldering. The guards she did not disturb so clumsily, clambering halfway over the outer wall and stepping across corners to slide over the stair railing. Then it was a moment's work to reach the room at the top of the small tower

Three armoured women were watching the scene beyond the gate. Medair crept across the room to a vantage point against the far wall, and then stopped to stare south.

Fire, everything was fire. Finrathlar and Pelamath must by now both be ash, and Athere would follow within a decem. There was no smoke, but the hot wind dried Medair's face. She had to clench her teeth to stop herself from making any outcry.

The Silence of Medair

Kier Inelkar stood some considerable distance out from the wall, her back to the fire. Her head was bowed in concentration and she slowly moved her hand in a repetitive pattern. A faint blue glow of gathering power was visible around her, but she looked puny, impotent against that backdrop of flame. Near the gate, her troop of guard were having immense trouble controlling their horses and as Medair leaned forward to get a better look, one of their number gestured them back inside the city. Even blinkered and enchanted, the animals would go completely mad when the fire was closer.

"A full-measure or less," said one of the women, the one furthest from Medair, who wore three entwined sickle-shapes in her right ear. Das-kend. A Kend was, simply, ultimate commander of an entire army, answerable only to the Kier. A Das-kend was a Kend's second, handling mainly administrative details, but also regarded as a 'chosen heir', much as Avahn was to Cor-Ibis.

"Less," said the woman standing between the other two. The Kend, according to her ears. She was, so far as Medair could tell, entirely Farakkian, and her black hair and eyes contrasted remarkably with her two pale subordinates. Her pronunciation of Ibis-laran was soft and measured, her stance weary, facing something she had no way of fighting. "It's gaining speed with size."

"They won't be able to judge the arrival," the Das-kend murmured.

"Will they finish in time?" the third woman asked, in a small voice. Medair was mildly surprised to hear her speak, for she wore the sigil of a kaschen, the most junior officer in an Ibisian army. It was not her place to offer opinions. But this girl barely out of her teens was watching the Conflagration race toward her, and neither of the older women looked inclined to discipline her for the question.

The Das-kend smiled reassuringly. "They have almost completed the individual castings, Mira. See, the Kier makes the passes of *shel-toth*, to bind what she has been creating, so she need not release it at once. The joining of their casting, that will take a matter of a measure or two more, and the shield will manifest without great delay once they have joined. It is creating the shield too early, rather than too late, which poses the risk, for no matter how many rahlstones are involved, a shield covering all Athere cannot be held for more than a handful of ten-measures. It would need the intervention of the AlKier to make it permanent, even if we wanted that."

"We don't?"

"No matter what the condition of the land after this fire has passed, we will wish to venture beyond the confines of the city gate at some point," the Das-kend said. The kaschen looked down, a faint flush colouring her pale cheeks.

Leaning forward, Medair was able to see Avahn standing in the same pose as the Kier, far to the right of her position. She still did not understand how they proposed to link over such a distance. Avahn would barely be able to see the Kier, let alone the other mages who must be stationed at, presumably, equal points around the city.

The Kend straightened, turned and walked to the opposite side of the guard tower to stare up at the towers of the palace. The Das-kend joined her after a moment, but Medair and the young kaschen were captives of the burning horizon. Everything in the south was alight – there was no longer sky nor earth, only fire, swallowing the world. The wind was stronger too, hot and harsh. Medair shuddered. What would it be like when the flames were upon them?

Some tiny sound she had made caught the kaschen's attention and the young woman stared at the spot Medair occupied, frowning. A questing hand came out, but Medair leaned carefully beyond reach, watching the uncertainty on the young woman's face. Even if she had mage-gift, the kaschen would be unlikely to sense the murmur of the ring, drowned by so much ambient magic. Her glances toward her two superior officers revealed indecision.

"It is a fated name," the Kend announced, successfully distracting the kaschen from Medair's invisible presence. "It must be a grave matter to give it to your only child."

"A tradition of honour and sacrifice," the Das-kend replied. "But inapposite in this case, Ke, for dying during the casting would end the last hope of our people."

"The casting could easily overwhelm him."

"Yes."

The kaschen, after one final glance in Medair's direction, joined the Kend and Das-kend in examining the view from the other railing. The Kier also seemed to be gazing up towards the White Palace's towers, so Medair could do nothing but join in.

She could not see him. He would be on the viewing tower atop Fasthold, by far the highest structure in Athere, but the distance was too great to be sure of anything up there. Keridahl Illukar las Cor-Ibis, the solution to the problem of linking a massed spell across such a great distance.

Irrationally, Medair felt a surge of anger. She'd carted this man out of Bariback Forest, cleaned, fed and sheltered him, just so he could kill himself. The idea bothered her, and she linked it to her dislike of the concept of being 'fated'. But then, as the Das-kend had pointed out, he would have to go against the tradition of his name and survive while saving the lives of his people. This was not the simple shield of pure power he had used against the blast of fire. A massed spell, precisely focused and hopefully enduring, would have to be cast perfectly, or there would be nothing to hold back the flames. If the focus of the spell crumbled during the casting, it would fall apart. And probably take Athere with it.

Medair thought of the message Cor-Ibis had sent her through Jedda las Theomain, and heard his voice saying goodbye to her last night. She remembered how angry she had been to be geased by a White Snake, and had to turn away, only to be shocked by how much further the fire had advanced while she had been gazing up at Fasthold. She stared, mesmerised, at the wall of leaping red-gold, orange and yellow until a distraction appeared in the form of a small cloud of dust on the southern road.

People from surrounding farmland had fled into the city. Medair had heard the crowd on the wall discussing arrivals, and those who would not be able to make it. This, it seemed, was one of the latter. A person on a horse, too far away for clearer detail.

The fire was still at least a full day's ride from Athere, but that was by far too close. Would they have time to cast the shield?

"The signal!" gasped the kaschen, and half Athere turned from the fire towards the point of light which had appeared on Fasthold's apex. A heartbeat, two heartbeats, then a shaft of blue rose from beyond the western reach of the city. It was joined by eight others, a many-sided pyramid whose apex burned and flamed like a sapphire sun. At the heart of the blaze was a soft-voiced man whom Medair had bathed in a horse trough, and she found that she preferred to watch their destruction bearing down upon them, rather than their prospect of salvation.

The wind had become a gale, harsh as a desert in drought, drying sweat as soon as the heat conjured it. The flames were closer again, leaping miles in moments. And then the shield solidified and shut the world away. The gale vanished, blocked by a transparent blue wall. So did the noise, the roar of the fire and the wind. Instead, it seemed to Medair, she could hear an entire city take in unison a single, sobbing breath.

"Thank the AlKier," the Das-kend said softly, her voice shaking. She returned to the outer side of the watchtower and craned forward for a better view of the shield. Medair could see the Kier unhurriedly walking toward the city gates.

"But will it keep the fire out?" the Kend wondered. "Stupid to ask, I know, since we won't know the answer until it's here. Ah, I could kill that man!"

The southern king, Medair assumed. Had he had a moment to understand what he'd done, before the fire took him? Had he at least regretted the gamble?

"Mama, I'm scared," said the kaschen in a small voice, and was folded into the Das-kend's arms.

"We all are, Mira. But we have done what we can, and perhaps the shield will hold. It will be a hard future, with Farak's Breast burned away, but we will face it together. Else...at least it will be quick."

On the southern road, the person on the horse, still too distant to be recognisable as male or female, made a despairing, desperate motion with its hands towards the translucent blue pyramid which covered Athere. Then it was lost, a mote swallowed up by the fire which swept relentlessly across the land.

The shield would have stopped anyone else from getting in, anyway, Medair thought, and sent a silent prayer to ravaged Farak as the flames, a burning fog, flowed over Athere.

Sixteen

Incredible as it seemed, in the teeth of the Conflagration they would probably all die of suffocation. The shield kept out the fire, the wind, most of the heat. And the air. The exclusion had been deliberate. It had been important that the shield be complete, not semi-permeable like the one Medair had used in Finrathlar. After all, there was nothing beyond the shield but fire.

She wasn't sure how long it had been. The soldiers had left the watch-tower soon after it was certain the shield would hold, and Medair had stayed to watch the flames. They took on a greenish tinge, through the blue of the shield, and showed no sign of abating. Enough heat came through to keep Medair sweating, and there was not so much as a hint of breeze.

Medair's first concern had been that the shield would not last as long as the fire, but she'd had time to think it through, now. How long would it take for a city full of people to use up all the air trapped within the shield? How long before Athere became an expensively preserved tomb?

Even if they survived the Conflagration and the shield released before everyone suffocated, what would they find? Anything at all? Charred earth, the scorched beds of rivers? No crops, no stock, no wild game to hunt. There should be, in Athere, stores enough to do some planting. There might be horses to breed, but few cattle and sheep and birds. Frogs? Dragonflies? Let alone the fodder to maintain what survived. Faced with the prospect of starvation, Medair thought of the Bariback violet, tiny and delicate, and lost forever.

"The sky!"

A single voice from the crowd still lining the walkways. It sparked a series of outcries as eyes sought the apex of the glimmering pyramid and found, as proclaimed, the sky. So commonplace a sight to inspire such a groan of unbridled relief. The shield still held and the fire was waning. Athere had survived the Conflagration.

Like water, the fire drained slowly down the sides of the shield. Medair followed its progress sadly, not wanting to see what it had left behind, not wanting to see the–

–verdant hills. Manicured woodlands. Fields of gently waving corn and wheat. A road paved with stones of lambent silver instead of the familiar, worn grey. In the distance there was a rider, racing towards the city.

Medair, who had suffered many shocks in the last day, swayed invisibly in the watch-tower. She had looked upon the land around Athere countless times, and this was somewhere else. Five hundred years had changed certain features of Palladium, but it had still been the same place. This sculptured landscape of quiet hills and soft curves was... She shook her head.

In the far distance, the mountains which formed the eastern reaches of Farak's Girdle rose as they always had, yet they seemed higher and darker than before. The glitter of the Tarental River curved to the east, but surely that bend shouldn't be there? And that bridge, an elegant arch which led to the beginnings of a dark forest where farmland should be? Everything was different and oddly familiar.

"I finally have run mad," she whispered.

The verdant world did not go away. The shield remained, locking out the scene like an image behind glass. It was better, surely, than the ashen char everyone had been expecting, but Medair still stared in blank dismay. She could hear cheers from the wall below, but they were muted, nervous. Frightened.

There was something strange about the rider still racing toward them. No, not the rider, the steed. It took only a moment to isolate why: not only was the animal travelling faster than any horse Medair had ever encountered, it was doing so at about a foot above the ground.

It *looked* like a horse. A black horse which cantered along with great, smooth strides. Its rider was a woman, dressed in green, black hair flowing in a mass down her back. Long before horse and rider were in hailing distance of the shimmering blue shield, Medair knew she wanted a much closer vantage point.

The Kier's armed escort, their own horses missing, were holding the crowd back from the open gates. Medair was quick to slip invisibly past and hurry out to the shield. The Kier, with the Keridahl Alar and a cluster of attendants, was standing before the shield, lost in casting. Even as Medair came up, the blue wall dissipated, and a cool, scented breeze swept over the city.

It was all real. Medair stopped where she was, only a short distance from the Kier. Beneath her feet, the grass was withered and brown, a testament to the heat which had beat upon the shield. A few feet away, beyond where the shield had stood, the grass grew lush and moist. She took a few steps forward and then knelt to touch it. Grass, cool beneath her fingers. It smelt real. There was magic everywhere, the lingering remnants of the Conflagration, but the grass was not an illusion. The fire had destroyed Farakkan, then remade it.

The rider on her floating horse was drawing close. Why its hooves should make any noise when they didn't touch the ground, Medair couldn't guess. And didn't try, as she had her first good look at the rider. She had Mersian features, almost exaggeratedly so. Her hair was a mass of thin braids wound with glittering threads. And she wore the uniform of a Herald.

Medair put her hands slowly down on the grass and simply stared.

It wasn't until the woman dismounted that she was sure it wasn't the same uniform. In outline it was almost identical to an Imperial Herald's, but there was no silver badge, no satchel, and there was a device of a tree stitched on the breast. And it was green.

Long before Medair been born, Heralds had worn a thousand combinations of colour to complement every kind of message. That was why the colour-change enchantment had been created. The system had been deemed overly complex during the reign of a former Emperor, and the Heralds had been restricted to three colours. White, red and black. Dark green would have been...marriage tidings? Medair shook her head, numbly. This wasn't an Imperial Herald. It wasn't.

"It was a marvel to look upon, *Ekarrel*," the rider was saying. Medair had missed part of their conversation, while she had crouched on the ground trying not to scream.

"Tell me more of Queen Valera," the Kier responded.

The Mersian looked frankly bewildered, but then, so did most of the Ibisians. "*Ekarrel*," she said, "I have carried messages between you and My Lady Valera these past five years. I was in My Lady's escort when she visited the White City two years ago. I do not understand what it is you wish to know."

The horse, a black mare, swung its head in a strangely alert fashion as Medair climbed unsteadily to her feet. The animal seemed to be looking directly at her, and Medair shifted uneasily, not certain whether to be concerned. At least the black's hooves were for the moment planted firmly on the ground.

The Kier's voice was as thin and cool as it had been when she'd interviewed Medair. But she looked tired. "This day has brought many strange things to Athere, Heleise of Tir'arlea. The memories you have I do not share. Nor, it seems, does the fire we watched overtake our land remain in your mind."

"Fire?" The Mersian's gaze rested on the withered grass, a puzzled frown creasing her brow. She shook her head, then continued urgently. "*Ekarrel*, my message is such that it cannot be delayed, even if it seems you no longer know the one who sends it. Estarion's armies mass. His mages work spells of great strength and speak of bringing down the White City at dawn. My Lady's spies send word of a new confidence in the Cloaked Lands. They whisper of a weapon of surpassing strength. Over such a distance a warning is all My Lady can send before the dawn, but if a battle is to be joined, the Lady of Silver-on-Water will not allow her presence to be missed for long."

The woman – the Herald – was sincere, impassioned. She was met by blank silence and her steady gaze faltered.

"The Cloaked Lands?" the Kier said, slowly. "Silver-on-Water? Keris N'Taive, I do not understand you. I do not understand you at all."

The Herald shook her head despairingly. "I know not what subtle magic has stolen your memory, *Ekarrel*," she said. "In the name of the Holy Four, I know not what to say to you."

Medair looked at the Kier's still face and wondered if she felt as Medair had, when she'd stumbled into Morning High. That stunning dislocation, that irremediable sense of loss. It seemed all Athere had joined her, out of place.

<hr />

Kier, Herald and entourage had abandoned their attempts to make sense of each other and gone into Athere. After a short pause, curious Atherians had begun to drift in the opposite direction. Hazed and confused, Medair wandered towards the bridge she could see to the east.

The Tarental glittered in the sunlight. The bridge was yellow-white faintly tinged with pink and apparently carved from a solid block of stone. Medair studied it dubiously. It was honeycombed with an intricate pattern of tiny flowers and she could see the water through the smooth arch across which she was supposed to walk. The little holes gave glimpses of sunlight flashing and glittering on flowing water.

Back where the Tarental curved beneath the wall the Ibisians had constructed, a mounted patrol trotted cautiously out of the nearest gate. People milled all about the city, but few were venturing very far from the walls. The sky was a brilliant, almost violent blue and the air was full of the scents of soil and pollen. It still didn't seem real; not the grey-white city climbing into the sky, the cool forest at her back, or the fields and hills. Or too real. She felt faded in contrast with this glowing world. Small and insignificant and unreal, a ghost of a woman from a past which wasn't even right any more.

Belatedly, Medair realised she was suffering the side-effects attendant to wearing the ring of invisibility. None of them were serious, but they went badly with her current state of mind. She immediately removed the ring, then grimaced. Doubtless a few thousand people on Athere's walls had seen a woman suddenly appear from nowhere at the bridge. Well, she was too far away for anyone to make out her features.

With a shrug, she set her feet upon the bridge, which showed no sign of collapsing or doing anything at all unbridge-like. She wasn't certain why she'd thought it would. The forest was the shortest of walks away, the trees weaving together into an arch over the path. It hardly seemed natural, it was so perfect. Everything looked so...created, placed for effect.

Dappled shadows and bird song. The forest was restful, with plenty of paths to follow among groves of oak and elder. Medair wandered randomly, climbed a small hill and discovered a tiny valley with a pool at the centre. The trees here were small and carefully tended. Medair stared at them for a long time, then plucked a round, dark berry. A black denan.

It was too much. Dropping the supposedly extinct fruit to the ground, Medair left the forest. By this time, others had reached the trees and she met a half-dozen groups wandering. She avoided speaking with them, and made her way back to Athere, to lose herself among the crowd.

<hr />

The sun was low. She seemed to have been walking in the woods all day, though it had not felt a quarter so long. Hungry, she found her way to a tavern within Cantry Wall, full of excited people, voices bright with relief and incredulity. She slipped into an empty seat and ordered a meal, then listened to the wild stories being exchanged about the claims of the Mersian Herald.

According to fifth-hand report, the Herald was from Ashencaere, from the Court of Queen Valera in Tir'arlea. That was stunning enough. The Mersians had not had their own court since before the formation of the Palladian Empire. Not since the Silver City, Tir'arlea, had tumbled in arcane war. The Conflagration had conjured Tir'arlea back to life. It was now an ally of Palladium against the 'Cloaked Lands'. Half southern Farakkan had been formed into an Empire by Xarus Estarion, who was a mage. And on the verge of invading Palladium.

"May I join you?"

It was the man who had been serving behind the bar. Young and neat of dress, very Ibisian, yet with a beguiling smile curving his pale lips. He took her hesitation as acquiescence and slid into the seat opposite.

"Your pardon for disturbing you, Kel," he said. "I was wondering if you had been on the southern wall when the Herald arrived, or perhaps had been outside the city after the flames had passed." He shook his head, laughing at her surprised expression. "No, I am no seer. I've asked everyone who's come in and have yet to find a single person who witnessed this woman's arrival, rather than having spoken to one who spoke to one who was standing behind someone who could see."

He was one of those people of infectious good humour, and Medair tried to smile in return. "I was on the wall," she said, and his face lit up.

"Then tell me, did this Herald really fly in on a winged horse?"

That made her laugh, a brief, surprised burst. "Close," she admitted. "It didn't have wings, but it, well, rode on the air. It's a bit hard to describe...its hooves didn't touch the ground and...it was a little like it bounced along. Effortlessly."

"The world remade." The bartender seemed caught between wonder and horror. "I went down to look, once the crowds had died away a little. It's eerie: familiar yet strange. And we are wrong here, because we were shielded from the fire. It will be a poor thing if Cor-Ibis has given his life only to make matters worse."

The jolt was palpable. Medair felt as if her pulse had stopped. "He's dead, then?" she asked, her voice tight. "I didn't know."

The man grimaced. "In truth, neither do I. Half of those who've claimed to know have assured me that he is. The rest agree he is merely blinded, his sight burned beyond recovery. Whether to believe them or those who claim he is spell-shocked or transformed or completely unaffected – when there are so many stories, I choose to believe none. But his name is fated. All who have borne it have made the greatest sacrifice to save the Ibis-lar."

Medair found herself remembering the time she had learned of Kier Ieskar's death, five hundred years after the fact. This same jolt, as if a prop had been knocked out from beneath the land. She had never really believed he was mortal, let alone slated for such an early demise. He'd only been twenty-three.

It felt just as impossible to picture Illukar las Cor-Ibis dead, that soft voice silenced and those mirror eyes dimmed. "That means Avahn would be Cor-Ibis, now," she said, slowly. Surely it was impossible.

"I heard tell he was one of those who cast the great shield. That's scarcely believable in itself. When did Avahn last study? But he has always been one who surprises. I don't think he'll be happy to come so soon to the title."

"You know him?" Medair asked, blinking.

"He comes here often," the bartender told her, with the pleased air of one who knows the benefits of illustrious patronage. "Or came. Who knows how being Cor-Ibis will change him?"

"Jaith!"

An urgent summons from the doorway. Medair's companion turned, frowning in confusion. Then he froze, jaw dropping.

"Esta?" he gasped, sounding not altogether certain.

"You know me, don't you Jaith?" the woman asked, a note of pleading in her voice. She was pure Ibisian, a few years Medair's senior, and in much disarray. White hair fell loosely over her face and there was dust on her clothes.

"Esta?" Jaith repeated, more loudly. He rose falteringly to his feet. "It *is* you, isn't it?"

"Who else would it be?" the woman replied, caught between exasperation and desperation. "Has *everyone* gone mad?"

"What *happened* to you?"

"To me?! Nothing's happened to me! It's all of you who've run mad! And worse. Jaith, I was just at mother's – I don't understand what–" The woman shook her head, lifting hands to press against her temples while the occupants of the tavern shifted uneasily about her.

"Tell me what happened, Esta," Jaith commanded, walking forward and, after a slight hesitation, taking the woman's hand.

The woman wrapped her arms around Jaith's waist, holding on to him like an anchor in a storm, not seeing the discomfort on his face.

"Mother's different, Jaith. I don't understand. I'm just back from Callamere – delivering the kabli-man's order, you know. There are all these people roaming about outside the city walls, looking as stunned as pole-axed cows. I avoided them, as best I could. And something has killed all the grass around the walls – at least a hundred feet out. Inside the walls, it was just the same – people roaming about aimlessly and talking all the while about something called the Conflagration and fires and who knows what? I thought Mother would explain, but she... she..."

"Is part Farak-lar," Jaith finished. He stared deep into the woman's eyes. "You were outside the walls," he said.

"Well, I could hardly travel to Callamere *inside* the walls, Jaith!" Esta snapped. "What does that matter? What's happened here?!"

"You – Esta, you are Farak-lar," Jaith told her, sounding miserable.

The woman frowned, looking faintly hurt. "My mother has some hot blood, it's true. You've always told me that it didn't matter, Jaith."

"It doesn't! Esta, Esta. Ah, AlKier, I don't understand this. Esta, you are not...as you were."

There was a stricken little silence.

"It's not me who has changed," she said, eventually, voice small. "Mother is different, and Tehan. And..." She trailed off, gazing at his face. "I'm not Farak-lar. Mother is not Farak-lar. We have that blood, yes, but so does half Athere. The cold blood is dominant, Jaith. You *know* that!"

Seeing only incomprehension in his face, the woman's self-control broke and she tore herself from his arms.

"It's you who have changed!" she cried, stumbling backwards. "*You!*"

Then she was gone, the bartender running after her. Medair left amidst a buzz of horrified speculation.

The cold blood was dominant. The girl had only been quarter or half Ibisian, but there had been no sign of Farakkian blood. She obviously remembered the bartender and her family and everyone within the walls, but all as slightly different people. What would Athere be like if the flames of the Conflagration had been allowed to sweep over it? Who would Medair be now?

Lassitude had claimed her by the time she found an inn with a spare room, the same deadly apathy which had followed her visit to Athere the previous year. She went to bed, and lay thinking of the Conflagration and black denans and the threat of war. And a soft, eternally courteous voice.

Seventeen

Another pale and beautiful dawn. The dew-studded hills were stained with jewels of colour beneath a sky of streaked pastel. It slowly brightened to reveal what had been moving in the shadows for a full-measure or more. Black specks, like a flock of crows which had settled on a meadow. But no flock of birds was so orderly, or endlessly numerous. Or so formidably armed. The hills south of Athere were blanketed with an enemy army, come to lay siege in the night. Their black and white pennants fluttered in the wind.

Magic had again woken Medair and she had travelled back to the watchtower, joining the same kaschen and Das-kend in a silent vigil in the pre-dawn dark. They could all sense the distant throb of power, and could only wait to see what daylight would bring them.

"It isn't possible," the kaschen suddenly said, speaking for the first time since Medair had entered the watchtower.

"Of course it is possible, Mira. We have done it ourselves, in a time of great need."

"Not without aid. Not to make war."

Yes, to make war, Medair thought, viciously. But no, the Ibis-lar had fled to Farakkan. It was only once there that Ieskar had decided to make the land his own.

"We would do it in war if it did not mean exhausting our adepts buildings gates." The Das-kend turned a brass-bound spyglass over and over in her hands. "To take the enemy unprepared, that is a great advantage. To overextend yourself in doing so, that is a great foolishness. Estarion – the Estarion we knew – could not build such gates. He had adepts, true, and could gate a sizeable force, just as we can. But we could not do this. At the fall of Sar-Ibis, we drew on the very magic which was destroying the island, but the Conflagration is already fading. He should not have the strength to gate an entire army. We certainly do not."

"Then how?"

"The Herald spoke of a weapon. It may be what builds them the gates, or it may be that he has adepts which now surpass us. What can one say to this new world? Decia was by no means ready to make such a move, before the events of yestermorn. What I see here..." The Das-kend shook her head. "We may be outmatched."

"Almost I wish the Conflagration had left the world a charred ruin, rather than this."

The Das-kend looked at her daughter. "Do you really?"

"No. I wish it wasn't happening, though. We don't even know our home territory. Probably those who come against us have a better idea of these hills and that forest."

"Possibly. They at least know enough not to make their gates within reach of our adepts. Even if we had anticipated this move, used the warning brought to us, we could not have hoped to disrupt all of them. Not without covering the land with patrols able to bring down a gate as it formed. And they have protected themselves immediately against attacks from a distance. With what, I cannot say precisely, but likely the winds and mirrors, unless they have things we do not even know of. We will not be throwing sleep at them."

"The Cloaked South." The kaschen made an angry, exasperated noise. "It's as if all the rules have changed! What are we to do against so many, when we've lost the advantage of our blood? When they have equal power?"

"If not more." The Das-kend stroked her daughter's arm lightly. "We will fight. Have faith in our Kier, and those who serve her. The Ibis-lar have triumphed in the face of great odds before this."

The kaschen did not reply, but her look of doubt was answer enough. Medair, standing as far from the magic-sensitive pair as possible, felt sympathy stir through the lethargy which gripped her. This was the same as Mishannon. She had stood on Mishannon's walls and stared out at an Ibisian army. It was the first battle of the war and their tactics and their strength had been unknown. Mishannon's defenders had done what they could to prepare. They'd tried to guess how the Ibisians would do battle and had been wholly unprepared for what came next. A massed spell, cast by dozens of adepts. It had rolled over Mishannon as inexorably as the Conflagration. And that had been it. Battle over. Only a handful of Palladian defenders had been able to resist the sleep spell and they'd been immediately overwhelmed.

Now, the southern army was moving slowly forward. Towering over the leather-clad soldiers were what could only be giants, though giants had been gone from the world longer than dragons, were as much legends as...as Kersym Bleak and the Horn of Farak.

These figures wore armour of silver, with wicked horns projecting from glittering helms. They carried swords longer than Medair was tall. She could see no more detail from such a distance, and wondered what faces might hide beneath those helms. Would someone within the walls recognise a friend or relative, lost to the change?

The silver armour reflected incongruously roseate hues as they advanced beneath the strawberry dawn. She had counted no more than a hundred bright warriors scattered randomly among the thousands which marched towards the city, but a hundred of such proportions would count for a battalion of ordinary warriors.

New arrivals in the watchtower forced Medair to squeeze into the farthest corner. Holding her elbows in, she tried to avoid coming into contact with the short man who came nearest.

"Keridahl an Valese," the Das-kend said, inclining her head formally to a woman some years her junior, with neatly bound honey-blonde hair.

"Das-kend las Maret, isn't it? Tell me, can you make out the device on the pennants they carry? We have come in hopes of gaining a better view."

"It is Estarion's gryphon, Keridahl, though it seems he no longer cares for gold and blue." The Das-kend politely proffered the spyglass, and it was passed from hand to hand.

"Well-equipped, disciplined, protected by magic," was the Keridahl's assessment. There was no voice of dissent. The army which came against them was obviously not lacking in preparation.

"What's that they're doing now?" asked a comely young man who stayed awkwardly close to the Keridahl's side. "Changing direction?"

"Stopping."

The leading ranks had indeed drawn to a halt less than a quarter-mile distant.

"A formal declaration of war?" the Das-kend speculated, catching the Keridahl's eye with a frown.

"Considering their opening moves, I would not trust to it," the Keridahl replied. The moment stretched, as the Keridahl plied the spyglass and frowned more, then handed it back to the Das-kend with the innate courtesy of her kind. The kaschen, at her mother's side, struggled not to fidget.

"**INELKAR.**"

Half the watchtower's occupants jumped. Probably half the city did, as that word boomed and rumbled from the sky. Medair's eyes jerked involuntarily up, almost expecting the sky to be black with thunder-clouds. A lone fluffy splotch bundled itself away behind the castle towers, as if in a hurry to disassociate itself from the voice which again made the very air tremble with its volume.

"**INELKAR. WILL YOU COWER BEHIND YOUR WALLS? DO YOU FEAR TO MEET ME?**"

A long pause, as if the voice were somehow waiting for an answer, though the Kier would hardly be likely to emerge in response. It must be Estarion, the Decian King. The voice was so strong that Medair imagined she could feel it making the bones of her chest vibrate. A calm, deep voice. This Estarion sounded utterly certain, and that was perhaps the most chilling thing of all.

"**WE HAVE TRAVELLED A LONG WAY TO THIS, INELKAR,**" Estarion went on, as the Keridahl turned to whisper some message in the ear of one of her aides. "**CENTURIES OF DISPUTE, OF DRAWN KNIVES, OF BLOOD SPILLED IN THE NAME OF HONOUR. YOUR HONOUR. WHITE SNAKE HONOUR.**" He sounded sad, which felt out of keeping with his reputation. There were few in Palladium who were not convinced the southern king was a greedy, ruthless man thirsting for power.

"**The sins of the past can not be forgotten, Inelkar. You call this land your own, but it was stolen from those to whom it truly belonged. Time will never wipe away that crime, nor make you more than what you are: the child of a thief, a bandit who cut the hand held out to offer aid.**"

An angry murmur filled the watchtower, but Medair shivered and turned her face into the stone. This was the very thing which cut her deepest: the reason behind the fall of the Palladian Empire. Ibisian honour, Ibisian pride. There had been no need for the war which had shattered the Empire. Grevain Corminevar had been willing to shelter the refugees, but they, in their pride, had brought down Medair's world rather than accept such charity.

"**In younger years,**" the voice continued, a thoughtful rumble vibrating through Medair's breast, "**I vowed to scour Farakkan of your blood, of all the pale thieves who shattered the Golden Age. But time offers the grace of mercy, and your race will benefit from mine. I will allow your children to live, White Snake. They will not sit high on stolen thrones, Inelkar, but I will not hunt your race into nothing, for all the anger of my forefathers urges me on. They will serve, but not die.**"

"He would make slaves of us!" spat the kaschen, meekness forgotten.

"**There is, of course, a condition,**" Estarion rumbled on, heedless of the instant opposition his mercy inspired. "**A stolen prize, another piece of thievery to add to the accounts. Give up to my protection the woman of the Isle of Clouds, before the sun sets this day. Else, my anger shall know no limits, and there will be no hole a single one of your spawn can crawl into that I will not find. Dawn will bathe in your blood. The choice is yours, Inelkar.**"

The Silence of Medair

Thunder died to silence over a city seething with fury, confusion and fear.

※

As soon as she could escape from the crowded watchtower, Medair had retreated to Odessa Park. She was lying in the grass, watching the clouds and pretending she wasn't paralysed. She didn't know what to do, did not want to do anything, but could not force thought from her mind so that she was able to do nothing at all.

~Medair?~

Jerking upright, Medair stared about, but Ileaha did not suddenly appear to accompany her voice. A wend-whisper, she realised, as the wind carried her more soft words.

~Medair. Please meet me in three ten-measures at the Bravi Fountain. I will wait.~

Of course they would be looking for her. Especially after Estarion's demand. Medair waited a moment more, to be certain Ileaha had not whispered anything else to the wind, then lay back down. She breathed the scent of clover, with damp earth lurking beneath. An ant ventured onto one hand, and she twitched it off. Only the calling of birds disturbed her peace. Lying there, Medair could forget about wars and oaths and the army at the gate.

With a curse she climbed to her feet, and shouldered her abandoned satchel. Of course she could not.

Bravi Fountain was within Remembrance Wall, near the southern gate. The fountain filled the centre of the square, which was actually more of a curved rectangle. It had been newly constructed in Medair's time, in an area which had once been a slum, but was now a prosperous place. The fountain was a magical construct: round, rising four levels, with a sculpture at its peak which had a suspicious resemblance to the White Palace. It spurted water in almost every conceivable direction, a fine mist providing cool delight in Summer. She wondered if they still held parties there on warm nights, to watch the tinted pastel colours which appeared beneath the stars, and argue about whether something so frivolous as colouring water was a waste of magic.

There was something about large, open squares with fountains which attracted birds. A flock of grey and white pigeons landed a comfortable distance from the people clustered at one end of the square, then immediately took to the air once again. The crowd centred around a group of young women and a youth who would better be called boy than man. They were having a white-faced and tight-lipped discussion with unhappy parents about whether it was better for them to go join a battalion of reserves or stay to defend their homes in the event that Ahrenrhen and Ariensel fell. Ileaha, very plainly dressed, was seated quietly on the far rim of the shallow pool around the fountain, her attention on the crowd.

"No shouting," Medair said, having made her way with deliberate silence to the younger woman's side. "No raised voices, no shoving or struggles. Even those with no Ibisian blood behave this way. Not unemotionally, but fantastically restrained. It takes something like the Conflagration to really jar all these careful good manners."

Ileaha, who had started violently when Medair first spoke, gave her a strange look in return for her brief lecture on Ibisian social demeanour. "You came," she said after a moment. "I did not believe you would."

"Didn't you?" Medair sat down, cool mist soothing the back of her neck, a hint of mildew and pigeon dung tickling her nostrils. "Why send the wend-whisper, then?"

"Because I could not search all Athere, and you wear that set-charm against traces. But I knew you would hear a wend-whisper, and I needed to find you."

"You needed to find me." Medair frowned, for she had expected more of a search than Ileaha alone. Had they not–? "Why?"

Ileaha looked down at her hands, almost guiltily. "I...perhaps you might not care to know it, but finding you was a test. At least, I think that is what he meant."

"A test?"

"I don't know what I would have done if you had not come," Ileaha went on distractedly, clenching her hands together. "I could not think of anything to do when he asked me to find you. Sitting here, praying that you would produce yourself, I have been searching my mind for ways to find a single person in all Athere. Nothing I can imagine was possible without the aid of a dozen, a hundred others. And I thought to be a Velvet Hand."

"It could be said that it took some ingenuity to think of a wend-whisper," Medair remarked, hiding her impatience. What mattered Ileaha's career, when Athere itself might have no future? But then, Medair was trapped by people dead for centuries. At least Ileaha was looking ahead.

"That is different altogether. You found yourself. I don't think he would consider that I had proved myself."

"He? Who sent you to find me?"

That finally pulled Ileaha's eyes from her hands' attempts to strangle each other. "Cor-Ibis," she said, with an unspoken 'of course'.

"Ah. With rumours of dead and blind and spell-shocked, I should have known that he would be completely unaffected by the casting," Medair said, her voice sounding as if she were angry because she had found that she was boundlessly glad, and hated herself for it.

"Not unaffected," Ileaha said, carefully. "He was, in truth, blinded for a short while, but that...passed. Wielding so much power – no, it did not leave him unchanged."

"Cor-Ibis sent you to find me, to test you," Medair said, thrusting emotional turmoil to the background again. "Don't tell me you finally announced that you weren't going to be las Theomain's secretary?"

"At such a time. Selfish, I suppose, but if this is to be the end, I don't want to spend it running errands for Jedda las Theomain." Ileaha grimaced. "I didn't mean to say anything. The entire Court has been chaos since they returned from Ahrenrhen, and running errands would probably be the most useful thing I could do. We are not ready for this war, and the Keridahl had better things to do than debate my wants and needs."

"Debate?" Medair stood up, a sharp, violent movement. "I doubt it, Ileaha. That one rarely needs to debate things. I have encountered his kind before, and know enough to recognise the methods." She smiled stiffly, her eyes on one of the young would-be warriors, who had gone so far as to pull her arm from the grasp of an elder and was now pushing her way steadily out of the confines of the crowd. "He tests you, certainly. Keris las Theomain was your test. I suspect the task of finding me was by way of being a reward."

Ileaha rose, and smoothed down the linen robe she wore as if it would somehow grant her control. She took a deep breath, but still sounded woefully young when she spoke.

"Why are you angry, Medair?"

By this time, Medair was no longer angry. If she were able to sustain such an emotion for any appreciable time, she would be able to focus herself around it. She continued to watch as the crowd began to break apart.

"Do you think they should stay, or go, Ileaha?" she asked, as the small group marched resolutely away from home and family. "Who preaches wisdom here? Do the young chase glory, or are they simply better able to make sacrifices?"

"I think both of them are right," Ileaha replied, with the air of one unable to follow the conversation. "There is no clear path, and wanting glory does not lessen the fact that they are needed."

"Or change the impossibility of the task." Medair offered the confused woman an apologetic smile. "We are alike, I think, Ileaha, for neither of us trusts ourselves. Did Cor-Ibis tell you merely to find me, or to bring me back?"

"To find you. But returning with you was implied, I think. You don't wish to come back?"

"Not really. But I don't suppose it will make much difference."

"No." Fear and sorrow chased personal concerns from Ileaha's eyes. "There is little hope, though few dare to say that the end is a forgone conclusion. The world has been remade, it seems, to Estarion's specifications. He wanted victory over us, and the fire of wild magic he caused has given him just that. And made him monstrous."

"Do you think he knows?" Medair asked, following Ileaha as she started out of the square. "Perhaps being the cause of the Conflagration will have allowed him to escape the changes."

"I don't know. There's so much we're ignorant of, in this new world! We cannot even guess who this person is he seeks."

"What does the Mersian Herald say?"

"That the Isle of Clouds is a sacred place in the Shimmerlan, where, as far as she knows, no-one lives. Or, rather, it is the home of Voren Dreamer, Lady Night, also called 'Lady Death', and that no mortal would dare go there."

"Lady Night?"

"One of this Four she keeps talking about. Maddening, the way things have been reshaped. The AlKier and your Farak have been joined by two others gods. Just conjured up, for everyone to believe in. There is, and always has been, only one God. The AlKier has no equal, and shares Her burden with no others."

Ileaha sounded personally offended by the suggestion, and Medair was forced to smile. She had never heard of the Isle of Clouds, let alone Voren Dreamer, but had little doubt who it was King Estarion demanded be surrendered to him. Possibly, Cor-Ibis had made a similar deduction, though he could not understand how important the woman he had geased might be to the coming battle. He had not heard the result of the Decians' true-speaking.

She didn't know why she was willing to go back, or what her answers would be if he questioned her. How could she judge the right thing to do, when her feelings were so suspect? They were all Ibisian. The pale invaders. White Snakes.

She wished she wasn't so glad he was alive.

Eighteen

"Kel ar Corleaux."

Medair looked up and found Avahn standing in the doorway of the sitting room. "So formal?"

"I didn't know if you'd still allow me use of your name," he replied, with a solemn smile.

Listening to Telsen's perfidious song seemed aeons ago. "I'm not angry with you, Avahn."

"No. Disappointed." He sighed, and sat down opposite her. It was necessary for him to make a minute adjustment to the sleeve of his robe of shimmering dark blue before meeting her eyes. "I apologise, Medair. I'd told you that same day that I wouldn't keep treating you like a puzzle it was my privilege to solve, and then did precisely that. I'm not ordinarily so ill-mannered."

"No?" she asked, then shook her head. "It doesn't matter, Avahn. We will forget it happened. Perhaps, instead, you can explain to me why the Ibisian Court tolerates a song with such a subject? Waiting for the hero of the conquered to return and drive you out? Even if it is Telsen's masterwork, I find it difficult to understand why it hasn't been banned in Athere."

"Tradition," Avahn replied, his eyelids drooping as he studied her. "You must have lived a sheltered life indeed, never to have heard the song or the story behind it."

"You can't help but probe, can you?" she chided, and the faintest flush lent a delicate violet to his cheeks. "I suppose you believe that bizarre tale Cor-Ibis produced, of me being raised in isolation to pretend to be the past reborn."

"He told you that? Well, we have not found any other explanation which fits. I don't suppose it really matters any more. So much else has changed, I wouldn't be surprised if they no longer even have that legend, outside Athere."

"I sincerely hope not. Have you spoken with the Mersian Herald?"

"Tried to. But many others wish to claim her attention, and I am not able to pre-empt them."

"Not even as one of those who shielded the city?"

He made a dismissive gesture, but looked pleased. "That disconcerted a few."

"Your act won't be as convincing, any more."

"Perhaps not. I think I shall have to abandon it, though it would be possible, I imagine, to have some believe that high-adept casting was mere luck."

"Just stumbled into doing the right passes. I'm sure." Medair sighed, and rubbed her left temple. "Tell me the story behind that song, Avahn," she commanded.

"Without trying to provoke revealing reactions," he said as if put-upon, and smiled charmingly. "Very well. It's a short tale, after all. Telsen, with typical daring, asked the *Niadril* Kier for permission to play the piece, and a dispensation was granted. Speculation over why was naturally rife, but the *Niadril* Kier was famed for keeping his own counsel."

"Ah." Medair shook her head, feeling ill. "No wonder your cousin thought nothing of suggesting an affair. It would have become almost an accepted fact, for those who did not understand." And those who had known Medair would have berated Telsen for those inferences, seen Kier Ieskar's silent acceptance, and wondered angrily if it could be true. The Ibisians of the time would have known it wasn't possible, but those of her friends and family who had survived her might well have believed she had betrayed them. Consequences unrolled in her mind and she sat staring at her knees, not caring about Avahn's steady gaze.

Hero or traitor? She felt like she'd been led through a series of decisions where she'd had no choice at all, just so she could betray her people. It seemed fitting that her name had come to represent both things. Doubtless "The Silence of Medair" was guaranteed to make any Medarist foam at the mouth, for the implications of both its lyrics and history. How a woman raised to believe herself Medair an Rynstar reborn would react was another question.

"Most do not believe as Adlenkar does," Avahn offered, in a conciliatory tone. "The *Niadril* Kier's motives are unknown, and you were right to point out the stain it would be on his honour, if the speculation was true. Perhaps he shared my admiration for Telsen."

Medair tried to picture Kier Ieskar allowing such a lie to be spread, no matter how prettily presented. It seemed terribly unlikely, and spawned possibilities Medair did not care to think about at all.

"I have long since given up trying to comprehend the motives of Ibisians," she said, almost too softly for him to hear.

"We are just like you at our core, Medair," he replied, solemnly.

"That's probably what's so frightening." She sighed, and sat a little straighter. "Could I bring you to believe that I am no-one in particular?"

"It is a possibility we have considered, Kel," said Cor-Ibis, from the doorway. "But one, like many, we have dismissed. You may leave, Avahn."

Avahn, dismissed like the many possibilities, rose without protest and offered his cousin a slight inclination of the head as he passed him at the door. Medair, who had been convinced that seeing Cor-Ibis again would answer some of her most difficult questions, watched as he crossed the room and found no solution within her. That she cared about this Ibisian she had no doubt. Something which had been clenched painfully in her chest had relaxed when Ileaha had told her that he lived, and since then Medair had doubted her every motive, her every action.

As he arranged himself opposite her, she tried to sort through what she was feeling. Apprehension, mainly, for she had too much respect for his mind not to know that this interview would be difficult. She had come in part hoping that she could make herself hate him, see him as an adversary still, as a White Snake, as wrongness made flesh. And to see for herself that he was uninjured.

If possible, he was even more impeccably presented than usual. She tried without success to isolate what it was that seemed different as he withdrew a slender cylinder of parchment from one sleeve of his robe. Not a hair was out of place, not a single crease marred his full robe of pale green and blue. She wondered how he made it shimmer so, whether he had the vanity to use magic to enhance his appearance. She was distracted from such speculation when he leaned forward and offered her the parchment.

Unsure what this signified, she accepted it cautiously and unrolled the tight cylinder as he settled himself back with that characteristic absence of expression. A map, not much wider than her two hands side by side. Drawn in detail with a fine hand, it was immediately recognizable as Farakkan. And all wrong.

Medair noted the forest grown larger in the north-west and the dark border which surrounded most of the lands south of the Girdle of Farak. She frowned over the absence of borders between Farash, Kyledra, Mymentia, Corland and Northern Histammeral, unable to understand the significance of the irregularly-shaped blobs outlined in the midst of these lands. "The Shimmerlan" was written across the entire area. Then she gasped.

It couldn't be. Medair counted the scattering of blobs, most numerous where the western reaches of the Girdle of Farak...had been.

"Islands," she whispered.

"Just so," Cor-Ibis agreed. "I asked Keris N'Taive, the Herald from Ashencaere, for a map to ascertain the location of the Isle of Clouds. I imagine you will not be surprised to learn that we were not long ago very close to it."

At that moment, Medair was less concerned with his attempt to shock her into an admission than the fact that her homeland was covered with water.

"What about the people?" she asked, still stunned. "Has everyone drowned?"

Cor-Ibis made a complicated gesture with his hands: negation and lack of knowledge combined. "Keris N'Taive speaks of beings called Alshem, who dwell in the waters of the Shimmerlan and trade with those on the islands. Mer-folk, if you will. Many of the islands correspond with the cities of the lands which have vanished: Thrence, Varden, Sarenal."

"Dwell? Mer-folk?" She shook her head, studying what little detail such a small map was able to give of this inland ocean. "Half Farak's Girdle seems to be gone."

"But not Bariback," Cor-Ibis replied, returning to the point. "The Isle of Clouds, where Lady Night, Voren Dreamer, makes her home and the Four have been known to hold Council. Kel, why does Estarion hunt you?"

"Out of idiocy, it seems to me," Medair said, twisting one side of her mouth. She studied this man who owed her his life, who was the blood of her enemy and innocent of their crimes. Who held to the same Ibisian honour which had destroyed the Empire. He watched her in return, his eyes silver mirrors, his demeanour too like one she hated for comfort.

"I would be on Bariback Mountain now, if it were not for Decian interference. Or the Isle of Clouds, whatever it's called." She glanced with some awe at the parchment she held. "I don't care to think what I might have become, out there. Mer-folk and flying horses."

"Despite the Conflagration, you are still hunted."

Medair shrugged. What could she say to this Ibisian who was important to her? Should her undefined feeling for him make any difference to the greater question? "Do you hold out hope of surviving this attack, Keridahl?"

"There is always hope. Athere faces a great threat – her walls are strong and woven with magic, but we deal with an unknown quantity along with strength of numbers and casting to equal our own. The fruits of wild magic, as yet not fully known. Why does Estarion hunt you, Kel?"

"Not to fire his troops with tales of Medair an Rynstar reborn," she replied, sourly.

"No. Answer my question, Kel. I am not able to allow you the luxury of continued evasion."

This was better. Threats would make it easier. "Would you force me then, Keridahl?"

"If you were allied with Estarion, then I would be wise to at the very least restrict your movements."

"I've never met the man," Medair protested. "Besides, why would he hunt me, if I worked for him?"

"Why would he offer you protection?"

"I doubt it's concern for my health and well-being."

As an attempt to rile a White Snake, Medair's answers failed miserably. He just looked at her, pale eyes stripping away her veneer of carelessness to the confusion beneath.

"Kel, we face a battle beyond the scope of any before brought to these walls. War to be waged on young and old alike, with the promise of slaughter without mercy. We will not bargain with Estarion, for the reward he sets upon your life is none we would care to accept. But such a demand can only mean that you have a value we have not yet realised. If there is some knowledge you hold, I would ask that you share it."

"I have no knowledge of Estarion," Medair replied.

"You know why he wants you," Cor-Ibis countered, with complete certainty.

Medair hesitated, then nodded minutely. "Yes." She stared down at the map in her hand, found she had crumpled it, and carefully smoothed it out again. She knew that she needed to give him something and let out a breath. "A True Seeing. Estarion has no idea who or what I am, but follows a Seer's pronouncement that to possess me is to gain some advantage in this war."

"And is this true?"

"Where would Athere be without the rahlstones, Keridahl? Arguably, the Seeing is already proved. Estarion's magics may be formidable, but the rahlstones have ever made Ibisian mages an army in their own right."

"He seeks you still, and you no longer possess the rahlstones, Kel." But Cor-Ibis had been struck by this twist, she could tell. His eyelids had dropped completely for a moment, and now were open much wider than before, as if he had suddenly woken.

"Does he necessarily know my role in that misadventure?" she asked, the picture of reason.

Cor-Ibis rose to his feet with slow grace, and stood looking down at her. "Perhaps not. This is not the whole truth, Kel. If it were, if you were that blameless passer-by you posited, you would not have any reason for mystery." He held up a pale hand to arrest speech. "You need not try to convince me you have a love of playing games. It is not so. Tell me this, Kel ar Corleaux. Will you remain silent as Athere's walls fall? Are your secrets worth so much?"

"This is not my war, Keridahl." A tight, small, obstinate voice.

"You are here. It is your war." As soft and calm as ever.

"No."

"Will you maintain this stance as you watch children cut down in the streets, Kel? It will not only be warriors, not only Ibis-lar, who die after dawn."

Medair could only sit silent, angry and ashamed and frozen by vows to the dead. And the part of her which could not forget that Kier Inelkar sat a stolen throne. Cor-Ibis studied her face, his own a mask which betrayed no emotion. Then he turned and walked away, pausing at the door to look back. In the shadows, away from the window, the subtle difference which had teased Medair's perception earlier suddenly became clear. Faintly but surely, Illukar Síahn las Cor-Ibis was glowing.

"I thought better of you, Kel ar Corleaux," he said, cool voice turned to ice. Then he was gone.

☙

"Medair?"

This time it was Ileaha. Medair raked the girl from head to toe with a searching glance, then closed her eyes. "Would you ever betray your Kier, Ileaha?" Her voice was harsh.

"I–" Ileaha took two steps forward, then stopped. "No," she said flatly, as if Medair were inviting such an action rather than asking a question. "Inelkar is Kier. I would give my life for her."

"Even if it seemed the right thing to do? If it would prevent deaths?"

"What seems the right thing to do is not always the best path, Medair," Ileaha replied. She was uncertain of the ground she was venturing onto, but sure of her convictions. "On my name day I gave oath to serve, to obey, to protect. There are no ifs or buts or half-measures. That is like being a little bit pregnant."

Medair lifted the corner of her mouth in a weak smile. "Partly a traitor. You are very certain. And if your Kier were killed, and the survivors surrendered, would you serve Estarion? What do you do when everything has changed but you, Ileaha?"

"If my Kier were killed, my life would already have been spent."

"Matters do not always arrange themselves so conveniently."

"Perhaps not." The young woman stood behind the couch recently vacated, trying to find hidden meaning in Medair's questions. "We will not surrender, Medair, even if the opportunity were offered to us. If I survived my Kier, I would avenge her, or die in the attempt."

"Like a Medarist, fighting on when the cause is lost?"

"That's no comparison," Ileaha objected. "The Medarists fight over something long past, something they did not participate in. Like Estarion, they ground their violence in the dead, lay blame on the living, and have motives based in greed rather than justice."

"Some of them think it just," Medair said, and frowned down at the paper in her hands, not truly seeing it. Cor-Ibis hadn't changed anything, except by making her feel a little unhappier. Baiting Ileaha as a way to lash her own wounds was pointless. She couldn't decide how her oath bound her, could not resolve the conflicting voices of conscience. She wanted so much to give in, to relinquish the burden she carried to those who needed it, but could not bring herself to take a step she knew she would always regard as a betrayal. Give the salvation of the Empire to those who had destroyed it?

"For you have to ask, Ileaha," she said, wearily. "What is justice? Whatever Estarion's motives, can you deny the very core of his arguments? That the Ibis-lar stole Palladium, that an Ibisian on the Silver Throne will always cause dissension, that the hatreds will not die?"

"I stole nothing, Medair," Ileaha replied, skin splotchy with anger, hurt in her eyes.

"No."

Medair retrieved her satchel from underneath the couch, then handed Ileaha the crumpled map. "This is the Mersian Herald's, I believe."

She left without farewells, tired of talking to people who could not understand because she dared not explain. Ileaha did not try to stop her, and the guards did not seem to know she was not supposed to go.

With no help amongst the living, Medair decided to search for it in the halls of the dead. Her oath had been to Grevain Corminevar. She would seek counsel from his grave.

Nineteen

Even stone ages.

The Hall of Mourning was a place of high ceilings and dark shadows. It covered several echoing chambers, tiered and separated by balustrades. Telsen had called the Hall the Gallery of the Dead.

Centuries had added hollows to the shallow stairs, and stains of damp on the walls. She bent to touch the depressions in the cold, grey stone and marvelled at the number of feet which must have passed this way since Telsen took her on tour.

Gazing out over the sarcophagi of generations of Corminevars, Medair saw that the Hall had been extended. Through a wide new opening to the right of the second tier she could dimly make out stone railing and marble. Built to house five hundred years of Ibisians who had ruled from a stolen throne.

The Hall was not permanently lit, and she felt suddenly uneasy about venturing among the dead. Waiting for her eyes to adjust to the gloom, she hesitated at the foot of the entrance stair. Light reflected past her off the polished floor of the Hall of Ceremony, where several large mageglows provided a steady, clear illumination. It only served to make the shadows deeper.

Voices prompted her to edge to one side, where must and dust waited to assail her nostrils. The palace seemed overfull of guards today. They had watched her suspiciously as she'd made her way down from Cor-Ibis' rooms. She'd had half a mind to don her ring, but was tired of the vague sensation of illness. Besides, there was no ban of which she knew against visiting the Hall of Mourning. Skulking around invisibly would only make her seem guilty of something.

The source of the voices proved not to be guards, but a group of young nobles, walking in a tight cluster. She couldn't make out what they were saying, and waited until they had passed through the

Hall of Ceremony. Then a series of careful gestures served to conjure a bobbing mageglow bright enough to keep the shadows at bay without drawing the attention of passers-by.

Her footsteps echoed as she walked across the first tier, where the earliest kings and queens of Palladium lay in stone-wrapped state, their likenesses carved by hands long turned to dust. The second tier was larger, but held fewer sarcophagi. It had once been considered fitting for the coffins of monarchs to be more than a container for their bodies, for their lives to be reflected by some tribute. So there were friezes, columns, crypts within crypts. They ranged in complexity from the wrought iron fence around Iriane the Just, to the miniature palace which housed the remains of Varden the First.

She paused momentarily at the entrance of the new extension. A corner of pale stone was visible in the light of her glow, but the rest was little more than black shapes in darkness. Ibisian dead: she had no wish to look upon them. Gritting her teeth she went onward, to the third tier. This was where Grevain Corminevar's mother had been laid to rest, where the last true Palladian Emperor would surely lie.

White, pure, unembellished. Her mageglow heated its milky depths. Medair stumbled to a halt, having discovered not the resting place of her Emperor, but the one who had destroyed him. There were no markings of any kind on the tomb, not even his name, but Medair knew it could be no other. Standing alone at the very end of the Hall, an achingly simple box of near-translucent marble which held the mortal remains of Ieskar Cael las Saral-Ibis.

Twenty-three and dead. She refused to think of it, of him. He had destroyed the Empire and deserved no thought at all.

With grim determination she dragged her eyes from the soft marble, sought and found the carved, grey face of the man to whom she had sworn her life. Grevain Corminevar's sarcophagus lay in the shadow of two of Farak's handmaidens. The statues towered some seven feet high, leaning out of the wall at the head of the sarcophagus, each holding a stone arm forward, hands resting on the shoulders of his image. Their heads were bowed in sorrow or contemplation.

A lump lodged itself in Medair's throat and she went to one knee in the traditional obeisance. He had not been a handsome man. Stocky, bearded, dour. Whoever had been set the task of recreating his likeness had been skilled: the prominent Corminevar jaw was visible beneath the curling outline of beard. The stone face was at peace, despite the sword clasped to his chest to indicate he had died in battle. Medair could not remember ever seeing him wear such an expression. He had been a brisk, impatient man, used to dealing with problems quickly and efficiently, always thinking on to the next trouble brewing on the horizon.

"I'm sorry," Medair choked out, inadequately. She brushed at tears suddenly streaking her cheeks. The enormity of her failure overwhelmed her and she was barely able to hold her ground, wanting to collapse into wails, to crawl away in shame. "One stupid mistake," she told indifferent stone. "I – it could have been so different, if I hadn't – Excellency..."

The futility of it all strangled further words. Grevain Corminevar was dead, the Empire had fallen, and nothing Medair could do could change that. She could not even ask his forgiveness.

Did death release the bonds of oath? Medair was running out of time in which to struggle with her own conscience. She did not want to stand by and watch the inhabitants of Athere slaughtered, for all they were Ibisian. But to give the Horn of Farak to those whom she had originally sought to use it against? No, that was beyond her. She would not betray her people to the benefit of another. She would rather...

Medair placed her satchel on top of the stone hands of her king, and slowly opened it. Reaching in, she found a heavy silk cord and pulled it gently, not enough to expose the Horn, not yet. It was so rich in power that every Ibisian in the palace would likely be able to feel it. Instead, she found the bone handle of a knife, a sliver of metal which would cut flesh cleanly. Fear and uncertainty washed over her, but she pushed second thoughts to one side. It was better this way.

Winding the cord about one wrist, she closed her eyes and sent a silent prayer to Farak. The Horn would be pulled from her satchel when she fell, and she would be free of choices she did not want to make.

"*One last place to run, Keris an Rynstar.*"

Medair gasped, entire body jerking with shock. She stared around her at the shadows lurking at the edges of her mageglow, but could not see the source of that entirely too familiar voice. It couldn't be him.

She cautiously unwound the cord from her arm and took a step forward, knife held at ready. Another step and she was able to see the stair, and the tall man watching her. His eyes were serious, his pointed face the same grave mask he'd worn for an entire war. Pale hair fell neatly over the shoulders of a shimmering robe of Kier's white.

The knife fell to the ground with a clatter. Medair backed away until her ribs connected painfully with a corner of white marble and she stopped, trapped.

"*A most convincing display of horror.*" Kier Ieskar descended the last few steps into the room and paused.

"How–?" Medair rasped, lifting one hand as if to fend him off. At the same time she began sidling sideways, to remove herself from the vicinity of the white marble which she had thought housed his body.

He inclined his head to one side, lids lowering as he followed her progress. White Snake. When he spoke again, it was in Parlance, a concession he had not made since their first meeting.

"Wild Magic," he said, and looked down at himself, as if to confirm his own existence. "The shield held off the reshaping of the Conflagration, but the world is still saturated with unfocused power. It collects in pools, sinks into the ground, is carried on the wind. It will be a long time before there ceases to be unpredictable changes."

"*Changes!!?* The dead coming back to life is not–"

"Not what has happened here. Calm yourself, Keris an Rynstar. You have summoned my shade from beyond the veil, not returned me fully to this world."

"I –?!"

"Yourself."

He came forward and she managed not to cringe, or even leap to snatch her satchel to safety as he approached her Emperor's sarcophagus. His long fingers touched the blood-red cord which trailed from the satchel's mouth.

"I did not summon you," she whispered.

"You did. You know that, within yourself. Do not argue against it." He lifted the tasselled end of the cord. "You sought this to kill me and my kind. To revenge yourself for what we, what I, had done to your Empire. And I was not here. You cannot assuage your sorrow in belated apologies. You want justice, a clear choice, for it all to be right again, and, failing that, you want to rail at me for my role in your loss."

Silence. Medair could not answer him.

He looked at her, cord still in his hand. "You do not like to face certain truths, Medair an Rynstar. Unwilling to help my people, unable to ignore their plight, you decide to kill yourself. And, not wanting to die, you reach out to pull me here, to convince you not to. It is an unusual form of cowardice."

"I don't want to live," she protested, numbly. "There's no place for me here."

"You do not want to lay claim to your name, yet you refuse to give it up. You do not want to face the world as yourself, to have history record the breadth of your failure, but nor are you willing to create a new identity for yourself."

It was a cold, precise, unforgiving denunciation of her faults. Medair turned away, hugging her arms around herself.

"Go away," she said. "If I summoned you here, then surely I can banish you. You have no reason to stay – the power of the Horn will alert your people to its presence, and they will be saved. It is not necessary that I personally hand it over to them. I want to die more than I fear death."

"If that were true, I would not be here," Kier Ieskar countered, calm as ever.

"I don't even know if you are what you seem to be," she replied, trying to rouse anger, hurt, anything but numb fear and apathy. And shame.

"My identity is not at issue." She could hear him moving, and looked cautiously over her shoulder to find him gazing pensively at the marble which encased his body. "I did not wish to live," he said. "To struggle against the wounds of my body, the losses I had incurred, to lead my people in war. But the easy route is not often the best."

"An unnecessary war," she accused, still searching for anger. Why was it she could not feel as she should, when she looked on him?

"Not so."

"The Emperor offered you safe haven. You *chose* to make war."

"Tell me, Keris an Rynstar," Kier Ieskar said. "Why do you imagine my people refused the offer made to them this day – why pass up an opportunity to ensure their children, our race, survived?"

Medair frowned. "If you are trying to make a comparison, you over-reach yourself, *Ekarrel*. Grevain Corminevar would not have enslaved your people. He was an honourable man."

"He was. He would have aided my people in any way possible, given us shelter, provided us with food. And we would have been lost, a pauper race with no land to call our own, feared for our strengths, hated for our differences. Chained by our own laws. Our culture has been irretrievably altered through exposure to the peoples of Farakkan, but it would have shattered us, or been lost altogether if we had allowed ourselves to be separated, broken apart as we would have been as petitioners."

"That still doesn't make it *right!*" Medair groaned, finding that this was an explanation she would rather not have heard.

"The salvation of my people to the detriment of my honour. It is a price I would pay again, and willingly."

"I hate you."

"I know." Impossible that there could almost be a hint of humour in his voice. She stared at him, at that perfect mask and the blue eyes which could still look straight through her, despite his death. "Tell me, Keris," he went on. "Why did you seek out this Horn, so unexpectedly? The odds were against your success, and it is not a task usually given to Heralds."

Medair did not answer.

"Keris?"

"What does it matter? If you are here to convince me not to kill myself, why don't you do that?"

"Because I do not need to, Keris. The moment has passed, and you will not take up the knife again. You will go from this place of the dead to the halls of the living and admit your name and your past. Because you know that that is right."

"Is it?" She shook her head. "From your perspective, just as, from your perspective, it was better to invade Palladium than be its pensioner."

"Your replacement was much less adept with Ibis-laran."

He said it in the same even tone that he'd used to condemn her, and she felt it just as strongly. It was beyond comprehension, how she could be standing in the bowels of Athere having an argument with Kier Ieskar. Medair, moving away from the man or ghost or whatever he was, carefully collected her satchel from the hands of her Emperor. Tucking the cord inside, she sealed it gently. She could feel Ieskar watching her.

"Why did you allow Telsen to play that song?" she asked, in a tiny, thready voice.

"A question for a question?"

"If you wish." Medair closed her eyes. She could not think about this.

"An interesting man," Ieskar said, with unshakeable equilibrium. "Soulless, turning the hearts of others into music. His saving grace was the skill with which he did so. That song – Telsen may not have felt it, but eternal longing for the impossible has never been better expressed."

Medair started, blinked, but his face was still a mask, and before she could react further he continued. "I believe, at the time, it was a form of apology."

"Apology?" She seemed able to do nothing but stare at him. He was still gazing down at his tomb, as motionless as the statues which guarded Grevain, but at that he lifted his eyes.

"Not for making war, Keris. When a new Herald brought me Corminevar's next message, I sought your location, and learned that you quested for an artefact which might well cost me victory. I sent a handful of my best to find you and ensure you did not return."

Medair laughed, unable to stop herself. She clamped her jaw when she heard an edge of hysteria. "How appropriate," she managed, through quivering lips. "In attempting make amends for murdering me, you succeed in destroying my reputation."

"I learned, later, that they had not found you, but by that time my end had nearly come and I could only charge my regent to be on her guard." He did not appear in the slightest way remorseful about ordering her death, his voice thoughtful, introspective. "It is perhaps appropriate that it is now my people who wait upon the silence of Medair."

"They can wait forever, for all I care," she said, hotly.

"You are too just for that, Keris. Answer my question now. What sent you on this quest?"

She looked at him from the corner of her eye, wondering why he wanted to know. What he had meant, about Telsen's song. He had tried to have her killed. He had died. And she couldn't begin to tell him something she refused to admit even to herself.

"Your brother's daughter," she replied eventually.

"Adestan? Ah, of course. The last game of marrat. It is hard to hate a child, is it not?"

"It is hard to hate."

"All too easy." He walked towards her, measured, implacable. "This is your war, for this is Palladium, Athere, which you are sworn to protect. This is your war, because you cannot stand by and watch innocents slaughtered alongside warriors. This is your war, because you are here. Give me your hand."

Medair stared, fingers curling into fists. She had never touched him. It was forbidden, and even if it were not, she would never have been able to bear such contact. He lifted his hand, and she flinched.

"Give me your hand, Keris an Rynstar. Consider it my price. Perhaps I could even haunt you, if you deny me. In this new world, it may well be possible, and I do not think you would like such a thing."

Not at all. She stared at him, at the pale blue eyes glittering behind hooded lids, and could not ask why he wanted this. There were some things that had to be left unspoken.

Tentatively, she lifted one hand and placed it against his, palm to palm. Her hand looked small and muddy against his white flesh. Icy fingers, colder than death, closed around hers and she shuddered.

That soft, imperturbable, unbearable voice went on. "It revolts you to touch me. That is hate. Remember this feeling, Keris, for it is not what you feel for those who live in this time, who had no part in the downfall of your Empire. There is no betrayal in alliance with them."

She stared at slender white fingers, livid against her skin.

"Take your place in this world, Medair," he said, very softly. "Goodbye."

As she watched, the pale fingers blurred and changed, became smaller, more delicate. She gasped, and went to her knees as the person attached to that hand sagged against her. She found herself holding a boy of fifteen or so, in the throes of shivers so violent they were practically convulsions. White hair spilled across her arms as she tried to hold him still, and she could hear his teeth chattering. Awkwardly she pulled open her satchel, dragged out the lambs' wool cloak which she resorted to on the coldest days, and wrapped it around his shoulders.

He clung to her, decidedly disconcerting until she realised how warm her body must be in comparison with his own. So she held him close, this Ibisian boy she suspected must be a descendant of Ieskar, and wondered if the *Niadril* Kier had known this would happen. Deliberate contrast. Like the attempt on her life, it would be characteristic.

"Who are you?" she asked, when his shudders had finally subsided to the occasional quiver, and he lay exhausted against her chest.

"Islantar." His voice was a breathy sigh.

"The Kierash."

"*Yes.*" He spoke in Ibis-laran. Eyes rose to peer at her through a disordered fringe. "*You are Medair an Rynstar. That was...*"

"Kier Ieskar."

"*Yes.*" The boy hid his face against her chest, trembling. "*He was so sad,*" he whispered.

Medair could not think about that. She disentangled herself and found her feet. "*Can you stand?*" she asked.

"*No,*" the Kierash replied. Then, with her aid, he levered himself upright, swaying.

"Medair an Rynstar," he repeated, as she began to guide him towards the exit. She did not reply. "Forgive my weakness, Keris," he continued, switching languages.

"Hardly your fault," Medair replied, shortly.

"The centuries have been kind to you, Keris," was the boy's next foray into conversation, as they crossed the second tier of the Hall of Mourning. A round-about Ibisian way of asking how she came to still be alive. She wondered how much of the conversation he remembered, what else he had learned from briefly housing the *Niadril* Kier.

"You don't know how wrong you are," she replied.

Islantar shook his head, then made an effort to stand on his own, and failed. The chill which had gripped him had faded, but he was as ungainly as a newborn colt.

"What were you doing among the crypts?" she asked, at least in part to stave off further questions.

"I don't know. We were going to ask permission to go to the wall, then..." He frowned. "I don't know."

Medair thought she should probe him on how much he remembered, but found she didn't want to know. Such was the pattern of her life.

Emerging into the Hall of Ceremony, she winced at the sudden, alarmed shout of a guard and waited, resigned, as one of the patrols rushed towards them. The Kierash made an effort to stand upright, gripping her arm tightly. His change of stance must have made some impression, for the approaching guards stopped looking quite so inclined to cut her down, and slowed their charge to a merely hurried advance.

"Kierash?" The young woman in the lead pressed a hand to her chest in salute. "Do you require assistance?"

"I would be obliged if you would lend me an arm, Kaschen," the Kierash replied, very dignified.

"Kierash," the kaschen murmured. Taking over the role of vertical support, she assumed a weirdly cross-eyed and awed expression. It served to remind Medair that this was the heir to all Palladium and that even now there were protocols about whom he could touch. The man and woman at the kaschen's back were eyeing Medair, ready to spring into action if their Kierash in any way indicated that she was the cause of his sudden indisposition.

Looking at the boy properly for the first time, Medair was unsurprised to discover a distinct resemblance to his distant ancestor. There were also marked differences, including a more determined jaw-line, possibly a remnant of his Corminevar heritage. He was considering her in return, blue eyes a shade or two darker than Ieskar's.

"I would like to accompany you, Keris," he said. "But fear I would be a distraction." He attempted to shrug, and swayed perilously, sending a momentary flash of panic across the face the woman trying to support him without intruding on the royal person. "I can only...thank you."

He wasn't referring to her assistance in his attempts to stay upright. He inclined his head to a more than courteous depth, without further allusion to her secrets. Then he handed back her lambs' wool cloak, turned, and led the trio of highly confused guards down the length of the Hall of Ceremony. Medair watched them go. Then she looked down at the satchel depending from her right shoulder.

She could do nothing but accept her fate.

Twenty

A light tap on the door.

"Medair?"

Avahn's voice. Medair paused in the middle of fastening her tunic.

"Yes?" she asked, stalling.

"You *are* here." He sounded relieved. "I've been sent to collect you. Can I come in?"

After a glance at the bed, Medair closed the last three buttons, and said: "Yes."

As the door opened, she picked up the cloak. When she'd first been given the uniform, she'd made a great play of swirling it about her when she dressed. Now, as a startled Avahn took in her clothing, she merely arranged folds of pearlescent grey properly to cover one shoulder, and clipped the two ends together with the strangle-knot clasp.

"A rare occasion indeed," Avahn managed, though there was shock in the voice he meant to keep light. "Illukar is hardly ever wrong, and he did most particularly believe you were not going to declare yourself Medair an Rynstar reborn."

"You've stopped calling him 'my esteemed cousin'," Medair said.

"He gave me his name." At another time, Avahn would not have hidden his pleasure. Now he was merely distracted.

"Mm. I am not going to declare myself anything reborn, Avahn."

Carefully, she lifted the silver badge from where she had placed it on the bed, and fastened it to her chest. It gleamed dully, this sigil of her office. Two crossed crescent moons, one etched with a scroll, the other with the Corminevar triple crown. She touched the crowns lightly, then glanced up at her audience.

"Herald Savart," she whispered, and black clouded the grey pearl of her uniform, like a thimble of ink dropped into a glass of water. A handful of heartbeats and she stood swathed in unrelieved night, her badge shining like a beacon on her breast.

"In wartime, we were Sanguine," she told Avahn, who was staring at her, caught between astonishment and disbelief. "The red of drying blood, words of threat and anger. Savart was for death, for the ending of things. For surrender."

"Medair..." he breathed.

She did not respond, afraid that if she stopped to explain she would not be able to go through with this. Closing and sealing her satchel, she drew it over her shoulder, its weight firm against her hip.

"Who sent you to collect me?" she asked.

"The Kier." Avahn eyed her doubtfully, but visibly decided to keep his thoughts to himself. "That map – Bariback is this Isle of Clouds and the Kier wants to question you after she has finished addressing the Court."

"She is in the Throne Room, then? Good. Take me there, Avahn. It is time to end something."

Avahn hesitated. "I am sworn to my Kier, Medair," he said, carefully. "If you mean her harm–"

Medair laughed, a short, bitter sound. "I am not an assassin, Avahn. I will not raise a hand to her."

"No, you are..." He trailed off, delicate white brows drawing together. Then he smiled, a glow of sudden delight in his eyes. "You are most unexpected, Medair. I am glad to know you."

It was a reaction purely Avahn, and almost won a smile from her. He was Ibisian, but she couldn't help liking him, any more than she could help being attracted to Cor-Ibis. They were Ibisians, and some part of her was never going to forgive that, but they were not her enemies. The war was over, was centuries past, and she would not put her hatred over her duty.

It was evident that many of the palace's current residents had somewhere seen a depiction of an Imperial Herald. Their reactions ranged from dismay to anger, and Medair found Avahn's presence a useful pass as he waved away two separate patrols inclined to intercept her.

All the doors of the Great Hall were open, but Medair was careful not to glance left or right as she strode down the marbled floor. The crowd in the Throne Room was densely packed, spilling out of the ebony doors. Typically, they were also completely silent, listening intently to the words of their Kier. Only the guards, who faced outwards, saw Medair's arrival. They stirred, exchanged glances, then slid swords slowly from their sheathes.

"When have the Ibis-lar drawn weapons upon Heralds?" Avahn asked, in a clear, carrying voice.

Several of the courtiers at the rear of the crowd turned at his words, and made shocked comments. The guards hesitated.

"My bond," Avahn said, with complete assurance, and smiled faintly at Medair. An Ibisian, willing to vouch for her. It felt strange.

Stepping forward, she wondered how she was to reach the Kier, and was foolishly conscious of her dignity. A Herald should not have to push her way through a crowd.

But, whether out of ingrained Ibisian protocol, or a desire to witness a confrontation, the men and women nearest her began to move aside. There were more Farakkians in the room than she'd expected, and they stared at her with particular shock, but none chose to bar her way. As Medair continued to walk forward, a corridor formed through the centre of the Throne Room, accompanied by the whisper of silk and startled voices. The Silver Throne rose above the room on a small dais, and Medair knew the precise moment when the Kier saw the cause of the spreading commotion in her Court. The clear voice which had been addressing the gathering paused, continued briefly in a softer tone, then was silent. Waiting.

A tiny droplet of sweat launched itself the length of Medair's spine, and she gulped air as inconspicuously as possible as she passed into the circle of space around the Throne. She focused on those members of the Court fanned out on either side of the Kier like an honour guard. The only faces which caught her eye were las Theomain's, stiffly affronted, and the Mersian Herald, wide-eyed.

The rest were a blur, insignificant at this moment. The Kier was everything, blood of both usurper and the one who owned Medair's loyalty.

"You bring a message, Kel?" Kier Inelkar asked, her voice cool, her eyes cautious. She was wary, not ready to react with immediate hostility to what must appear to her as a threat, but by no means welcoming of this woman garbed in the past.

Medair had been trained to deliver the words of others, not proclaim her own thoughts. She felt a need to justify herself for an act of betrayal, but words crumbled to dust before they reached her lips. But she would not fail her Emperor now, not this last time.

"I bring no messages," she said, before the Court could grow restive. She lifted one hand and plucked her badge from her chest, bursting open the clasp. It cut her hand, but she did not care. She looked one last time at her most prized possession, then let it fall to the floor of the Throne Room. The colour drained from her uniform, even as the flames had drained from around Athere.

"There is nothing to say," she continued, hollowly. "The past is dead. And lost in fire. I will not watch Athere fall to invaders, no matter who sits her throne."

She opened her satchel, to the accompaniment of a half-dozen swords drawn. She ignored them, all her energy focused on an effort to keep control. Her fingers tangled in a silken cord, and she drew it into sight.

The Horn of Farak was fashioned from grey-yellow bone, banded with black greshalt. It was long and narrow, a bell of dark metal flaring at one end. The other end was slightly knobbed, with no shielding mouthpiece. It looked like a piece of someone's leg, fashioned into a musical instrument. And it sang.

Medair had heard tales of singing swords and always found the idea a little ludicrous. She had never conceived of such a sound as now filled the Throne Room. Waves breaking on endless shores. A bubbling brook. Rocks clattering down a slope. The deep vibration of rock, grinding in the bowels of the earth. The wind: in trees, through fields, down lonely ravines. Roaring at the heart of a storm. The essence of Farak, expressed a thousand different ways, all in a single whisper which deafened and was impossible to deny.

How this barely audible, wholly inescapable cacophony became melody, Medair could not explain. But it was a song truer than any that Telsen had ever crafted, and its effect on the Court was like a physical blow. They rocked on their heels, these proud, cold nobles, gaped stupidly and broke into cries of protest and wonder. Medair took two steps forward and held the Horn out to Inelkar, taking care that the Kier would grasp it by the cord, rather than the Horn itself. She had made that mistake, on first discovering the artefact, and was kind enough to not inflict such sensations on another.

The Kier brought her free hand up to the shaft, let it hover within touching for moments, then lowered the Horn so that it rested on the floor. The thing Medair had quested for to destroy the Ibis-lar, now in the hands of their leader.

"Medair an Rynstar." A statement, not a question. Inelkar's voice was mild, but the part of Medair which hated herself for this deed heard it as an accusation, and shame washed through her. She had betrayed her oath, and delivered the Horn into the hands of the White Snakes. All the altruistic motives in the world would not excuse that.

"*Ekarrel*," murmured the Keridahl Alar, "we should shield the Horn. It would be well not to alert those who wait at our gates of this turn of events."

"Truly said." The Kier stood, as if the Keridahl's words had freed her to action. She gestured peremptorily to two Court officials – Gantains, if Medair remembered the term correctly – and in a few short moments a large, disappointed portion of the Court was filing obediently out of the Throne Room. Medair wished she were going with them.

Avahn moved to Cor-Ibis' side, presumably so he would not be swept out with the rest. Cor-Ibis was gazing fixedly at the Horn, but lifted his head when Avahn reached him, and asked a question Medair could not hear. Avahn shrugged and they both looked at her, wearing mirrored heavy-lidded masks, their shared blood very apparent. Medair averted her face, and found herself looking at Jedda las Theomain, who was in turn staring at Cor-Ibis. The woman's expression was set, as if she'd just seen a threat confirmed.

The ebony door thudded shut. Questions waited upon the arrival of an iron-wrought chest spelled to dampen magic in the same way as her satchel. The Horn of Farak was carefully lowered inside and a few words said to activate the dampening effect.

A look of palpable relief crossed the faces of the handful who remained. The song made the blood rise up to dance in the body's courses, and none who heard it was left as cool in heart as Ibisians strove to be.

"Medair an Rynstar." The Kier now addressed her more purposefully. "Our debt to you is beyond reckoning, Keris. This is an act of greatness."

Medair looked at her, then dropped her eyes to the bauble of silver she had discarded. She shook her head, denying the words and her actions equally.

"An act born of lack of alternatives."

"Perhaps. How came you to be here, Keris an Rynstar? Centuries have passed."

Medair made a gesture toward the chest. "The Hoard of Kersym Bleak slumbers outside time," she said. "As did I." The words sounded pretentious and false, an attempt to hide the simple fact of falling asleep in the wrong place. "I erred," she continued, trying to make herself clear. "Chose to rest where I should have had better sense, and found the–" Her voice broke, and she inhaled sharply, as if she had been forgetting to breathe. "– I found that the war had passed me by."

It was not condemnation she read in their faces then, but pity. These White Snakes pitied her for failing to defeat them. That at last seemed a good reason to hate them, but she did not have the energy.

"All Athere has joined you in being displaced from the world, it seems," the Kier commented, bringing Medair's past tragedies into perspective. She turned her eyes to her Keridahl Avec and Alar, standing to either side of her throne. "What say you? Will the changes which have been wrought by the Conflagration effect the Horn?"

"Impossible to know, *Ekarrel*," the Keridahl Alar responded, immediately. "It is claimed the Horn will summon an army sufficient to defeat any foe. That it has power of immense proportion is obvious to us all. More exactly we will not know until it is..." She hesitated, then continued less confidently. "Until it is used."

When his Kier's attention turned to him, Cor-Ibis raised a hand in agreement. He seemed to be glowing still, though it was difficult to be certain in the bright light of the throne room.

"If the Conflagration has indeed caused the rise of two unknown gods," he said. "And brought together the AlKier and Farak as part of this Four, then there can be no guessing as to the consequences of using the Horn. The consequences of not using the Horn are clearer."

"Keris N'Taive, do you know the legends of the Horn of Farak?" Kier Inelkar asked the Mersian Herald, who had been staring at Medair with something like awe.

"*Ekarrel*, of course!" exclaimed the Herald. "Did we not discuss–" She broke off, frowned and shook her head. "Well, perhaps we did not discuss those very tales, at our last meeting. It seems to me incredible that you have no memory of the past, or that my memories are false within this city, but I can only accept and try to remember. Yes, *Ekarrel*, I know of the Horn of Farak, fashioned from the body of the Living World at the end of her sojourn among mortals. I know of the Hoard of Kersym Bleak and the quest of Medair an Rynstar. Who does not know the Silence of Medair? I can scarce believe I witnessed its breaking." She turned wide, tilted eyes on Medair. "Have you then been on the Isle of Clouds all this time? Dwelling with Voren Dreamer?"

"Has it occurred to you," Medair retorted, stung by the apparent enjoyment this woman took in legend made flesh, "that you might venture out from the walls of Athere and find that the world does not correspond to your memory of it? That Tir'arlea fell into ruin a thousand years ago, and there is no Isle of Clouds?"

A flicker of surprise crossed N'Taive's face, then the compassion which grated so on Medair's nerves. "Yes, it did," the Herald said, softly. "When my every statement was met with a blank stare and endless disbelieving questions. But then the South obliged me with confirmation, and I knew that the world I had grown up in was out there, and it was everyone here who was wrong. A rare occurrence indeed, for one of Tir'arlea to greet the advent of darkness with relief, but the presence of the Cloaked South means that Tir'arlea shines to the north-west. I think I would like to tell Estarion that, if ever the chance is given to me."

Medair looked away from the tilted eyes. She found the Kier was waiting for her to answer the question posed, and gritted her teeth. She had given up the Horn. What more did these White Snakes need?

"I went to Bariback after I – found Athere as it is."

"How did Estarion know of you?" the Keridahl Alar asked, sharply. "Is he aware of what you carried?"

Medair shook her head, then shrugged. "Vorclase was there to fetch me," she told them. "Estarion had sent some unfortunate to his death bringing forth True Speaking. All they knew was–" She stopped, and glanced at the iron-bound box which shielded a legend. "That to hold me – or whoever it was living on Bariback – was to hold victory. Twice over, I suppose, if the rahlstones are to be counted. They must have decided the location for the exchange to complement Vorclase's expedition." She frowned, and looked again at the Mersian Herald. "What are the consequences of using wild magic?" she asked.

The Herald seemed mildly startled, and glanced uncomfortably at the Kier.

"That is surely known, here above all places," she replied. "Sar-Ibis died in wild magic."

"Yes. But do you know what the Conflagration is?" Medair asked. She was thinking of Esta, the woman at the tavern.

"I am told it was a great fire," Herald N'Taive, began. "I saw no fire, but..."

"But had you heard of the Conflagration before you came to Athere?"

"No."

The Ibisians, having listened to this exchange with mild confusion, finally saw Medair's point.

"If there is no warning against the Conflagration," asked the man who Medair thought was the Keridahl Alar's son, "what weighs against using wild magic?"

N'Taive was clearly perplexed by their sudden tension, but answered anyway. "The Creeping Dark, Kerin. That which overwhelmed Sar-Ibis. The Blight."

It was not new information, for no Ibisian could be unaware of Sar-Ibis' loss. "Estarion has already used wild magic," Medair explained to the Herald. "And brought upon us the Conflagration. Remade Farakkan. Now, if he loses the coming battle, past behaviour suggests that he may again turn to wild magic. Even if he does remember the past as we do, he might again be willing to risk trying to control summoned power. And this time, if he fails, no shield will save Athere."

"Or the rest of Farakkan," the Herald responded, looking doubtful. "Estarion is not so stupid, surely? Did he not put to death a mage in his realm who was experimenting with power beyond herself?"

"He may very well have," the Kier said, taking back control of the conversation. "But the possibility that Estarion might turn to wild magic when he is on the verge of defeat is one we will not overlook. There is also a great deal of unbound power loose in Farakkan, which will complicate any casting we wish to do. We will need to draw again upon your knowledge, Keris N'Taive, for there are obviously many aspects of your world which we have yet to cover."

Kier Inelkar lapsed into a moment's thoughtful silence before addressing Medair:

"I cannot adequately express our debt to you, Keris an Rynstar," she said. "There is a great deal more I would know, and I hope that you will agree to discuss matters with me at another time. Until then, you will remain our guest." She gestured to Avahn. "Escort Keris an Rynstar to her chambers."

Medair had no objection. She wanted to leave this room of Ibisians, and the thing she had just done, behind her.

Twenty-One

"Am I under guard, Avahn?"

Avahn hesitated, then lifted his hands, fingers uncurling.

"It is probable," he admitted. "I will ask Illukar, later, exactly what the Kier's wishes are. They will discuss you, of course."

"Of course." Having dropped her cloak on the divan by the door, Medair sat on the bed, holding her satchel on her lap. She turned the strap over and over between her fingers, surprised at how little she felt. Only exhaustion.

"I had not really thought of what would come after. The choices don't go away. I'm not what the legends describe, but there are those, I suppose, who would rally to me. Your Kier will not want me free to roam."

"You could be a unifying force in Palladium," he offered, diffidently. "Mend the fractures."

She snorted. "Do I need to do that? The cold blood is dominant, in this world. Mix-bloods are born almost as Ibisian as you are. Surely the Medarists don't exist any more."

"Mix-bloods were never Medarists. I don't see why the Hold or any other faction would cease to exist, simply because the object of their hatred stands out the more." He pulled a chair from beneath an elegant writing desk and sat down on it. "How do you know that the blood of the Ibis-lar is dominant?"

"A woman at a tavern – she was outside the shield when the fire came, and went from mostly Farakkian to indistinguishable from Ibis-lar, and spoke of the cold blood being stronger. She was very distressed. Her home is here and she no longer fits it." Medair shrugged. The parallel was obvious, but unlike Esta, Medair could no longer call Athere her home. There was no place for a former Imperial Herald. An unpredictable piece on the marrat board, as Avahn had once said, with too much cause to hate to be trusted.

Avahn, however, had other things on his mind.

"You knew Telsen, didn't you?"

Medair grimaced. "Telsen really wasn't a person to emulate, Avahn," she said, lowering her satchel to the floor and kicking it gently beneath the bed. "He–" She thought about it, choosing her words. "He lied, to the benefit of his music and the detriment of others. He created this legend of Medair which makes my position frankly impossible, and, because he loved hidden meanings, managed to ruin my reputation to top everything off. Does the brilliance of his talent excuse the untruths?"

Avahn, abashed, made a gesture of apology with one hand.

"Could he not, could we not be inferring more than he intended? There is nothing said outright."

"More than enough for me to claim injury before a Council of Peers," she replied. "Yes, I knew Telsen. I was briefly his lover. He made up the part about his eternal unfulfilled devotion as well." She frowned at the caustic note in her voice, and went on more equably. "He was a generous man, full of life, but he was also carelessly cruel, and nothing took precedence over his music. Not truth, not loyalty, certainly not women."

"I don't know what to say."

"Have I ruined all of your illusions, Avahn? It doesn't change the music. He had a marvellous voice and his songs will be remembered, well, as long as I am."

He smiled at her sadly. "I must do something to restrain this talent of mine for asking the wrong questions. Do you want me to leave you in peace?"

"No. Yes. I suppose so. I feel a little...beyond conversation, just now." Her bones dragged at her, and she struggled with overwhelming fatigue.

He nodded, stood, then suddenly assumed a formal stance.

"My thanks are as inadequate as all others, Keris Medair an Rynstar," he told her, gravely making the three gestures of debt Cor-Ibis had also once given her. "But know that I am yours to call upon in need."

He bowed and turned before she could respond, as if he were embarrassed by the sincerity behind his words. When the door had closed behind him, Medair drew her knees up beneath her chin and tried to think about her future.

That the Kier might try to control her in some way was certainly possible, despite the debt they all owed her. Confine her to the palace, keep her under observation. A life of luxurious semi-imprisonment. But safe.

For she would be hated.

The longed-for hero had become the grand betrayer. Among any who opposed the Ibisians, those who had paid a moment's attention to foolish legends about the past reborn, and most especially the ones who had taken Medair's name and turned it into a banner – there would be no understanding, and no forgiveness. It was quite probable that the Ibisians were the only group with both the will and capacity to keep her alive.

Kier Ieskar had told her she didn't want to die, but in sacrificing anonymity Medair had made anything but a caged life impossible, with death a constant threat. If she abandoned White Snake protection there would inevitably be an alley, a mob, a beating she could not escape. Poison, a knife in the back, open execution. There were so many ways her story could end, if she did not cling to those she had hated, did not cower in their shadow.

Proud little herald, brought so low.

At sunset the battle with Estarion would begin – and end. At sunset, when the city's attention was on that battle, Medair had to leave. The plan to return to that place out of time, to sleep and perhaps wake when her name was nothing more than history, had now become a question of survival, and she had to take that option before anyone remembered that Kersym Bleak had been renowned for a hoard, not simply the Horn of Farak. Or even that she still had a charm against traces.

She nudged her satchel further under the bed, then went and locked the door. Briefly, she considered wedging a chair below the handle, then shook her head. They might want to confiscate the satchel, but she did not think the Ibis-lar had changed so much that they would sneak in and steal it.

Removing her boots, she lay down on the bed, trying to work out how long it was till sunset, and when the Kier would see fit to use the Horn. It would be necessary to move before then, and she would rest while she could, because she had a long way to run.

"One last place to hide."

Medair laughed, then shook, as she touched the palms of her hands together. She supposed she *was* a coward, but she would certainly not be summoning any ghosts to prevent this escape. Nor would she linger long enough for Cor-Ibis to have any attention to spare, because she doubted she could face or fool him. He would make this decision too hard.

Or not. It would hurt to see him, to have to work against him, but there really was no choice. She had given up the Horn, and now had no further role to play, only a future of pain and hatred and people looking at her in a way she could not bear. She would not live that.

She was done here.

Concluded in Medair: Part 2
Voice of the Lost

Glossary

AlKier	The god of the Ibisians, ruler of 'everything' and considered able to manifest as anything, but most commonly depicted as a transparent, idealised hermaphroditic figure visible among clouds.
an	A Farakkian naming custom designating the maternal line. 'an Rynstar' means that Medair's mother was of the Rynstar line.
ar	A Farakkian naming custom designating the paternal line. 'ar Corleaux' means that Medair's father was of the Corleaux line. However, since she was not an acknowledged child of her father, granted heir rights, she should not use the name.
das-Kend	The Kend's second in command.
decem	A Farakkian unit of time a little more than 70 Earth minutes. A single day is divided into twenty decems.
Ekarrel	The form of address given to the Ibisian Kier.
Farak	The incarnation of the continent of Farakkan, believed to have actively created the people who dwell there. Usually depicted as a generous female shape fashioned of fruits and flowers.
Farakkan	A large continent, fashioned into a single Empire known as the Palladian Empire by the Corminevar rulers of Palladium.
Farakkian Farak-lar	People native to the continent of Farakkan.
Ibisians Ibis-lar	The People of the Land of the Ibis. Uniformly tall, pale-skinned and white hair, Ibisians believe that they are by inherent nature 'cold-blooded' (self-controlled). Although they do have a blue line marking their spine, their blood temperature is the same as humans. Their culture is extremely mannered and rigid, with a strong emphasis on following laws and controlling impulse.
Kel	An Ibisian courtesy title for anyone not of the nobility.
Kend	The Commander of the Ibisian armies.
Keridahl	An Ibisian title (translating roughly to 'High Lord of the Cold Blood'). Keridahl command large regions known as dahleins (including Ibsa, Holt Harra, Laskia and Iskand, which maintain a different national identity to Palladium). They often have a particular 'seat' which a Kerikal manages in day-to-day matters, but are expected to spend their time advising the Kier and settling regional disputes.
Keridahl Alar Keridahl Avec	Two Keridahl are designated to sit at the right (Alar) and left (Avec) hand of the Kier, to act as particularly trusted advisors. In the event of the Kier's sudden death, the Keridahl Alar would assume control of Palladium as regent until the Kierash was of age.
Keriden	An Ibisian title. Keriden are an exalted level of Kerikal, controlling the larger cities.
Keriel	An Ibisian title. Keriel control a small area of land (an elein) which may constitute nothing more than a large farm and a single village. [Best equivalent: "Lord of the Manor".] Serves either a Kerivor or a Kerikath.
Kerikal	An Ibisian title. Kerikal rule large towns (somewhat equivalent to mayors). They commonly also hold the title of Kerikath. They owe service to either Keriden or Keridahl, depending on the region they are in.
Kerikath	An Ibisian title. Kerikath command any Keriel and Kerivor which fall within their 'kathilein'. The holders of the title Kerikath usually also hold the title Kerivor, and have their own area of land to manage.
Kerin	An Ibisian courtesy title for male members of the nobility who do not hold a specific title.
Keris	An Ibisian courtesy title for female members of the nobility who do not hold a specific title.

Kerivor	An Ibisian title. Kerivor control a moderate area of land (a vorlein) up to several villages and small towns. May command one or two Keriel. Serves a Kerikath.
Kier	Ruler of the kiereddas. Formerly the Kier went through a binding ceremony to ensure the health of the land, but since the fall of Sar-Ibis this has not occurred.
Kierash	The only title given to an heir, the Kierash is the Kier's designated successor (usually the first-born child, unless the Kier has specified otherwise for reasons of incapacity).
Kiereddas	Previously Sar-Ibis, which was a large, narrow island with no near neighbours. 'Kiereddas' translates to 'the land' and did not originally envisage that there be other lands. The Kiereddas of the Ibisians now encompasses Palladium, Ibsa, Holt Harra, Laskia and Iskand.
las	An Ibisian naming custom indicating the 'clan' the person belongs to. Members of the Cor-Ibis 'clan' are referred to as 'las Cor-Ibis'. The only exception is the current head of the clan, who is referred to simply as 'Cor-Ibis'.
Niadril	A word used to refer to Kier Ieskar after his death. It combines a meaning of 'great', 'eternal' and 'doomed'.
Sar-Ibis	The Land of the Ibis. A large, narrow island with no near neighbours, it was mountainous and fertile, with relatively mild winters. It was consumed completely by a combination of the Blight and earthquakes.

Printed in Great Britain
by Amazon